Kuhlken, Ken.

The loud adios.

DATE DUE		
JUL 2 4 2007		

© THE BAKER & TAYLOR CO.

THE
LOUD
ADIOS

By the same author:

MIDHEAVEN

THE LOUD ADIOS

KEN KUHLKEN

ST. MARTIN'S PRESS

NEW YORK

Design by Dawn Niles

Library of Congress Cataloging-in-Publication Data

Kuhlken, Ken.
   The loud adios / Ken Kuhlken.
      p.   cm.
   "A Thomas Dunne book."
   ISBN 0-312-05951-5
   I. Title.
PS3561.U36L68   1991
813'.54—dc20   90-29881
                                                CIP

First Edition: August 1991
10 9 8 7 6 5 4 3 2 1

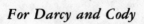

For Darcy and Cody

1

As Clifford Rose came to, the first thing he recognized was the stink, like a drainpipe running out of hell. Then he remembered.

"Wendy," he screamed. This time no one answered.

The big mestizo thugs dragged him through the doorway of the Club de Paris into the fog, across the dirt sidewalk and down three high steps to the muddy street. They flipped him over, threw him facedown into the mud. The biggest one kicked him with a pointed boot in the neck. The chest. The forehead. Finally the one they called Mofeto, who had sliced the gash in Clifford's cheek, sauntered out of the club. He looked like the runt of the litter, with a sharp face, pinched mouth, starved eyes. He wore a felt hat and a baggy dark suit. His hand with the switchblade swung beside him.

Through the fog you could hear invisible gringos talking and whooping, uphill toward the main boulevard. Neon from across the street red-tinted the fog.

Clifford lay curled in the mud, waiting for the next blow. When he saw the runt step closer, he heaved himself up on one arm. Slobbering blood, he croaked, "You give her up now, hear. I got friends. You'll see."

The runt straightened his coat and gazed both ways again. From the side of his mouth, like a parrot, he squawked, "Oh, you got friends. Sure. We don't want trouble." Lazily, he folded and pocketed his switchblade, reached beneath his baggy coat, then his hand shot out, gripping a long-barreled .45 revolver. "I better kill you now."

Clifford dropped and covered his head with his arms. He tried to push off with his legs, but they slipped in the mud and the biggest mestizo stomped and held his ankle down, while the runt bent closer until the gun barrel touched the base of Clifford's skull. He let it rest there, then glanced up the hill.

The U.S. Marines came like a stampede. Their boots squished and sucked out of the mud, and one yelled, "Whee hoo!" while another tried to whoop like a mariachi. They materialized out of the fog just ten feet from where Clifford Rose lay pressing inward with all his muscles, as if he could make himself tiny as a soul. The runt drew back to a crouch while the mestizos snatched up their guns. They turned on the wall of gringos. The Marines skidded to a halt. All white boys, straight out of boot camp with burr heads and no weapons except the bravado a gang and tequila guarantee. One of them snarled, "Move on, greasers." His pals seconded with grunts and a volley of threats.

Beneath the biggest mestizo's foot, Clifford started writhing. Large drops of blood ran down his face and he felt his mind trying to lift out of his body and lose itself in the fog. Holding onto life, he squirmed so frantically it looked like a seizure. Everybody turned to watch him.

A deep voice shouted from the door of the Club de Paris. The patrón, a Latino, in his cream-colored pin-striped suit, stepped across the sidewalk and aimed a finger at the runt. "*Basta*, Mofeto," he commanded, and whipped his arm toward the door.

The thugs slowly packed their guns away. Glaring at the Marines, they kicked mud off their boots and disappeared into the club. The Latino folded his arms and gazed disgustedly from the writhing soldier to the Marines. Finally he said, "You better keep that one out of Tijuana."

2

Over both cities lay thick, drizzling clouds. No moon or stars shined through. Streetlamps stood dark. Old neon signs hung in disrepair. North of the line, even the headlamps of cars stayed unlit or dimmed by thin coats of paint on their lenses. The only lights flickered behind window shades.

From the border you couldn't see either city. But you could smell Tijuana. As the wind shifted, smells would change from burning rubber to gasses, to nose-biting whiffs of chile fields, to sewage in the river, to whores' perfumes. And though San Diego lay ten miles north, if you listened closely you could hear a steady noise, the low howl of wheels cutting over wet asphalt as trucks carried supplies to another day of war. It was April 1943.

Tom Hickey stood on the border under the shelter between a lane for cars and a turnstile and passway for walkers. A sentry. His mouth was set in a scornful way. The blue of his eyes held no gleam. His blond, gray-flecked, scraggly hair inched over his ears and his uniform was a mess. No top button on the shirt. The white helmet lying on the ground beside him. The gun and holster he wore shifted around behind so it wouldn't get in the way. His sleeves were rolled up almost to the white MP band.

A carload of officers who pulled to the line reeked of French perfume and whiskey. Officers didn't come back smelling like Tijuana. They carried the scents of classy whores and gambling spots down the coast at Playa Rosarito.

The civilian border guard, Boyle, alias Diamond Bob—on account of his flashy rings, two-toned sport coats, the alligator brogans he wore off duty—stood chatting with the officers. The cars stacked up behind them and horns bawled, but Boyle still commiserated with the officers while they bitched about card-cheats, gravel roads, the goddamned Japs and their bombs that made things so you had to drive lights-out. Boyle never asked what they were smuggling. He just made friends, gave out favors, took money. Hickey slouched against a post and waited. Finally he stepped forward. The officers showed him their passes.

Hickey said, "Sirs, if you were approached by anyone who may have ties to a foreign government, I'll take your report. If you copulated with a Mexican, stop at the clinic over there."

A Marine lieutenant leaned out the window, squinting to look Hickey up and down. Then the car jumped forward into the darkness.

Hickey threw them a mock salute. He checked the time. 11:45. In a few minutes the next watch would show. So he could cross the border, tramp through the mud down by the river to Coco's Licores where he'd grab a short bottle of mescal, and head back to meet Lefty for the ride—fifteen miles in the open Jeep with dimmed lights to the MP barracks near the harbor downtown. The border platoon could've been stationed at Ream Field, only three miles from the line. But that would have made sense and saved money— not the military way. Or maybe they had reasons. Hickey didn't ask, because he didn't care; the war had gotten squeezed out of his mind by troubles all his own. He'd drink on the ride, then lie in his bunk and hallucinate. Maybe he'd sleep and dream of Elizabeth.

The wind blew a few drunken whoops his way as a gang of sailors started over the river bridge just beyond Coco's Licores. In a few minutes they came dimly into sight, holding each other up as they staggered alongside the road, splashing through puddles and laughing boastfully. They wore dress whites stained with mud,

4

fruity rum drinks, and splatters of blood. One held his arm in a sling. Water streamed from their caps and hair down their faces.

Every night a few hundred military guys crossed the border. Most of them Hickey could've busted or led to the dungeon shack to sleep it off, but he didn't bother. He only detained the mean ones and guys so drunk they might stumble into the dark road and get crushed.

When these sailors reached the gate, Hickey took a pass from the first in line, checked it, then stared into the boy's eyes and asked, "You screw anybody?"

"Yes, sir."

Hickey aimed the boy toward the clinic shack and gave a little shove. Then four other sailors passed through the gate like that, except the last, a redhead with a bloody gap where his front tooth ought to be, said, "No, sir. I didn't screw anybody. I got ambushed by a Jap. He come out of this alley."

"You want a Purple Heart?"

"No, sir. I wanta make a report, 'cause there's sure a lot of Japs down there. I bet they're spies, sir. And there's this bar called 'Hell', I hear a Kraut owns it."

So Hickey led the sailor partway to the office shack and told him to go in there and wait, and went back to the line, to let through more sailors and a few civilian shipyard workers.

He didn't see Clifford Rose step up behind him. The kid slumped like any second he'd lose to gravity. When Hickey finally turned, Clifford stood gawking at him. A golden-haired, handsome kid, breathing raspily, his eyes full of the glazed, pained look Hickey knew well, since not so long ago it appeared every time he spotted a mirror. Before he squared off against his demons and drowned them in booze.

"You made it. Swell," Hickey said.

A week before, the kid had showed up mutilated, dragged by a gang of Marines. He looked like somebody had rolled him down the muddy street, then dipped him in a vat of blood. He was so bad Hickey had walked them clear across the compound to the clinic shack before he recognized the kid as a fellow from boot camp,

5

somebody he'd liked and shot a couple games of pool with. For three days, until he heard different, he figured the kid might die.

But now he stood there in a sport coat, slacks, and a hat, rentals from a downtown locker room, his face only marred by a few small scabs and a Band-Aid on his cheek, an inch below the right eye. Hickey asked what he was doing out of uniform.

"There's some guys in TJ might not recognize me in this stuff," Clifford muttered.

"Going back down, huh?"

"Yessir."

"Hope you aren't going the same place as last time."

"Pop, reckon we could talk a little?" Clifford asked.

Hickey studied the kid, who looked so wretchedly sweet and innocent only a creep could've sent him on his way. Besides, Hickey was curious about what had fallen on the kid in TJ. Every night somebody tripped the switch on his curiosity. From the stories he heard, Germans were pouring into TJ—but probably anytime a jarhead caught a word of German, a bar fight errupted and the losers claimed they'd got beaten by a dozen Nazis. Anyway, Hickey might persuade the kid out of going back for more. He called over to the next gate, reminded Lefty he was going south for a bottle. Five minutes later, when the next watch arrived, Hickey and the kid stepped across the border and walked through the drizzle toward Coco's Licores.

Hickey bought two short bottles of mescal, gave the change to a beggar woman, and they started back. Their feet plopped and sucked in and out of the red clay mud as they crossed the knoll along the river. The riverbed was a hundred yards across, a sandy plain cut by a stream full of algae, mosses, the froth of sewage. The water poured like syrup through the narrow arroyo.

Along the riverbed, beyond the stream about five hundred Indians camped. Their fires smouldered in the drizzle. Many of them slept uncovered in the sand. Some lay beneath cardboard and scrapwood shelters. Haunted people walked like shadows near the riverbank, or squatted alone, staring at the rain.

These Indians had come from the deep south, from Zacatecas,

6

Yucatan's jungles, the mahogany forests of Chiapas, from drought or pestilence to live on scraps that war left behind. But there weren't many scraps for Indians after the poorest refugees from Europe, waiting in Tijuana for their turn to cross the line, took their share. Most of these Indians lived off handouts and garbage. Among them were the sick, the freaks, the deformed and unclever. Their children prowled the streets and bars begging from drunken troopers, training to be whores and thieves.

Hickey motioned toward the settlement, hoping Rose might notice the misery and think less of his own, whatever it was. He screwed off the bottle cap, took a long pull of mescal, and passed the bottle to Clifford, who stared across the river, keening his eyes through the dark. Beads of rain hung on his nose and round cheeks. Wisps of golden hair lay pasted to his forehead. He took a gulp of mescal and coughed.

As they turned and started walking again, Hickey nipped from the bottle and watched the kid. Finally he asked, "You about to ship overseas?"

Clifford nodded and looked up. Tiny sparks glistened in his eyes.

"Where to?"

"Maybe the Solomons. But they ain't saying."

"You're scared." Hickey's voice was strong, rich like a general's ought to be. "Sure you're scared. Anybody who's not, he's just looney or stuffed full of hero dreams. Or he doesn't give a damn for living anymore. Anyway you twist it, he's a loser."

Clifford stopped and squinted through the dark at the man's face. Hickey passed the bottle. The kid took it, gulped, coughed again. Finally he said, "Thanks, Pop. Sure I'm scared. But not so bad." He glanced toward the river, then turned back. "It's okay I call you Pop?"

"I don't give a damn," Hickey muttered. They'd been calling him Pop the last three months, since he was the oldest guy in boot camp, and looked at least his age, thirty-seven, especially when he frowned and the lines cut deep across his high forehead.

While they turned and walked the last fifty yards to the border,

Hickey realized that nobody else had asked if he minded being Pop. He decided he liked this kid. No swagger or bluff about him. A rare find. An honest man.

They passed through the gate and turned toward the Jeep. Lefty was there and he shouted, "Get the lead out, Pop. There's dames waiting on me up in Dago." Lefty, a pretty boy, had the jaunty style and slick voice to go with his dimples and slate-black hair.

Hickey climbed one step into the Jeep, and got jerked back out. His arm cinched in the fierce grip of Clifford Rose, like the kid was some brute who didn't know his strength, Hickey wheeled around and said, "Let go—" before he noticed Clifford's eyes.

They had swelled and whitened. "I wanta show you something. Okay, Pop?" His voice had cracked, and he dropped Hickey's arm. "Reckon you'll go back to TJ with me?"

"No," Hickey said. "I'm tired, going to be drunk soon as I can get there." He took a swallow of mescal. "Only a stooge shows up in Tijuana that way."

Clifford's eyes closed and the skin of his face drew up tighter. "There's something I gotta do," he said, "and it ain't liable to be easy. But you and me could do it."

"Do what?"

"Can't tell, I gotta show you, and I mean to pay." He fumbled in his pocket, pulled out a brand new fifty, and held it between them. "See, I heard you was a detective. It can't hurt to look, ain't that right?"

"Hell it can't," Hickey muttered. But futilely. He wasn't going to leave the kid to get massacred again, at least not without knowing why. He cussed under his breath. His night was sure wrecked. No quiet. No sleep or good dreams. He grabbed the fifty and said harshly, "The thing that's got you down, is that what you want me to see?"

Clifford nodded just as Lefty fired the Jeep, raced the motor, and yelled at them to get on board.

"It'll keep," Hickey said. "Tomorrow afternoon, before my watch, we can go down there."

"I'm shipping out tomorrow."

"Okay, then what's in Tijuana won't matter anymore."

"Sure will."

"Why? What's the big deal?"

The kid stared at his feet, and folded his hands over his head, while Lefty roared the motor and cussed loud. Then Hickey said, "Aw Christ, c'mon." He turned and waved Lefty away.

3

They plodded back across the line and down the road to a coffee and taco stand where the cabs always waited. There was only one taxi at this hour, a ten-year-old, battered Chrysler limousine painted shiny red and pink. The driver sat in the rain on the hood, munching from a sack of salted peanuts. A deep knife scar, diamond-shaped, ran from his right cheek down to the lip, which he tried to cover with a mustache, but hair didn't flourish on the scar. So his mustache was mostly on the left side, below the patch on his eye. He wore a black Texan hat, old and crumpled as if he'd found it smashed on the road, and a long black zoot coat.

Clifford said, "Please bring us to the Paris Club."

With a grin, the cabbie leaped to the ground. "You going to see La Rosa." They climbed into the limo and he kept talking. "That one's an angel, man, I swear to you, I see her lots of times. Hey, you guys want some reefer, I know where it is. Man, I know where everything is in TJ."

While Clifford sat rigidly glaring at the cabbie, Hickey folded into the rear seat and tried to ignore the springs that gouged him. He sipped mescal as they bumped and lurched over the ruts and potholes across the bridge and into central Tijuana on its one paved road, Avenida Revolución.

Parts of the sidewalk looked like a dark midway, where the men wandered and yelled—soldiers, sailors, dockhands, displaced Jews, Japanese merchants walking skittishly, Bohemians, Gypsies, Chinese. Some walked holding hands with the flashiest Indian whores, argued with the big mestizo pimps. Or they staggered into the alley to piss and came out robbed, beaten, or maybe handcuffed, if they didn't have money to bribe a cop who prowled on the take. Just enough light spilled out of the doorways so you could see drunks lying on the sidewalk and dark women who squatted, begging, with babies cradled in their arms. Children in rags stood on the corners selling gum and benzedrine. The doormen outside Club Eros and the Climax Bar grabbed at everybody, trying to show them inside. Two Marines came flying out of The Long Bar, and threw curses back at the door.

Hickey screwed open the second bottle of mescal, took a snort and passed it to Clifford, then to the cabbie. He kept wondering what could be so important at the Club de Paris. Maybe the kid just wanted another poke at the guys who'd thrashed him, but he guessed there was more. You could tell by the stiff slowness of his every move that Clifford was deep in pain, all the way to his heart. Probably he wouldn't talk because words can cheapen the pain—Hickey knew the feeling.

"You looking for pills, opium, I know where that is." The cabbie wheeled left off the paved road and crashed down a hill on washboard. The limo clattered like a jackhammer but he drove relaxed with one hand and at the same time turned back and grinned. "After you see La Rosa Blanca, man, you wanna chica for your own, I know where she is. You got all the shit in the world right here, man, there's even spies and you don't know what else, right here in TJ."

As they pulled to a stop in front of the Club de Paris, Clifford sat with hands gripping his thighs and his eyes fierce on the cabbie. Then he grabbed a pair of rimless specs out of his coat pocket, fitted them on, and tugged his hat low.

Hickey stepped out of the limo. Clifford paid the fare. Then Hickey walked with an arm around the kid toward the club. It was bordered on the east by warehouses running a few blocks to the river, on the west by a lot full of high weeds and rubble. The stucco was soot-dulled blue adorned with sketched silhouettes of dancing girls. Two thugs stood at the door. The big one welcomed them heartily, while the scrawny one they called Mofeto stayed quiet with his arms folded. Until suddenly his hand shot out and grabbed the pistol from the holster at Hickey's side.

Hickey stared, gave a wry smile, reached into his pocket and handed the runt a quarter. "Keep an eye on the gun, amigo."

He walked behind Clifford who paid the one-dollar cover charge. As they stepped inside the stench hit. Like dead things boiled in formaldehyde. It blended from the smoke and vomit and spills that caked the floor and spotted the walls. The place was lit only by a blue neon light above the stage. There a skinny Indian dancer gyrated. She wore high heels, dark stockings, black panties, and a top hat, and balanced herself with a cane.

The club was one large room, all wooden, high-ceilinged. Every footstep, voice, and scrape of a chair leg echoed and mixed with the music, a droning alto sax, somber and lowly, and the conga drum like a dying pulse. There were about twenty small, round wooden tables, half of them vacant, with many of the chairs overturned, kicked around, broken. But along the three sides of the stage tables were filled by gringo troops. The Mexican Army must've been on alert tonight, Hickey thought. Cárdenas—the ex-Presidente who'd returned as a general to tighten the border and shoreline defenses—kept his troops on a tight rein. Not one of them was here.

Some gringos lay passed out with heads on their arms. Others shot drinks, whistled and hooted. A few of them hung over the low rail of the stage and tried to goose the dancer as she passed by. She teased, wiggling close in, sprang back,and smacked at them with her cane. Then she ran the cane back and forth, in and out, between her legs.

Hickey followed the kid and sat at a table away from the stage, on the dim side of the blue light. He gazed around the room, noticed three large bouncers leaning against the side wall, then stealthily took out his bottle and swallowed a long pull. He sighed, at better ease now that the drink had started to take him. And mescal didn't send you into a drunken fog—it carried you to a bright place where a picture on the wall might suddenly change to a window in Rome or the face of somebody you loved could appear out of nowhere. Just far enough from the real world, it sent you. He reached the bottle toward Clifford. But the kid sat in a trance, his face more pallid than ever, under the blue light. When Hickey shook the kid's arm and finally got him to take the bottle, as he lifted it toward his lips his hand shook wildly. Mescal dribbled off his chin. Yet he managed a long swallow, coughed, and killed the bottle.

Hickey flagged a waiter, signaled for two beers. He looked around the room and wondered again what the kid had brought him here for. He watched the skinny dancer as she peeled down her panties, took them off and used them to wipe the sweat from her face, then pushed out her behind and shook it around just beyond the reach of the grabbing, whooping Marines. She turned and stuck out her tongue, shimmied her pointed breasts, strolled off through the silver-blue curtain beside the two musicians at the rear of the stage. The music fell away, a moment of silence passed, and slowly the room filled with drunken talk. Hickey turned to the kid. "Where is it?"

Looking up vaguely, Clifford gazed around as if the question had escaped him. Finally he muttered, "She'll be out next."

"She?" Hickey bolted up straight—this punk had lured him down here on account of a whore. *"She?"* he growled. Clifford stared intently at the stage. Maybe the kid was stoned on some Mexican plant, Hickey thought, and it made him feel immortal. Or he was a natural goon.

The beers came. The kid paid. Hickey decided to leave about one minute after he got an eyeful of this Rosa broad, who must be the piece that Clifford was swooning over. The one the cabbie had got poetic about.

Soon the old humpbacked conga drummer appeared on the stage and rasped, "Okay, troops, now we going to see the beautiful virgin, *la chica mas hermosa* in all TJ. We going to bring her out now. La Rosa Blanca." The customers stomped and whistled. The announcer sat down and beat a lazy roll on his drum. As the curtain parted, a hush fell over the room. Out stepped the girl.

She was purely naked. No shoes, no beads or ribbons, and her skin shined the color of ivory, only brighter, moonlike. All the men gaped, including Hickey. He got up, stepped closer, put on his glasses, while the kid stayed back in the dark.

She was small, with most of her height in the legs. Long, rounded calves and thighs. The hips were smooth but muscled, slender, tapering gradually up to her waist. Her long sleek arms made circular patterns in the air, and even her long, floating hands wore no rings or polish. The breasts were round and small in profile, the nipples tiny as flowerbuds. Her shoulders sloped gently, her neck was long. And the face, haloed in shaggy golden hair, soft and glowing, stunned you most of all. Her face made Hickey's breath go shallow.

The skin was pure, the eyes glistened blue then emerald, and darted shyly from the men to the floor. Sometimes they closed. She had round cheeks and pink lips, the bottom one fuller, and it curled up just slightly on the right side, caught between a pout and a little smile. There was no trace of anger, guile, smugness. You might not find a face more innocent in all the world. She looked about fifteen.

And she danced with grace, flowing across the stage, until she caught sight of something in the dark behind Hickey. Then she began to move stiffly with arms at her sides, bouncing woodenly from the knees. Finally she stepped to the rail and looked down at the men who crowded there. She stood still until the first man touched her. And, letting each man touch her in turn, she moved along the rail, her troubled face gazing up from the men to the darkness beyond them.

A giant Marine ran his fingers down the curve of her thigh. A sailor cupped his palm on her behind. Two soldiers did the same. Next a soldier got brave and brushed a finger through her muff of golden hair. A fat blond civilian beside him wedged his whole hand

14

palm up between her legs and squeezed. He laughed and then laughed harder as the girl raised her fists to her eyes.

"Dumb fucking German," yelled a Marine who sprang up wielding a bottle, and while the other man cheered him, he flew across a table and crashed his bottle over the civilian's head, but the fat boy still clutched one hand on the girl until she broke free and ran to disappear through the curtain behind the stage. A dozen cheated gringos attacked the civilian, yelling and pounding him good before all ten or so fellows from around the bar, most of them shouting in German, jumped the Marines. Bouncers flew from out of nowhere, mestizos and two large blonds, lashing with blackjacks and clubs.

Hickey'd stepped back out of the light to sit with Clifford and watch the brawl. In a minute the bouncers were herding the troops toward the exit.

The blue light started to flash on and off. The musicians began to pack up. Hickey drew a long breath of the stinking air and shook his head clear enough. He checked his pocket watch. Almost 3:30. He groaned and glanced at Clifford. The kid sat rigidly, right hand clutched around his beer bottle, left hand squeezing the table edge as if the brawl had spooked him.

"Whew," Hickey said. "She's a beauty all right. I guess you got reasons to fall for her." He put his hand on the kid's shoulder. "But, see, she's not real. She just looks like an angel, Clifford. You know she's gotta be a tramp."

Clifford's lips pushed out and he snarled something that got lost in the noise of waiters clearing tables, throwing glasses into the trays. Hickey leaned closer, figuring he'd been cussed. He wouldn't take any guff from the kid, not after he'd dragged himself down here for no good reason. "What's that you say?"

"She's my sister," Clifford hissed.

And Hickey fell back into his seat. He slapped a hand across his eyes while the kid pulled from under his coat and belt a little .22 pistol, sneaked it under the table and pressed it onto Hickey's leg.

"Sister," Hickey muttered.

The kid lifted his hand. The .22 started slipping between

Hickey's legs. At the same time Clifford sprang up with a bigger gun of his own, a .45 that had been strapped to his armpit and now hung at his side as he walked stiffly, over fallen chairs, around tables, straight as he could toward the stage.

As he leaped up, Hickey grabbed the .22. He bounded over chairs and caught Clifford by the scruff of the neck. The kid tried to shake him off, lunging for the stage rail. "Wendy," he screamed. "Let go, Pop! Wendy!"

A flash of blue light stopped everything. Out of the light, a mestizo and a German appeared, with raised arms and sticks that slashed down on the gringos' skulls. A shot boomed and echoed. Somebody howled. Three or four blows glanced off Hickey's neck and head before he fell with a pain that stabbed down his back and loosed a storm in his brain. Yet he got the little .22 into the deep pocket of his MP trousers. Then he let himself get dragged away, towed along on rubbery legs, knowing these guys couldn't hold him up and smash him at the same time. He caught a blurry side-glance of Clifford. Out cold. As he staggered through the exit, Hickey saw a little brown hand fisting around a short length of galvanized pipe. Then the fist, wearing a golden ring with a big saint's face, a jagged intaglio, crashed his right jaw. It jolted all the way down to his knees, and they gave out again. For a minute things only buzzed and sputtered. No pictures or thoughts cleared until he heard Clifford yell, "Pop, where'd you go?"

They were on the sidewalk now, moving toward an alley, with El Mofeto in front, then the two big thugs dragging Hickey, and finally Clifford. He crawled between the bouncers, who had his arms wrenched backward.

The last thing Hickey wanted was into that alley, but he couldn't break loose yet. They dragged him there and let him drop, onto his belly with his right arm underneath. Slowly, he wormed his hand down until it touched the .22. He found his grip. Nudged off the safety. Slid the pistol free of his belly and slowly rolled over. The first guy he saw was a bouncer just letting go of Clifford's arm. Hickey jerked up the gun and squeezed. A blast echoed down the alley. The man heaved back over a stack of cardboard and into the stucco wall.

Rising to his feet as if the ground were a rowboat at sea, Hickey spotted nobody with a gun drawn. He waved the pistol and ordered them to face the wall. The shot one still lay on the cardboard, moaning and squeezing his thigh, but the others did as Hickey commanded. Except El Mofeto. He crossed his feet, scratched his ear, curled his lip, and squawked, "What you going to do now?"

The chambers of Hickey's brain kept misfiring randomly, which made thinking tough. And suddenly the kid stood beside him, then leaned on his shoulder as he swayed, drooling blood. "Make 'em get Wendy, Pop."

Hickey stared, listened, kept trying to think. "No time. In a minute there'll be cops."

"I gotta try, though."

Before Hickey found the sense to grab him, the kid went stumbling toward the street. Hickey lunged that way, on impulse. But he couldn't at once chase the kid and hold these guys back.

"Whoa!" he shouted. "Get back here, give me a hand, anyway. Grab their guns, will you?" he shouted.

One Mexican shot his arms for the sky and pleaded mockingly for the kid to spare him. His compadres sniggered.

Clifford slowed, finally stopped, leaned on a garbage can a second, then turned back and marched to the three Mexicans against the wall. He quickly frisked them, snatched their guns, and slipped them into his pockets under his belt. At last he turned to Mofeto. But as he got near, the runt snapped his teeth and croaked, "No, boy. You touch me, only that, I'm killing you. My pleasure."

"Go on, get the girl," Hickey shouted. "Hold it—before you go in, find a cab. Make sure he's waiting by the door."

The kid weaved out of the alley, into the street. Hickey stepped closer to El Mofeto.

"Pass it over, la pistola, chico."

The runt didn't stir. One of those punks made tough by a death wish, Hickey thought. The kind you don't even try to reason with.

But he'd try anyway. "Here's the deal. My nephew, he's the girl's brother. That makes me her uncle. And her dad, my brother, he's General Bradley. Comprendes?"

"You a liar."

"You oughta believe me, chico. Aw, the hell with you. Where's the guy that owns this joint? El Patrón."

"Maybe asleep. I bet that's where he is."

The runt started whistling a jazzy tune, an upbeat number you might hear at a parade. He gazed up at the sky and smiled. One of his boys tittered, just as Clifford ran into the alley and wailed, "Pop, she ain't there."

The kid bent forward, hands on his knees, and rolled his head in tight circles. Turning back to El Mofeto, Hickey raised his left fist, wanting to knock the runt's teeth out of the rear of his skull. But not so much as he wanted the girl. "Okay, here it is—tomorrow you're bringing La Rosa to the line. We'll give you twelve hours. That'd be two o'clock. Comprendes?"

El Mofeto looked down from the sky and kept smiling. "Sure. We going to bring her. We're swell guys."

"Yeah, I'm betting on you. So we're leaving now. I'll take my pistola, huh?"

When the runt didn't move, Hickey raised the .22 and sighted at the pointy nose. Then he winked. "Aw, you got my number. I'm not going to kill somebody, not even you, for a gun. There's about a million where that came from. You like the rod, it's yours, pal."

The runt gave a hard, squeaky laugh. Hickey smiled grimly, turning to Clifford. He told the kid to guard their front while he watched the rear.

They made the street that way and got surrounded by a gang of spectators who'd been hiding behind cars, yet nobody challenged them. They piled into the rear of an old Ford taxi and Hickey commanded, "Frontera."

The drizzle had stopped. Hickey smelled a wave of sea air. He wondered how much of this night was real, how much a mescal dream. Surely the girl wasn't so perfect as she appeared. Nobody who'd spent an hour in a slime pit like the Club de Paris could be so undaunted and pure as she seemed. He leaned forward to see Clifford's face. The kid had rolled down the window and was staring out into the wind. He and the girl had the same pouty lip, the same golden hair. But Clifford's eyes were gray and frantic, and hers, until she saw her brother, had looked almost serene.

"You wanta tell me how she got there?"

Clifford turned and faced him. "Uh-huh. I don't mind." Suddenly his face clenched up in a fury, he grabbed Hickey's arm in both hands. He squeezed and yelled, "What'll I do, Pop? They ain't gonna bring her."

For a while, Hickey sat feeling the dull pains all over and the sharp one that burned from his eye nearly to his bowels. He silently cussed Clifford Rose for risking their lives without giving him the whole story. But again he thought of the girl. And before long he remembered his daughter, about the same age, and knew that if she was in the Club de Paris he might not care a damn about anybody else in the world. Not until he got her back.

Clifford tugged on his arm.

"I'm gonna pay you more," the kid pleaded. "Me and Wendy got this place on the beach up to Lake Tahoe. Ain't no buildings, but it's an awful pretty place, out on a foresty beach there. I'm gonna deed it to you."

"Sure," Hickey said gently. "Take it easy now. You've got a war to fight."

19

4

■ ■ ■

As always—drunk, sober, or beaten up—Hickey washed, then read himself to sleep. He read a page, conked out, and dreamed again. There was his daughter, fourteen years old, tall, grown up fast like her dad, with the black wavy hair and black eyes that made her mother a beauty. But her pale skin that reddened easily and the long, ascetic-looking face came from Hickey.

Wearing a flowered hat and a sundress, Elizabeth jumped off the train and ran to him. As they embraced, suddenly they stood out front of the hillside cottage in Hollywood where they used to live. They began walking and soon they reached the ocean, at Long Beach near the oil field that once was a ranch Hickey's father owned. The beach led them all the way to Tijuana. But as they passed through the gate, instead of finding hunger, filth, all kinds of meanness, they discovered a city more beautiful than any place. There were fountains around bronze statues, flower gardens, eucalyptus groves, boulevards lined with orange trees, shiny white buildings. Nobody was poor or sad in the Tijuana of Hickey's dream.

And, from here you could reach all the world. This time they walked a trail beside the river and saw that it emptied into the Seine. The water turned violet, at dusk. The air was full of apple blossoms. Hickey bought his little girl crepes, dark sweet coffee, ribbons for her hair.

Then he snapped awake to the pain down from his eye meeting one shooting up from his jaw. Together they bellowed like a pair of tubas. He got up and swallowed a few aspirin. But he couldn't drift off again, with the night in TJ come back to haunt him.

He should've known better than to get near any messes, the way this whole year had gone. Nineteen forty-three had sunk to hell about a day after it started, when he came home from work to his place on the bay, and found a letter folded into H.G. Wells's *Outline of History*, which he'd been reading.

Dear Tom,

It's not that you're a bad guy. But I'm 34. I need another chance before it's too late. See, we've got nowhere in 15 years. I give up. I mean, you're a three-time loser.

First the orchestra. You were a damned good bandleader, except you had to play what you liked instead of what the crowd wanted to hear. And of course you wouldn't kiss the right behinds. Then, you could've been the richest cop in L.A., a guy with the smarts and charisma like you had, who knew all the nightclub boys, but you wouldn't play the game. We could've had that mansion you used to promise me. No, you throw in your cards with old Leo, the next biggest loser, and drag me and Liz to this hick town. Two years we live like peasants. Then you get a shot at the steakhouse.

When you met Paul Castillo, it could've been the big break. Finally you get teamed up with somebody who knows how to beat the odds. I mean, what in hell does it matter if Paul had to pay off some guys and use a little muscle to get you the best meat in town? Rationing's just a setup. Another way the smart boys make their fortunes. And it could've made *us* rich too. But you are so damned noble. Like you always have to show off, lending money, buying people things so everybody will slap you on the back and say Tom's a prince all right.

Well, maybe you are, but this time it cost you dear. Today Paul sold the steakhouse, building and all. I'm leaving you our house, to help cover your losses. You can raise a few grand for the dump,

enough to get that sailboat or mountain cabin you always dreamed
of.

Sure, you'll want to kill me. That's one reason I'm staying with
Paul, he's at least as tough as you, and twice as shrewd.

Well, good-bye, my darling. It's too bad. We used to make
beautiful music. Of course I'm taking Liz. Where I go, she goes.

Love,
Madeline

Hickey would've fought back for his daughter. But he hadn't
even finished a two-week drunk when Uncle Sam jumped in. Saw
him down and figured it was the right time to kick him. January 10
his draft notice came. Even though a year earlier, the week after
Pearl Harbor, he'd tried to enlist—even knowing it might keep him
from Elizabeth for the six or eight months everybody figured they'd
need to smash the Axis—but they'd turned him down. He was a
borderline diabetic, thirty-six years old. But when enough boys had
died, by 1943, when the supply of young sacrifices became less than
the demand, Hickey's faults got forgiven.

It might've been history's ugliest year, with half the world
burning and shooting at each other, and kids like Wendy Rose
getting preyed on by rats like the one Clifford said had brought her
over the border and dealt her into some kind of slavery there.

Or, Hickey thought, maybe the kid was lying. Maybe his sister
was down there on her own.

5

Hickey woke up groaning at 10:15. After he'd fallen back to sleep, he'd kept waking in a sweat and seeing visions of Wendy Rose under the blue light in the Club de Paris, his heart gripped by something—maybe lust, or compassion.

The drizzle rattled on the barracks' tin roof. A few other MPs snored at the far end of the room. They'd woke Hickey, stomping in drunk a couple hours before—just as he'd got back to sleep from when the stupid bugle woke him—and it wasn't the first time they'd blighted his sleep. On his way to the shower he kicked each of their bunks hard. After a shower, he finished dressing in his MP uniform, gathered what he needed into a bag, and walked out.

In Hickey's gear bag were a couple of guns, swiped from the Mexicans outside the Club de Paris, his holster, nightstick, and a brown wool suit, bleached white shirt, and a tie with a painted macaw, his civilian work clothes.

At the Pier Five Diner on Market Street, he swallowed two rolls, an egg, and four cups of black coffee. Then he took out his old briar and smoked for a while. When his head felt clear enough, he went to the rest room, changed clothes, and walked a few blocks up Market Street, turning down 5th. He passed a line of service boys that stretched a half-block from the Hollywood Burlesque theater.

At the corner of 5th and Broadway, he entered an old brick building. He climbed three flights of stairs to an office door lettered HICKEY AND WEISS, INVESTIGATIONS, opened it with a key, walked straight to a desk, took out a Browning .45 automatic pistol in a shoulder holster and put it into his gear bag. From the same desk drawer he pulled an address book. He found the number of a German guy, a friend of Leo Weiss. The German was a devout Lutheran who detested Hitler more than he hated the Pope, yet who belonged to the German-American Bund, a gang of Nazis and sympathizers. Hickey sat down and phoned the man, told him enough about Wendy Rose and the Club de Paris to get in return the address of the German's best friend's wife's nephew, who had been living in Tijuana a few months now. A coffee planter from Chiapas. Juan Metzger.

Hickey scribbled a note, left it on the desk, went back down to the street, and turned up Broadway.

Even in the rain some derelicts hung out by the fountain at the bus plaza, and dozens of newcomers wandered around, wrinkled and aching from thousand-mile bus rides. More of the hordes who came drifting and trucking southwest, at least twenty thousand each month, to live in tent cities on the beaches or in rickety fourplexes built last week, to be welders, riveters on planes and battleships, or stevedores loading the gray ships that filled the harbor.

At 12:30 the bus for the border arrived. Hickey got on with a trio of teenaged pachucos in khaki trousers, and heavy shoes in case they had to kick somebody, and two Mexican women dressed in shabby black dresses and veils. They were going home from a burial, carrying a sack full of personal effects and medals of a Mexican boy who had gone to be a U.S. soldier.

The bus clattered along, splashing, skidding to a stop near the National City shipyards to pick up Mexican workers, and next at the trailer parks on the south bay waterfront, to let off citizens. Soon the road narrowed and the bus had to ride the shoulder or else crash into northbound Mexican trucks hauling onions and potatoes. On both sides of the road, to the sea and the mountains, were farmlands, and all over the fields Mexicans walked around, stooping to plant vegetables in the rain.

He got off the bus about 1:30.

The border lay at the base of dark mesas capped with dense black clouds. Hickey plodded through the rain to the office shack next to the clinic shack. The door was unlocked, but he found no one there. Inside, he took the Browning and shoulder holster out of his gear bag and stuffed the bag into a locker. He strapped on the gun and put his sport coat over it. Then he went outside, sat on a step, and watched the gate. By 2:15 he gave up hoping a car might show and drop off the girl.

With his hat pulled low against the rain, Hickey walked across the border against traffic through the U.S. entry gate. He sloshed down the road, leaping over mudholes, to the red-and-pink Chrysler limo beside the coffee and taco stand.

Tito the cabbie sat behind the wheel reading a comic book. The mustached, unscarred side of his face looked almost handsome with the sunglasses covering his patched eye. As Hickey stepped close, the cabbie jerked with a start, then yawned and motioned for Hickey to get in front.

He came around, climbed in, took out his wallet and passed Tito five dollars. "For a couple hours. Let's go back to the Club de Paris."

The big engine revved. Tito said, "No uniform today. Hey, what you thinking about La Rosa?"

"I think she's a little girl," Hickey snapped.

Tito raised his hand. "Sure, man. That's what I think too." He sped away, flying through the mudholes, roaring over the bridge, but he got stalled in a jam of trucks at the turn onto Revolución. He took a Hershey bar out of the pocket of his bright yellow Hawaiian shirt, nibbled while he honked and cussed, finally turned to Hickey. "Why you going back down there?"

"You're the guy with all the answers."

"You got that right."

"Who runs the Club de Paris?"

The cabbie lifted his eyebrows. "Hey. Easy. That one's Señor del Monte."

As they swerved around the double-parked cars, then turned and crashed over potholes and rocks on the way down the hill toward the river, Hickey asked what he knew about del Monte.

The cabbie said, "Not this del Monte, but his papa—he's a big one. Very famous. It's him that brings Coca Cola to Mexico. Maybe he's the richest cabrón in all Baja. Or maybe Lázaro Cárdenas is richer. Who knows?"

"How about this guy, the son?"

"Not so much," Tito said. "Except maybe he's a Nazi. In Spain, where he was going to college, he joined Franco's army. He comes back with a German wife. She's still here, up in Las Lomas. Maybe it's a reason why General Cárdenas don't send the Germans to the Capitol like he's supposed to. Because these ricos are all friends, you know?"

Hickey thought a minute. "What about the Japs? Why doesn't Cárdenas round up the Japs like he's supposed to?"

"They're paying somebody, I guess."

A block before the Club de Paris, Hickey told the cabbie to stop, let him out, and wait.

There was no pavement or sidewalk, only red mud, rivulets and pools. A hard wind came up, blowing the drizzle into Hickey's face as he waded around a ramshackle hotel, El Ritz, with most of its windows boarded up. He crossed a vacant lot. A few children playing there pelted him with mudballs, then laughed and ran. Hickey only glanced their way, turned up the road that led around back of the Club de Paris.

In the rear of the building were two doors facing a vacant lot with large piles of rubble. He noted that the left door must've let out of the back room that opened onto the stage. He finished circling the building, to the entrance, which was unmanned. No sign said open or closed. He drew the automatic from under his coat, held it in his outside coat pocket, pushed the heavy door, and stepped through.

The club was dark as ever. Windows were high and blackened.

26

A blue light over the stage glowed dimly. The only sounds were murmurs from the few customers, all Mexicans, a few of Cárdenas's soldiers at a table in the middle of the room. Behind the bar two men stood watchfully, a mestizo and a German. Each had clobbered him at least once the night before.

Hickey gazed around through the dark, looking for the runt called Mofeto. At the bar, he ordered a shot of mescal though he usually only drank the stuff at night. When the mestizo brought him a double shot of the brownest, thickest kind, he gulped, and asked, "Where's Señor del Monte?"

The bartenders looked at each other, and the German grumbled, "What for you wanting him?"

Hickey glared until the German got skittish. He stepped around the bar, went to a door on the left of the stage. The mestizo smiled at Hickey and poured another shot of mescal.

El Mofeto stepped out of the back room first, in his same dark baggy coat with padded shoulders and the hat down to his eyes. The boss followed. Tall, skeleton thin, about Hickey's age, with wavy black hair, pale flesh. Something about him didn't look Mexican or Spanish, and there was a nervous, haunted presence about him. He reached out a bony hand, which Hickey didn't shake as his right was occupied, still resting on his gun. Del Monte leaned on the bar.

With a glance at El Mofeto, Hickey said to the boss, "First thing, I'm an MP, and my partners know just where I am right now—so I'm not worth killing. Second, there's a girl who works here. A kid. Una chica."

"All our girls are young, Señor." Del Monte sighed, bored already. "We grow up young in Mexico. We die young. *Asi es la vida,* no? . . . I expect you are meaning La Rosa."

"Yeah. I wanta talk to her."

"Every man wants to talk to her, Señor."

Hickey seethed, then slapped his wallet onto the bar, in front of del Monte. "I got a hundred and twenty in there. You got a family. I wanta take her to her brother, that's all. Then we'll disappear."

Del Monte straightened up, wearily like an arthritic, rolled his eyes, and turned to walk away.

"Whoa!" Hickey said. "How much?"

The man turned back. "Her brother, three times he comes here. She never wants him. He scares her, that's all, and I don't want to see that anymore."

"She needs her family, pal," Hickey demanded. "She's like a little kid."

Del Monte forced a contemptuous smile. "Sure, she's not too smart. But she's human, no? She can do as she wants." His hand sliced the air to signal the end, goodbye. He turned and hustled to the back room. El Mofeto stayed just long enough to cackle before strolling after his boss.

Outside, Hickey caught some breaths, clearing the stink of that dive from his lungs. To the east it looked like the clouds might break someday. The limo was parked across the street. He jumped mudholes, slid into the cab, and asked, "You know that creep who wears the big hat and a mustache?"

Tito stiffened and his lips curled. "Sure. El Mofeto, that means he's the skunk. I know him plenty. I used to have two good eyes, before I knew El Mofeto."

6

■ ■ ■

The limo spewed mud, pulling away. They bounded up the hill, crossed Revolución, and stopped at the telephone office on Calle Cinco where Hickey struggled with the language and finally got a line across the border, to his partner. He asked Leo to check out this del Monte and to help figure an angle he could use on the Tijuana police, either the locals or the Federales.

When Leo talked back, he sounded underwater. "Ha. Where you been, son? You can't scare 'em, can't blackmail 'em, if they steal right out front. All you can use on a Mex is in your billfold."

After the call, Hickey asked the clerk for a listing on Juan Metzger. There was no private phone, only a message number, at Groceria La Portal, on a road Hickey knew was out past the Playas.

He walked outside and stood in the drizzle grumbling. Four days without sun. He thought of one more drink but his watch read 3:20; he wanted to make another stop before looking up this Metzger, and at 6:00 his duty began.

The police station was a rickety wooden building in the shadow of the Jai Lai palace and the bull ring at the south end of town, two miles from the border, at the foot of Las Lomas where the big shots lived. Cops sat on the long front porch, glaring at the rain, then at Hickey.

Inside were Indians, refugees, all kinds of poor, evil, or luckless folks slumped in chairs or resting on the floor. Some waited for sons or brothers to be released. Others loitered there, out of the storm. The room smelled like pestilence, as if you'd find dead people swept into the corners. Hickey stepped to the desk, gave the clerk a dollar, and asked to see the chief. Soon a fat, bleached secretary cooed, "Señor."

She clutched his arm and led him to the office where Chief Buscamente sat on his desk, wearing a cowboy shirt, a Stetson, and a big pistol on his hip. He was lean, smooth, all Spaniard. From the cocky lips and squinting eyes, Hickey made him as the kind of joker always wanting to help you play the fool. He gestured Hickey to a stuffed chair. Offered a cigaret.

Hickey lit up and started talking. The chief listened intently to Hickey's version of the story Clifford had told on the way to San Diego the night before, about this backward girl being tricked and hustled over the border, and turning up onstage at the Club de Paris. "So her brother tried to get to her, and the bouncers worked him over."

Buscamente dragged on his cigaret. "This is a terrible thing, you know. I think the brother is a mean one. He beats her too much. Or does something worse to her, huh? That's what you think too, no?"

Hickey riled, tapped his foot on the floor until it seemed he could speak without yelling. "The brother's a good kid. I'll give big odds he doesn't hit ladies. It's those caballeros at the Club de Paris who got her scared to death. Maybe on dope. Anyway, she's a prisoner there."

The chief leaned back and blew smoke, nodding earnestly. "Ah, now I see what you think. You must be a smart one to figure all this out. And you are the police from someplace. And you got a badge and everything, no? And that makes it okay for you shooting this hombre last night at the Club de Paris?"

After he cringed then recovered, Hickey took out his wallet, passed the joker his investigator's license, slowly brought out fifty dollars and held it between them.

But the chief dropped his hands to his sides. His face lunged forward. Hickey scowled—that way he wouldn't blush—and put the money away. "Look, the brother needs help, so we'll pay."

The chief walked to the door, put his hand on the knob, and said harshly, "How much do you pay, Señor?"

"Say, five hundred when you bring us the girl."

With a hiss, Buscamente opened the door and motioned for Hickey to pass. "This brother, this good kid, maybe he don't tell you about the murder she does. Now, you are going to stay on your side of the line. I'm giving you a big favor, see. Then you call me next week. Comprendes?"

The cop didn't get an answer. And when Hickey started to ask about this murder he'd accused Wendy of, with a final glower the chief said, "Ask the brother," and slammed his door.

Hickey left his business card with the fat secretary. *"Por el jefe,"* he said. Then he walked through the miserable crowd, out into the rain, ducked into the cab and gave Tito the address he had for Juan Metzger, southwest of TJ, between the coast road and the inland route to Playa Rosarito.

They clattered over about ten miles of gravel road all the way around Las Lomas, through olive groves and cotton fields, past a brick foundry, an orphanage, cattle ranches, and the headquarters of Cárdenas's army—a base of quonset huts, corrals full of horses, dirt lots jammed with trucks, cannon, artillery, a few tanks, a biplane taxiing along the dirt runway and two others gathering dust.

Hickey smoked his pipe, thought about the girl and murder. Sure, you couldn't always tell from looking which guy was a killer. But he'd bet this Wendy Rose couldn't be. There was no hardness to her, no masks. You could read all the feelings in her eyes, expressions, gestures, in the moves of her body. He thought she was the kind who'd cry about a run-over dog or from watching newsreels about the war. That cop had been blowing smoke, was all, playing for time.

One the west side of Las Lomas, at Groceria El Portal, they turned up Calle Huerta. Metzger's place was a middle-sized stucco, three or four rooms, flat-roofed, painted bright green. In the yard were citrus and avocado trees, a cactus garden, no goats, chickens, or pariah dogs. A middle-class neighborhood, rare as a blizzard in Mexico. There were screens on the windows and a screened front door. Hickey knocked at it.

A beauty appeared. Young, tall, a little stocky yet with good curves, and slender, with angular features like a Yaqui or Aztec, along with Spanish grace and hot eyes that met Hickey's straight on, telling him she was protecting somebody, or something.

Hickey asked for Juan Metzger. She opened the screen door cautiously, looked beyond him to the street. In perfect English she introduced herself as Consuelo Metzger. She ushered him to one of two padded chairs, and disappeared. Besides the chairs, a small table and desk were the only furnishings. Nothing on the walls. Two children peeked around a corner. Finally Juan Metzger stepped in.

He was a smallish, pink-faced, bulb-nosed man. He could've played the butcher or baker in a Dickens novel, Hickey mused. But his accent was thickly Germanic. He smelled of hard liquor, and carried a beer. Consuelo brought them each a Suprema and disappeared again, as if she only existed when they needed her, a guardian spirit.

"I got your name from Herman Frick," Hickey started. "Asked him for somebody who'd know the Germans around here. You guys probably stick together, being in a new place and all?"

Metzger took a long gulp of his Suprema, and tried politely to muffle his belch. Hickey began the story of Wendy Rose. He told about Clifford, the police chief, the Club de Paris with its German employees and clientele. He told Metzger he might need an insider's help. Say from a German who wanted his ticket north. If he'd help spring the girl, Hickey could buy him passage over the border, set him up with papers and everything—a guy who owed Hickey a favor worked for Immigration.

Metzger swallowed the rest of his beer, held the bottle out in front of him as if finding the table required too much thought, so he'd wait for the table to appear. He gazed at the floor and out the window, as though nothing Hickey said called for answers. Either the girl was no surprise to Metzger, or he was too drunk or weak to pity anyone but himself. Anyway, questions and propositions seemed lost on the man.

Just get him talking, Hickey thought. "What brought you folks up this way?"

Consuelo materialized, rescued the empty bottle from Metzger's hand, delivered him a full one. She stood with her back to the wall and listened to her husband launch his story.

In the remote Mexican state of Chiapas, on Metzger's coffee finca, New Year's day, he woke up thinking about Nazis. He'd tried to hold his thoughts far from Germany and its wars. But in December his cousin Franz had arrived, to give speeches for the Reich. New Year's eve, the German planters had gathered for a party, and Franz told them why the Reich would soon rule the world. He explained that their Fuehrer and the High Command had captured an icon, the sword that had pierced Christ's body the day of his crucifixion and had become, through Christ's blood, a vessel of power. It had belonged to Charlemagne, to all the Holy Roman Emperors. Now the Fuehrer held it.

While most of the Germans had laughed and derided Franz, many others praised him. By midnight, two fistfights and a near-brawl had started, and Metzger had drunk a gallon of beer.

New Year's morning, while Metzger's head still reeled, there came shouts from out front. The door rattled open. Boots stomped over the wood floor and the big, dark Federale, with whiskers like a bush, tromped into the bedroom. Perez, the jefe from Villa Flores. Consuelo jumped up and yelled at Perez to get out.

When they were alone, Metzger told Consuelo what she already knew, what they'd talked of many times in the last year. He said Perez would surely command them to leave the finca, to go and report to the Capital, where they'd be ordered to stay as long as the government willed. Their land could be stolen by the Indios and left as a socialist commune, an *ejido*. That was what had happened to Germans in Mexico, in one state after another. But Chiapas was the farthest state south, a land of its own, a wild place, and its Germans had been there for decades. Most had never seen the fatherland. So they'd been spared this far—until Franz arrived with his mad speeches.

Consuelo only wept for a minute or so. Then she lay with her cheek on her husband's lap and spoke of how, after six years she'd grown to love this place, the jungle, the smells of coffee, flowers, rain, and the mountain sky. But poor Juan, she said—all his life was here. She thanked God that he was a brave, wise man who knew how to protect her and the babies. Since last year, Juan had been sending the money they could spare to her sister in Baltimore. Now if, like the stories they heard about Queretaro and other places where Germans had been dispossessed already, the government allowed them ten days to settle business before sending them to the Capital, where they'd have to stay with other Germans in one neighborhood, under house arrest—before ten days, Consuelo, Juan, and the babies could get to a boat in Juchitán, and sail to Baja California. Where Lázaro Cárdenas would leave them in peace.

This fellow was like himself, Hickey thought, a drunken guy who'd worked hard, loved somebody, gotten kicked around. The German had only broken easier. Hickey wanted to stay for a couple more beers, console the man a little, but his watch kept ticking. At 5:40 he asked, "So can you help me . . . help the girl out?"

Metzger shrugged, sighed deeply, placed the heels of his hands on his eyes.

"Okay then, tell me about the del Montes."

The German shook his head, "No, it would be unwise for me to tell you anything."

"Unwise. You mean dangerous?"

"Unwise." Metzger looked at Consuelo. For another cervesa, for help sending Hickey on his way? Or both. Then he leaned back into the stuffed chair, stiffly as though he might as well die.

Hickey checked his watch, sighed and gave up for now. As Consuelo showed him to the door, he gave her a business card and left, thinking what a lucky fellow this Metzger was, compared to most, having a wife so rare, who kept him alive. That German better snap out of this funk, Hickey thought, before she walks, leaves him there to aim the gun at his ear, hitch his finger and pull.

Hickey asked Tito if they could make the border by six. The cabbie jammed the gas pedal. They flew over washboard, north between the hills and the sea.

As they neared the border and crossed the bridge, Hickey watched the poor squatters along the river. One guy stood all alone on the bank, shaking like he had St. Vitus dance. Many of them cramped together under cardboard roofs, five or six deep around low, smoky fires. Others were at work, heading out with gunny sacks to search for treasure, old batteries, Coke bottles, mushrooms that thrived in the rain. Hickey wanted a drink.

"You think this world's worth living in?" he asked the cabbie.

"Maybe," Tito said. "What you thinking?"

"Not when you're sober. Not this year anyway."

"Yeah. That's right, man. It's a stinking place. Hey, I got to tell you. I guess you owe me about seven more dollars."

"Stop at Coco's."

Hickey got a bottle, gulped enough to cut the chill he had, then walked back across the border with some time left before his duty. He went into the office shack, sat on the desk by the phone, and dialed Weiss's home number.

"What?" Leo snapped. Hickey could hear he was gobbling food.

"What'd you get on del Monte?"

"Guess."

"Naw. Tell it straight."

"Naw. Guess."

"Christ," Hickey muttered. "Be kind, will you."

"Right. Santiago del Monte's the richest guy in Baja. He's got eight sons. And they got cousins. The mayor, the police chief, the governor's right hand. And, Santiago plays cards with Lázaro Cárdenas, every Tuesday night."

7

The rain fell lighter. A few stars blinked above the Pacific and screeching gulls hovered over the borderland sloughs.

Hickey drank on duty for the first time, as he brooded about what to do, whether to go on chasing this girl. Besides the risk, it was costing him money. By tomorrow it might cost more than he owned. Then he could let the flyboy and his wife who'd rented his cottage buy the place. Like they kept trying to. Three times the flyboy had called saying he might go down overseas and he wanted to leave his wife a home. And maybe you ought to get rid of the place, Hickey thought. He couldn't imagine living around all those memories of Madeline and Elizabeth.

The kid was offering him some Lake Tahoe property. But even if that was real, it wouldn't be worth more than a few hundred, up there in the sticks.

Maybe he'd get the girl without paying any more, then sell the bay cottage and the Tahoe lot, and hold the money toward the day he could take Elizabeth back, somehow. He toasted that day with a taste of mescal, and for a minute his spirit glided free. Until reason complained it'd take a fortune to buy for Elizabeth what a slimy big shot like Paul Castillo could give her.

Hickey nipped the mescal, enough so that when Clifford Rose

appeared suddenly out of the dim brown light, at first Hickey thought the kid was a hallucination.

Clifford dragged a full duffel bag behind him. He wore civilian dungarees and a sweater. He gave Hickey a feeble smile, then heaved the duffel bag beside the post and squatted next to it. Looking at the ground, he asked, "You get her?"

"Not yet. You jumped ship, huh?"

Clifford let out a sigh and slumped forward, resting his arms and head on his knee, his eyes glancing up. "You won't turn me in, will you, Pop? Not till I get Wendy outa there."

"They hang deserters."

He didn't move except to shut his eyes. "Reckon they'll hang me?"

Boyle, the fink, stood nearby searching a car, maybe listening. Hickey shouldered the duffel bag, since it looked like the kid might collapse from lugging it. He pulled the kid up and led him across the two lanes around dark puddles to the office shack. Inside, Clifford flopped heavily onto the sofa. He curled up, placed hands under his head, and, shyly, he asked, "You mad at me, Pop?"

"Yeah. Mad's a good word. You're making a fool of me. First you try and get me killed. Then I'm chasing all over TJ. Now I gotta cover for a deserter. And there was a murder you forgot to tell me about?"

"Murder?"

"Yeah."

"George," he muttered. "I ain't told you about George." Hickey stared him down until the kid put a hand over his eyes. "Them guys are lying, sure. Wendy ain't killed nobody."

"What guys?"

"At the Paris Club. They said she killed that George, but it ain't so. Heck, you seen her. She never could."

"Who's George?"

"The rat that brang her down there, like I told you."

Hickey stood thinking, got out his pipe and chewed on the stem.

"You go down there?" the kid asked.

"Yeah. I tried to talk, offered to pay, but no dice. Maybe we'll grab her."

"You will, Pop? For real?"

"I'll think on it," Hickey said.

The kid's eyes dropped slowly and closed. In a few seconds his stiff body gave up and rested. And Hickey walked out, smoking, rubbing his temples, wishing he'd laid off the mescal.

He stood at his post and went through the motions but mostly let Boyle take care of business, with his hand out. A few times each night somebody would slip Boyle a favor. Between the war, with rationing and all, and the border's huddled masses seeking freedom, there was big money in law enforcement these days. Fortunes. Like toward the end of Prohibition when Hickey could've got rich as a cop in L.A. Yet while Boyle pulled in a few hundred, right beside him Hickey stood worrying about the fate of a dumb kid gone AWOL. They might forgive the boy, with the reasons he had, but you didn't count on anything from the military, except orders, skewed logic, death that didn't need to be. Just lately, in Tucson, since too many soldiers and flyers had gone catting around, families in Mextown had raised a fuss and the brass had put Mextown off limits. Then some private, drunk on the night of his eighteenth birthday, got pinched with a naked muchacha in her papa's delivery wagon. Papa owned a grocery. He screamed to the sheriff, who brought the MPs, who blabbed to some general, who ramrodded a court martial. The boy got his. Like a traitor. As if a person meant nothing except as a symbol, a lesson. The fools hung him.

Then Hickey wondered why he should stew about Clifford. He'd hardly known the kid until yesterday, and he wasn't worth any more than the thousands falling every day in Russia, or the people who dropped from malaria, pneumonia, or hunger in the Tijuana riverbed. He wasn't trying to save them, so why this Rose slut? She might be happy down there. And maybe she had killed a man. Her angel looks could sure be a lie.

One reason he worried about her was that she made him think of Elizabeth. She looked the same age, the same kind of innocent. He could've gone down Market Street or Revolución and found dozens of child-whores he could try and save. But then, nobody'd asked him to help those girls. Clifford had.

Maybe something in this business would stir his blues. Change his luck. Something had to break. So he started making plans.

Later he walked over to Lefty and said he needed a driver and the Jeep after their duty that night. He told about the girl and offered twenty dollars, but Lefty called him nuts, turned the post over to Hickey, and walked south toward Coco's licores.

At 11:00, Hickey went to the office shack, phoned Leo, raised the old man out of sleep and snapped him awake by saying there was a little girl in danger.

Leo groaned, "A charity case. Tell me I'm wrong."

"Naw, there's money in it. Say a hundred for you. And think about this. The lousy banditos snatch this little girl. Imagine what they're doing to her, then if you can go back to sleep, go ahead. If you can't sleep, get down here pretty soon."

"Night, night, Tom."

The kid lay on the couch with arms wrapped around himself, snoring softly as a purr. As Hickey walked out, he wondered if Clifford knew how to shoot or just how to wave a gun around. You couldn't be sure, the way they rushed them through boot camp and sped them off to war.

He went back to his post and stood figuring, laying off the mescal. Boyle got into a fight with two rowdy civilians. A big kid jumped on his back and rode him around. Hickey had to rap the boy with his club, though he would've rather conked Boyle.

The graveyard MPs arrived late, and not far behind them, Weiss's Packard rolled in. Carrying a thermos, a cigaret hanging from his lip, Leo got out and faced Hickey nose to nose. "I rue the day we met," he growled, then yawned and hacked a cough.

They walked to the office shack and Hickey told his partner about Clifford and the girl, and his plan. The old man lit a smoke, flopped into a chair. "Hearken to this, Tom. I'll go on down and take a look. If it's a sure thing, maybe we'll do it. Otherwise, I'm out."

Hickey nodded. He tapped the kid, shook him and kept

shaking harder. When Clifford finally roused and sat up, Leo handed him the thermos. They passed it around, while Hickey strapped on the shoulder holster and automatic under a pilot's jacket he borrowed off the shelf. Then he fitted Clifford with the big wooden MP coat so a Colt would stick under his belt without showing the bulge.

The kid eyed Leo warily. The old guy didn't inspire confidence. He looked slow, dumpy, with a graying walrus mustache and wrinkled eyes. His hat was cocked sideways.

A horn beeped several times before the others stepped outside and found the Jeep, with Lefty behind the wheel slugging down a beer. "Changed my mind," he said. "Give me thirty bucks and I'm in."

Leo eyed the Jeep. "Hell with this contraption. Let's take a real car with a roof and everything."

"We might need to drive back across the river. If del Monte alerts the cops, they might roadblock the bridge."

"Gimme the scoop once more, Pop," Lefty said.

"All you gotta do is drive." Hickey passed a twenty. They piled into the Jeep and Lefty wheeled south. They crossed the bridge, bounding at forty mph into the dark with the browned headlamps barely shining ten feet ahead, and turned onto Revolución. Suddenly the drizzle quit. For a second you could vaguely see a shifting of the clouds, before the rain came in great walloping gobs. They hunkered under their arms, except Lefty who sped up, cussing all the way. To beat the stalled traffic he ran over a curb, raced through a parking lot, an alley, another parking lot, and crashed back off the curb. Sailors, pimps, drug pushers, whores, and street kids all ran for cover from the rain, while Lefty zoomed into the wrong lane, hung a left on Calle Siete, and flew downhill toward the Club de Paris.

At the base of the hill where he pulled over, the mud reached the hubs of some cars. The four men jumped out and ditched under a balcony of the Ritz hotel. Leo coughed and leaned against the wall. He jabbed Hickey with an elbow and grumbled, "If I die of pneumonia, I'm taking you with me."

"Swell, now let's snatch the girl and get back on land." Hickey lifted his hat and shook it drier. "Okay—Lefty pulls the Jeep right over there." He stepped out into the rain and pointed around the corner, over the vacant lot to a point across the road from the rear wall of the Club de Paris. "Just wait there, make sure it'll start any second. And keep the seats bailed out."

"In the rain?" Lefty moaned. "I wanta go inside."

"Give the wimp a parasol." Leo lit a smoke, crumbled the empty pack and sailed it into the Jeep, fifteen feet through the rain.

"Leopold, you go in the joint and wait till she comes on for the act. She'll dance a while, then do this routine of letting everybody touch her. I guess she always does that, right, Clifford?"

The kid snapped around with fierce, red eyes, and studied each of the men. Finally he nodded and Hickey went on, "When she's, say, three guys from the end of the line, you slip out and get around back fast. There'll be a door on the west end of the rear wall. It leads to the back room, where the girls dress. We'll be in cover as close to the door as we can get." Hickey laid his arm on Clifford's shoulder. "By then she'll be in the back room. At least I hope to Christ she will."

"What if she ain't there?" Lefty asked. "Suppose she goes for a drink?"

"Then we hand it over to you, smart guy."

Leo turned and started lumbering toward the club but Hickey caught him. "Keep an eye out for a little tough they call Mofeto, the "skunk," big hat, thin mustache." With a nod, Leo trudged on.

"The old guy oughta drive," Lefty said. "I'll go in the bar. They'll spot him. He don't look like the kind that goes in there."

"Move it." Hickey gave Lefty a nudge. He led the kid out around the corner to the vacant lot, where their feet sank deep and squished loudly. A few times Clifford got stuck. Broad shouldered, a farmboy's arms, half Hickey's age, still he slogged through the mud like somebody decrepit. They might as well hang the kid as send him to war this way, Hickey thought. He'd lean right into the first bullet.

They stepped on rubble, broken hunks of concrete and old

adobe. A trail of concrete chunks laid into the mud led into a swampy little grove of tule weeds, where they came upon a family of Indians sprawled across each other, sleeping beneath a roof of woven tules. Clifford stopped to gaze at them but Hickey pushed him on. The path ended. They broke through the last wall of tules and stepped into the clearing behind the Club de Paris. The backstage door stood about thirty feet away. Clifford kept walking blindly ahead, but Hickey grabbed and held him back.

The closest cover to the door was a pile of fermenting garbage that even in the rain stank of ammonia. Hickey decided to stay where they were, crouching in the dark, a little sheltered by the tules, and try not to wake the Indians who slept about twenty feet behind. The downpour would help give them cover. He told Clifford to stay put. He crept out to look around the garbage pile, and caught sight of the front end of Lefty's Jeep. Between the garbage and the heap of another collapsed building lay a straight, clear run to the road from the backstage door. Only a hundred feet of mud to slow them down.

Hickey turned back to the tules and squatted beside Clifford. He strained to read his watch. 2:45. The night before, Wendy Rose had come on about now, and should've finished around 3:15. In Mexico, you didn't count on schedules, but she'd always be the last act, that was sure, to hold the spenders there.

They stayed quiet. The rain pelted and bathed them. Clifford drew loud, gasping breaths. Hickey had to stand often and straighten his legs. He wished for a smoke. He sipped mescal and passed it to Clifford. Time passed strangely. In a place that dark and wet, your senses lose contact and for a while each minute seems twenty, then your mind sails away and ten minutes can flash by instantly. When Hickey's mind sailed away, it flew to a brown city street in New Jersey. His daughter was out walking. Hoodlums slouched around, whistling the way they used to at her mother, pawing her with their eyes.

He snapped back to life and said, "You don't talk much."

"You told me to hush."

"Good soldier." He mussed the kid's hair. "Well, if somebody draws on you, then what?"

"I blast him, Pop."

"Think you can do it okay?"

"Can't wait," Clifford muttered, then sat a minute quietly. "Reckon that makes me a killer."

"Well," Hickey said, "let's don't start blasting everybody in sight. An eye for an eye, maybe you're not a killer. Some guys want two eyes, or three, or a bucketful."

"I never shot nobody," Clifford mumbled. "You done it a lot?"

"A couple times."

He drew his gun and checked it, holding it under his coat to keep it dry. Clifford did the same. Then they stayed quiet, listening, watching, until Hickey said, "Ol' Leo's probably in there with a muchacha on his lap. Drinking Irish coffee."

Clifford lunged toward Hickey. Up close he looked cross-eyed and deranged. Far different than yesterday. It seemed they'd better finish this business quick, before the kid cracked all the way and turned maniac, or dumb like his sister.

"The old guy won't mess up, will he, Pop?"

"Naw. He's sharp, you'll see."

The watch read 3:20. The rain fell softer. Hickey listened close for the saxaphone from inside, but all he heard was some men's rough laughter up the street, and the grinding of cars through the mud. A minute later he made out voices of gringos leaving the Club de Paris and taxi drivers shouting at them. Soon motors revved and tires whooshed away. Now he started to worry. In the distance a siren wailed.

He faked a chuckle. "Maybe one of those señoritas gave Leo a heart attack."

"No," Clifford moaned.

Hickey patted the kid's gun hand and they waited. A little past 3:30, he said, "I'm going to look out front."

Before he could move he saw a man walk fast around the corner of the building, and disappear behind the pile of rubble. Faster than Leo would care to move. Now the guy hurried across the street— Hickey caught a glimpse through the space between the garbage and the rubble. Maybe Leo was being watched, hustling to lose

43

somebody. But too long passed. Hickey drew the automatic. The kid pulled his revolver.

They ran to the garbage pile, stopped still, and heard footsteps sloshing around the other side. Moving toward the sound, Hickey tried to step with the noise of the other man's feet, but Clifford got out of time. The crunching of feet sounded loud as kettle drums. Hickey flashed his gun out and jumped around the pile.

With a bead on Hickey's nose, old Leo held his ground. And after a hacking cough, he muttered, "You oughta meet your doom for sending me into that stinkhole." Then he holstered his pistol. "On the other hand, I found out my critter's still alive." He looked over at Clifford Rose. "Easy kid, I didn't see her. She's gone."

Hickey stamped the mud.

"Yeah, I asked around," Leo said. "Gone, and nobody's saying where to."

The kid stood with downcast eyes and his pistol half-raised, pointed near Leo's feet, so the old man growled, "And that's only half the good news. You're gonna love the rest. Take a look over here."

They followed him across the road. The rain had lightened again, nearly to a drizzle. Hickey looked around, wondered where the Jeep had gone and why Lefty was sitting there on an old tire casing. Why he wasn't wearing his helmet or arm band. Lefty's head swayed loosely. He socked his own leg a few times then looked up and said, "I was sitting over there in that doorway, see. There was a couple greasers, nice enough-looking Joes. Class dressers. Spoke English. Had a bottle of some stuff. We got talking about muchachas. And then one of 'em had something you snoot up your nose. I give it a try. Pretty soon, bam." He put his hands on his head, slapped water off his face. "Let's get outa here. What'd you guys do with the Jeep?"

He sized up Hickey. Then Leo. And the kid. He gaped and threw an arm high. "Oh! Not the Jeep. Fuck! I'm dead. What'll I tell the lieutenant? Hey, they'll send me to goddamn New Guinea." He yelled, "Pop, you—" and lunged for Hickey—who shoved him face into the mud. Lefty rolled over and socked the ground.

44

The rain quit. A half-round moon appeared behind a shadowy cloud, straight overhead. The four men started wallowing up the road with Leo in the lead, past a few Mexicans who'd appear, then vanish fast as Consuelo Metzger, toward Calle Siete where the taxis waited. Hickey stopped once to check on Clifford.

The kid's arms were wrapped around his chest, squeezing his shoulders, and his head was cocked—he looked goofy and talked to himself without making a sound.

So Hickey gripped the kid's arm. "We'll find her. Mañana."

The cabs had left Calle Siete. Lefty spotted one, a couple blocks down, near the river. The red-and-pink Chrysler limo. They plodded that way, past the Club de Paris.

When Tito saw them coming he jumped off the hood, ran a few feet up the hill, and with a grin, he called out, "Hey, you heros. Give me a help here."

All five of them pushed, finally heaved the Chrysler a foot or so to higher, drier ground. Tito shook their hands. To Leo, Lefty, and the kid, he said, "I'm going to drive you for half-price, anytime, forever."

The other three climbed into the limo while the cabbie pulled Hickey aside, and whispered, "I can help you find La Rosa, man. For very cheap, you'll see."

8

Back in Kansas, in the dry spring of 1929, a doctor said Wendy Rose would never learn to think right. The prettiest child around was a moron—he said you could tell by her wandering eyes, and because at four years she'd only spoken a few words, and now she'd forgot them.

Her ma fell to the floor and bawled. Her pa went out to drink and that night he started cursing God the way he'd been cussing the bankers who were stealing his farm.

Clifford Rose was just six years old that year when his ma got quiet and his pa got meaner. He didn't understand much. He knew they left Kansas when they didn't want to and he had to be careful with Wendy and protect her from things.

Now he sat on a harbor dock right next to a tuna clipper just back from delivering gasoline, rockets, mortars, and vegetables to the South Pacific. Staring at the oily water, he finally understood what had happened to his folks, why they changed, why his ma gave up and Pa got worse. When you're supposed to keep care of somebody, he thought, and evil comes, you can try and shuck off the blame but it won't go. At least not when you know, like Pa and him, there was times you hurt her. You can cuss or do like Ma, get all squeezed inside, don't talk, just stand and bear the shame. You can swear to kill the rat that got Wendy. But the poison in you just won't go away.

As Clifford sat waiting for dawn, he wanted to jump and sink beneath the oily water. Even though he figured Pop would help him. He thought Pop was the best man he ever knew. You couldn't find a man in two hundred that would risk his skin for folks that weren't his, like Pop did. He'd get Wendy back. That was pretty sure. Pop knew how to do things. But him nor nobody could fix Wendy when they got her, Clifford thought. Nothing could fix what the rat and those Mexicans had done.

Clifford felt shamed to be a man. You put a man with a girl like Wendy—first, maybe he'd cherish her but then something would flip him over and evil'd pour out. So Ma got smacked anytime she disagreed, if Pa was in one of his moods. Clifford used to hear Ma weeping, Wendy howling, from the room where his folks and sister slept when she was still a baby. Pa loved his family, still he belted them whenever the devil said so. Anybody weak, gentle, men would protect her, knock her bloody, buy her fancy clothes or kill her, depending how they felt that day.

He remembered 1934. They moved outside Reno when Pa got steady work as a ranch hand. There was a neighbor girl called Laura Kelly. Ugly, with a pocked face, black hair all matted, old, grimy dresses. But she had a comely ass she'd switch around and give the men her cockeyed grin so farmhands walked her down the road. Folks talked like she was less than a dog when she never harmed a soul. There was nothing bad in her. Just dumb and happy, and nobody kept watch on her. Her ma and pa were like herself.

A few times Clifford's ma saw the girl and said, "That there's what Wendy's gonna look like, lest we keep her holy."

The Kelly girl had three babies. Nobody owned up. She carried the babies around, hugging and cooing with them. She never got mean to them nor anybody, Clifford thought, so it didn't figure how one day at the grocery men started pushing and slapping at her. They got crazy, bloodied her head, tore off most of her clothes. Busted some front teeth. After that you never saw her anymore—

47

just heard her moaning like a hound some nights as she walked the road.

That was a reason Ma used when she talked Pa into keeping Wendy back from school, because a girl like her wasn't fit to meet up with the world. Anyhow, Pa said schools were for regular people.

Wendy didn't leave the ranch except with her folks. They'd take her to the grocery, the feed store, the church, and once after Pa got an old truck they drove forty miles to Lake Tahoe where Clifford landed a brown trout long as his arm. Wendy gaped at the blue glass water and the green-and-black jagged mountains rising to the stars. It was during one of the good times, when Wendy talked some, held her mind on real things without always dreaming off. She asked if this place was Heaven, and Ma said yep, it must be. They drove around the whole lake and ate sandwiches on a beach and swam in icy water. They were drinking soda in Tahoe City when a man approached them trying to sell land. Wendy got so excited that Pa walked off with the man and came back in a minute saying he'd bought her a place. Wendy believed him. She didn't know about lies. It was the greatest day Wendy ever lived—she said that a lot of times after. Even two years later, when they were at church she told a preacher, "We been to Heaven, got us a piece of land there."

She always smiled, too much, Pa said. You could warn her that men got crazy but she'd forget and smile at most anybody who looked her way and if it was men they'd get ideas. Folks who didn't know her never could suspect she was a moron. She didn't act stupid. For weeks she'd be talking, learning things, keeping her eyes on what was real, until Pa would get raging over something and take her out back, out of sight by the river, to whip her, he said. He might've whipped her when she was little, before she got her figure. After that, Clifford believed, he punished her a different way too. Everytime she got punished, Wendy stopped talking again. Still, she didn't act stupid, or smart either, but just like Wendy, quiet as a sleepwalker and with the brightest eyes, the softest touch. Nothing goofy-looking about her.

She didn't have friends and Clifford supposed she got lonely, but she didn't act so. She puttered around and played with the cats and sang or hummed to herself and the horses while she brushed them down. She learned to cook some and to clean the house and tend the garden and Ma finally taught her to read one Bible story out of a book made for six-year-olds. Ma taught her an easy solitaire game. The problem with trying to teach her, she'd keep her mind on the learning awhile, then her eyes would drift and she'd be smiling about things nobody else knew.

Ma got TB in 1936 but dying took her two years. About halfway through that time Pa started getting headaches that turned him meaner still. One time, after Ma died, all Wendy did was not hear him yell, and he was leading her out back. Clifford tried to stop them. Pa smacked him, caught him with the bone of an elbow right beside his ear, so Clifford let loose, ran for the woodpile and grabbed up a board. When Pa chased him down and lunged to clobber him again, the old man got a rib busted.

It was lying there, crippled up, nothing much to do but think, which broke the old man's spirit. Made the rage go inside. A tumor started growing in his brain. It killed him, about a year after Ma died.

All he left was the rusty pickup and a brokendown tractor that Clifford gave to a neighbor in trade for the deed to ninety feet of rocky shore at Lake Tahoe. That was something Pa had had meant to do for three years.

Clifford was sixteen. He stopped going to school and took Pa's ranch job. Wendy followed him around. She rode along on back of the horse when he went out mending fences. In winter she rode on the wagon, helping him carry feed to the pastures. He taught her fishing and throwing baseballs and poker.

Most Saturdays they drove into Reno for a movie or a soda. He could've left her in care of the Meyers who owned the ranch, but he would've felt bad, leaving her there like a nobody. In town the men gawked at her. He told her not to smile at them, but she might forget. She got whistles and sometimes a fellow walked over and asked her for a date. Clifford had to say no and maybe the guy said dirty things about them. Then Clifford took Wendy home and came back the next day alone—his nose got bent so he only had one breathing nostril and his jaw still popped when he opened wide, from those fights.

Meantime, Wendy kept forgetting to be modest. Like she'd call from her bath and ask Clifford to bring more hot water, especially in winter when the water nearly froze as you poured. He could've said no or gone in without looking but he didn't because he wanted to see her, he dreamed about it, how she'd flutter her fingers on the top of the water and smile at him. Then his skin caught fever, his balls felt like jumping toads. Even so, for more than a year he didn't touch her, before the devil got his way.

A cold night, when you couldn't find a single place in their house where the wind didn't blow through some crack, he followed her from the bath tub over to her bed. She kept smiling, whispering sounds that didn't make words. As long as he touched her gently, rubbed soft and slow, she let him do anything. But if he clutched her, made a sudden jump or noise, she tightened into wood and whimpered.

It was only a few times, before he got too afraid she'd tell somebody, and he saw visions of a cavern where creeping and flying things attacked you in the darkness and the only ways out led to ditches you had to cross but they were full of boiling water. After that, even when she wanted him to hold her, he stayed firm-hearted. Two years before the Army called him.

They had no business calling him up, Clifford believed, and he told the draft board about Wendy. But they took him anyway.

He should've put her in the Catholic home except Ma was a Baptist. She would've sneaked back from the grave with fiery breath before she let her baby go with those nuns. Besides, Wendy begged to stay on the ranch to clean house for the Meyers and Mrs. Meyers was offering to give her a big room and teach her woman things, so Clifford could go off and fight the Japs. And home and Clifford were all she had. And it looked like she didn't believe him when he promised to come back. Probably in less than a year they'd finish the Japs and Nazis, he supposed. But Wendy didn't know time exactly—a month and tomorrow weren't much different to her. And what if he didn't come back? At the home they'd sure make her a nun and Clifford hated the thought of that. And she might tell the nuns about how Clifford used to hold her, how they lay cinched together all night those times. Besides, she'd always been half a prisoner. Maybe one day there'd come along a man to protect her and give her things that regular folks get. Somebody who'd cherish her and not mind too much that her brain wasn't just so, and who could forgive Clifford for losing to the devil. A man full of good. Like Pop.

He'd probably done right to leave her with the Meyers except that he shouldn't have left her at all. Most any man could fight a war but there was nobody like him to keep care of Wendy. That sure proved out. Not two months later.

Most of what happened he'd pieced together when he got leave, after Mr. Meyers called. Only a few parts of the story stayed missing, like he still didn't know what'd driven her away from the Meyers. Somebody scared her, that was sure, and made her need Clifford.

He hitchhiked to Reno and followed her trail, found she'd sneaked out one night and got on a bus. Then George sat beside her. He was tall and had skin way darker than hers but lighter than most Mexicans. He wore a bright red fancy shirt, and a baseball cap with the letters SD. In Bishop, the rat was drunk. The driver saw him slap Wendy. The driver said he'd have kicked them off except he figured it'd go bad for the girl, then they left the bus in San Bernardino. Four days later, somebody saw them getting on the San Diego bus.

The trail ended there. Nobody at the San Diego depot remembered seeing her get off, and folks most always remembered Wendy. He gave a photo to the dispatcher who showed it to all the drivers and finally one said, yeah, he saw her get off at the border, with a loud Italian guy in a silver shirt.

In TJ Clifford showed her picture to a cabbie—right away he said, "Oh, si, la Rosa Blanca."

Now Clifford took from his pocket the pint of mescal Pop had

51

left with him. He drained the last sip and threw the bottle hard into the water. Its ripple made rainbow colors. The bottle slowly filled and sank beneath the greasy water. He felt the sun on his back and he watched it flash on the harbor. He stared hard and soon Wendy's face came back like it was when they sat in the Paris Club two weeks ago. She was naked, right there beside him in a chair, and a hundred men leered at them. She had stopped in the middle of her dance and come down off the stage. She had sat beside him and touched his knee. The first thing she said was, "You are far away, my Clifford."

He gave her his coat. She laid it neatly on the table. He sat trembling with shame. "Put it on, Sis, and we'll leave, right now."

"Oh, oh," she whispered. "No, because George is dead."

"Well then, that's the only thing'll save him from me. You don't got some other rat keeping you here, do you?"

"My Clifford," she said patiently, "you forget—when George is dead somebody has to get punished. Don't you know—somebody stabbed George." Clifford shook his head, bewildered. She stroked his hand with one finger. "If you kill somebody, you have to stay in hell for—two years."

He jumped out of the chair, leaned up to her face. "Put on my coat, please, Sis."

He ordered her and begged. Her eyes just kept drooping sadder. She said, "The devil hates me, my Clifford. I can feel. Do you hate me?" Her eyes wandered up and she whispered, "There is a war, you know."

Finally he screamed, "What're you talking about?"

She moaned, sprang up, ran to the stage and away through the curtains. The moment he started after her, a stick whacked his gut, then his head, and the room started floating away. He kept yelling, "Sis! Wendy!" while the Mexicans belted him harder.

Then came days in the infirmary. But he still couldn't figure what held her there, and he sure didn't believe she'd killed the rat. Whoever killed George must've tricked her somehow. Taught her to lie and be secret like she never knew how before. Clifford wouldn't have a speck of mercy for the man that had deformed his sister—this Wendy onstage, who all these men got crazy for, she wasn't half as beautiful as she used to be. They must've loosed a new part of her brain and it came out bad, he thought. She'd never be like before. Clifford wouldn't either. For a minute he tried to raise the guts to drown in the oily water. But that was wrong. He couldn't die until they got her free.

9

Hickey liked to walk, hard, early mornings, to burn the poison out of him. He strode three miles inland and rested on a bus bench at the top of C Street where 25th crossed, on the outskirts of downtown.

From there he gazed east across the brown hills, canyons, rolling mountains, and valleys that looked like Hollywood when he was a boy, when they moved there after his old man lost a fortune on cattle, and disappeared, to kill himself in the last big war, when his mother was a seamstress to stars like Mary Pickford—before she started preaching Christian Science and ran her patrons off.

He thought about Wendy Rose and knew the Mexicans had more at stake than the few hundred a night the Club de Paris could make off her. Down there you had everything or nothing, and guys like del Monte had it all. Maybe she knew too much about something. Or del Monte planned to keep her for his own.

He considered going straight to the top. Lázaro Cárdenas. An ex-Presidente, hero of the revolution, now general of the army of the frontera—if Cárdenas ordered del Monte or anybody to set the girl free, the man would jump like a kangaroo. But Leo said Cárdenas was pals with del Monte. He might give a different order, and Hickey would disappear. Cárdenas had to be the last resort.

The air had gotten crisp, dry, and sparkling without a particle of fog or haze. Beyond the city, across the bay, sat the dock where Hickey and Leo once dropped their life savings into a dealership for new and used sailboats, the business that brought them to San Diego when Leo retired and Hickey quit the LAPD. In six months the business sank.

Hickey sighed, gazed at Islas Coronados far out to sea, which looked so close you could swim there. It was just past dawn, and the ocean beamed more golden than the sun. The light stung his eyes—he'd gotten only three hours sleep before the drunks came crashing into the barracks and he'd snapped awake. He needed food and coffee. Then he'd go down alone—the kid would just make trouble—and find out where the hell they took her. Tijuana wasn't so big. And while he was in the neighborhood, tonight he'd go see Luz.

The bus arrived and Hickey climbed on. At Horton Plaza he bought a pastry and transferred. In San Ysidro he chugged two cups of thick Mexican coffee. He changed, in the office shack, from his uniform to the gray suit. Then he filled his pipe and lit up, dialed the phone.

Sent from one number to the next three times, he finally reached Al Smythe—another ex-LA cop. When Hickey knew him, he was on the take from bootleggers. Now he was an Army lieutenant in ordnance, at the supply depot on the pier at the foot of Broadway. In charge of disbursing small weapons and vehicles.

Hickey said, "Al, this one'll give you a laugh. See, I misplaced a Jeep down in TJ."

When Smythe finished chortling, he said, "That'll cost you two hundred."

Hickey promised it tomorrow, then hung up, took paper from a drawer and wrote, "Lefty, If I'm not back for duty, sign me in and cover for me. Promise Boyle twenty dollars and he won't snitch. Do it good and I'll take the fall for losing the Jeep. Or else you better pack for New Guinea."

He folded the note, taped it to Lefty's locker, and stepped outside.

55

Beyond the sloughs lay a Swedish-flagged merchant ship carrying troops; soldiers hanging over the rails. It was probably bound for the Solomons. The ship Clifford ought to be on. You could almost see the soldiers' eyes through the sparkling air.

Already, before 9 A.M., the line of trucks had backed up near the bridge waiting to haul Mexican produce to the Navy ships. A cloud of seagulls hovered, cawing, diving at the open trucks. Hickey stepped across the three traffic lanes, turned south through the Mexican entrance gate, saluted the Mexican guard. Then he walked in tire tracks, where the mud had already caked dry, to beneath the river bridge where the red-and-pink limo waited.

Tito lay sprawled in back asleep. Hickey rapped on the window. The cabbie sprang up, gazed around and rubbed his eye. He put on his sunglasses and straightened his bright red Hawaiian shirt. Finally he rolled down the window. "I been working hard boss, making me tired." He rummaged through papers on the floor, came up with a stack of flyers. GIRLS! COCKTAILS! BEER! LA ROSA BLANCA! CLUB DE PARIS!—In the middle was a grainy, dark picture of Wendy Rose.

"I been asking around. Don't look like she's anymore in TJ. Maybe they take her down to Ensenada or over the mountains, but we can find her. Soon as you give me one hundred dollars." He eyed Hickey for a second. "Okay, sixty."

"Twenty."

"Hey, you don't get no other cabbies, just me. El Mofeto tells them already, don't talk with you, don't take you nowhere. So they don't. Nobody else can be that crazy. But I don't go crazy for twenty dollars." Hickey slipped him forty.

On the drive he worried about Clifford. Last night he'd told the kid they should meet this morning at ten by the tuna boats. The way Clifford looked, ragged and looney, the Shore Patrol could nab him for suspicion. Or he might run amok, shooting pimps on Broadway, out of twisted revenge. He might go looking for Wendy on his own. Hickey had taken the kid's gun away. But there were a million guns in San Diego.

He told the cabbie to stop at the telephone office. He went in and called Leo, reached him in bed, asked him to meet Clifford at ten and keep an eye on him.

"Only if you quit giving my number to jerks," Leo growled. "A sap name of Metzger woke me up an hour ago. Said to give Señor Hickey this message. 'Leave me alone and go to hell,' I think he said. The guy's a mumbler."

Something had got Metzger squirming, Hickey thought. The German could've woke from his stupor just long enough to panic and do something ignorant like call Hickey and give him orders. Unlikely, though. Neither did it sound like a trick to lure Hickey back down there. All Metzger had to do was invite him.

After a drink or two, and a look around, he'd pay the fellow another visit.

There were about thirty strip clubs in the two paved miles of Avenida Revolución. Between the curio and tailor shops. Beside the feed and tack store. In the cellar of a jewelry shop where you might find stolen diamonds you read about last week in the *San Diego Tribune.* Most of the clubs were dark, smelly joints. A few looked like pool halls or cafes; they had big windows from which the younger whores could wave at passersby. It wasn't the kind of street where gentle folks went strolling. Except on business, folks like the del Montes kept to Las Lomas. From where Hickey stood on Revolución, you could look over an open mercado and see the Lomas—the hot springs, mansions, and thoroughbred ranches, the race track with its palm trees high above everything.

At 4th and Revolución, Hickey stepped into the Climax Bar, ordered a shot of mescal. A half-dozen sailors slouched over a table near the stage where a leggy, orange-haired woman performed a belly dance with her back turned. Hickey didn't question the sailors. They looked too drunk to tell a white girl from a green, three-headed Martian. He gulped the mescal and showed a handbill to the bartender, who waited for a tip and said she might be at La Caverna, two blocks up the street.

The Cavern was at the bottom of a flight of crumbling steps. As you stepped down, the passage narrowed. The door looked like a small hole. The floor was caked with an inch of red dirt. You could see cracks in the walls where mud had poured in. The room was all underground, dark, clammy, and stinking of mold. The only drinkers were a few broken old whores who waved sadly at Hickey and motioned for him to come near. A short, skinny one with woolen hair climbed onto the little stage in the corner. To a scratchy honky-tonk melody, she started wiggling stiffly, pulling off her clothes. Her belly was a patchwork of bruises.

The bartender only shook his head at the handbill. Hickey ordered drinks for several whores. They dragged him to a booth and gathered around. One nibbled his ear. Another squeezed his thigh. When the music stopped, the skinny one who'd been dancing came off the stage, plucked the hat off Hickey's head and set it on her mop of thick hair. She kissed his bald place. Her pointed nipple kept brushing his shoulder.

"*Tu estas muerto,*" she whispered. "Dead man."

He questioned her with a stare, got a grin for an answer. So he passed around the handbill. The women studied it, gave him sour looks, made scornful clucking noises, and the oldest of them said, "You want a little white girl, cabrón, why you coming to Mexico?"

Hickey stood up just as Tito appeared in the doorway, and suddenly the dancer started yelling. She called Tito a queer, motherfucking goat. The cabbie only hissed. As Hickey followed him out of there, she yelled something after them. On the sidewalk, Tito grumbled, "*Puta loca.*"

"Friend of yours?"

"One time, she was. But I got to tell you, hombre, we better look out. That one's a sister of El Mofeto, and her brother don't like us both."

Hickey didn't mention she'd called him a dead man. But he felt a touch lightheaded. In the air he caught a whiff of something that smelled like doom. Maybe he needed a different medicine, besides mescal. They crossed the street to a grille with sidewalk tables and both ordered tacos al carbón. Up and down the block, gringo soldiers and sailors came surfacing out of the clubs, grimacing at the crystalline sky. Junk cars crashed over the potholes.

A gang of Indian kids stopped to beg. Hickey gave them a few dimes and they walked on, searching the gutters.

The waitress brought a stack of buttered tortillas, and Hickey asked the cabbie to tell him more about this Mofeto.

"Okay. I know that loco a long time. He's the worst, hombre, no lie." Tito ripped a tortilla and hissed, "I saw him cut the head off the Virgin—a little statue, you know. For no reason. At his mother's house while we eating dinner. It was Christmas, man, and he laughs. Ay, diablo."

At the end of the block, a two-year-old red Chevrolet coupe pulled up and a strange man got out. He might've looked at home in London, Paris, Berlin, but not here. It wasn't just the blondness that made him look unusual, but his shiny brown shoes and the fit of his brown cotton suit. Like a guy who combed his eyebrows. He glanced their way, then stepped into a curio shop.

Tito growled, "Aléman."

"Aleh what?"

The cabbie pointed over where the slick guy had been. "German, that's what I said."

"Don't point."

The tacos arrived. The slick German came out of the curio shop and stood, straightening the knot of his tie. A couple of minutes later, a white Ford Model A roadster pulled up to the curbside, hitting a puddle and spurting up mud. It almost splashed the German. He jumped back and barked at the Mexican who got out of the roadster and came around to meet him. The Mexican wore boots and a straw cowboy hat with the brim curled up the way gringos wore them. The German only said a few words, then turned and walked to his Chevy, and drove off. At the first corner he took a right. Up the road to Las Lomas.

The Mexican entered the curio shop. Hickey caught the guy staring at him through the window.

He dropped a few bills on the table, and he and the cabbie got up and strolled down the block toward the limo, keeping an eye on the curio shop. He didn't see the taxi until it screeched to a stop beside him.

Clifford Rose jumped out. He ran to Hickey and then pulled up short. His jaw quivered. "Why'd you leave me there, Pop?"

Hickey sighed and caught a deep breath of the fine air over the lump in his throat. He felt so sorry for the kid it shamed him. "I sent Leo to get you."

"Yeah, but he tried to keep me up there."

"Where is he?"

"I don't know," Clifford said meekly. "I socked him and got away."

"Hey, you don't sock an old guy. Understand?"

Clifford slumped and stared at the ground. Hickey gave him a shove toward the limo.

They cruised north on Revolución, and Clifford asked, "Where we going? You got a clue?"

Hickey didn't answer, but wondered how to tell the kid in a few words that to search you didn't just follow clues. Like in all pursuits, you kept your eyes drifting around, because the view straight ahead was only about a tenth of the world. Besides, Hickey wasn't only seeking Wendy Rose. Same as every man except the few content ones, he was looking for what had gone wrong, and the wild card that could set him free.

Hickey stopped at the Long Bar, which ran the whole block between Calles Uno and Dos and was jammed with gringo troops. He left a message for Luz, with her brother, a waiter.

Now they'd go see Juan Metzger. The cabbie turned right, started down toward the river, and cut back uphill at Calle Siete. A block past the Club de Paris, Hickey noticed the square two-story building, painted blistering yellow except where HELL was block-lettered in white over the open front door. He slapped Tito's arm, pointed to the curb.

Juan Metzger, he was thinking. The German had told him to go to hell.

Hickey stared at the queer sight and wondered how he'd passed here before and hardly paid it any mind. Finally they got out and started toward the door, but the kid halted, gaping at the big white letters. Hickey backtracked to get him.

"I hope she ain't here," Clifford mumbled.

Hickey nudged him along through the door and to a table. The air seemed reddish and full of incense. The place looked clean, with good light through high windows and from overhead bulbs. On one wall hung a giant portrait of some tough medieval king. A small crystal chandelier hung in a corner over a round oaken table. A heavy green curtain, fringed in gold, draped around a small stage. There were no dancers now and only one customer, a cop at the bar. Across the room sat two whores. A light-skinned mestizo in a wig of flaxen hair, and a real blonde. Maybe Dutch. But she talked fast Spanish.

"They go for blondes here," Hickey said.

The kid gazed up, glanced vaguely around. You reckon Wendy's a whore.

Hickey grabbed and squeezed the kid's shoulder. "Get that dirt outa your mind. Understand?"

Finally the kid looked square at him and drew back, let his frown ease away. "Yes, sir."

Hickey got up, went to the bar and stood beside the cop, a big, pale, stubble-faced guy with sour breath. When the bartender came over, Hickey ordered a mescal, a beer for Clifford. Then he laid a handbill on the bar, and motioned toward Clifford. "That's her youngest brother. She's got seven more. They're all Marines, and they got friends, and they're gonna ride through this town like Zapata unless the girl's back in San Diego tonight."

The cop growled in Spanish to the Indian bartender, who squinted at the handbill and finally said, "I going to get el Señor Zarp."

"Bring the drinks first," Hickey said.

While the Indian poured, Tito came in and sat alone near the stage. The whores moved to sit with Clifford. The Dutch girl touched his arm. He brushed her hand away. She laughed brashly but cut her laugh short when the patrón stepped into the room. He was a big man, dark in a nordic way—a hulking, brooding fellow—he reminded Hickey of something he'd read about the ancient Celts, that only in battle could their spirits, besieged on all sides by demons, find a sort of repose. He wore a soiled, rumpled white shirt, chino pants, the sandals of a campesino, and, on a leather thong around his neck, a cameo or something; Hickey couldn't make out the face, but it shone bright as its golden frame. His black hair, eyebrows, and mustache grew bushy and wild. His eyes were quick, small, dark green. He walked straight at Hickey, and his voice rumbled, "You are?"

With a scowl, Hickey reached for his wallet, passed a business card that the man looked over. Then Hickey motioned toward Clifford. "That guy's La Rosa's brother." He pointed to the handbill on the bar, and started talking—hoping the big man would take his side and use some of the power you could see he had on these Mexicans. Hickey spilled everything he could think of about Wendy Rose's mind, about how a rat named George had got to her, muscled her, scared her, hooked her into some kind of slavery at the Club de Paris, and maybe got himself killed. Hickey talked too much and knew it. When he stopped and gazed around, there was Tito watching from a dim corner by the stage. And Clifford, with his eyes fixed on Hickey, hands set to push off from the arms of his chair. The whores had stopped their business and stared at Hickey too. Then somebody came in from the street. The cowboy Mexican who'd met the German on Revolución stopped near the doorway, staring like the others.

Señor Zarp brought a big open hand down on the bar. He gave a contemptuous smile and seemed to expand until he looked like a dark god hovering over them. Then he roared, "You better do what el Jefe told you. Perhaps you think Mexicans are liars, Mr. Hickey? You don't believe there was a murder, the girl is a suspect, she can't leave Mexico now?"

"Naw. Sure don't," Hickey said.

"Someone must put you in jail then. El Jefe tells you don't come back till a week."

Clifford sprang up. But nobody argued when the cop opened Hickey's coat and took the automatic. When the cowboy moved on Clifford, Hickey told the kid to give his pistol over. He walked ahead of the cop and the cowboy, beside Clifford, out to the sidewalk and down around the corner to a police car.

The cop drove, the cowboy rode shotgun with his eye on Hickey and the kid all the way. They crashed downhill, turned and sped on the dirt road that ran along the river and passed above the shantytown, where Indians and children dashed off the road ahead. Some boys threw stones at the police car, while Clifford sat tight-lipped as though holding back a shout, and Hickey thought about the patrón.

That one could rape his mother and make tough guys squirm. His eyes had flashed a surety that you only look for in saints or madmen. For a minute Hickey thought how you'd find men like Zarp at the heart of all rottenness, pestilence, and war. Even when he quit simplifying, he hated the man. And wanted to fight him. Because every word Zarp had said came out like a challenge.

Hickey didn't crave power or victory. He liked equality best, until somebody threw him a boast or challenge. When he used to box, he couldn't get sparked until the other guy whopped him, then he caught fire, like with this desire he felt now. To floor Señor Zarp.

They zoomed across the bridge, swerved around cars and taxis approaching the border, pulled to the east side, and stopped at the walk-through gate. The cowboy jumped out, threw open Hickey's door. He made a bow and a pass with his straw hat, toward the line.

Hickey said, "Thanks for the lift." He took the kid's arm and led him toward the gate, where Boyle stood shaking his head nastily, picking his teeth.

As they crossed the line, Hickey turned to watch the Mexicans, and Clifford burst out, "Pop, that girl told me something. The blonde one, I think she told me where Wendy is, only she don't talk English."

Hickey grabbed the kid's shoulders to calm him down and lead him out of Boyle's hearing range. "What'd she say?"

"*Arriba,* she said. *Arriba con los ricos,* she said. What's it mean. Think you can figure it out?"

"Yeah," Hickey muttered. "It'll take me a minute, that's all."

10

As they walked to the office shack, Hickey turned far enough to see the Chevy still there. He led Clifford inside and looked out the window. He watched the Mexican cop get out of the Chevy and say something to Boyle. Then they stepped closer and money changed hands.

Hickey flopped down on the couch next to Clifford, pinched his eyes closed to block the lightheadedness that was spreading. When he opened his eyes, the room was a reddish blur.

"What the heck, Pop?" Clifford asked. "You okay?"

"Sometimes I drink too much sugar. Go get some peanuts."

"You get it figured out yet, where Wendy is?"

"Go on," Hickey growled.

The kid gave a grudging nod and walked out. Hickey dragged himself off the couch, over to the desk, and poured a cup of syrupy coffee out of the percolator. He sat in the desk chair and sipped and let those Spanish words loop through his mind. *Arriba.* Rosa. *Ricos.* Rosa. *Arriba.* Rosa. *Ricos.* Rosa.

Before long, Clifford was back with two nickel bags of salted peanuts. He opened one for Hickey, gave over both, and asked intently, "You figure it out?"

"Yeah. I think they got her up, *arriba,* where the *ricos,* big shots live. In the Lomas. Now I'm gonna doze. After Lefty comes at four, we'll go back down. But we need a driver we can trust and Tito's all we got. You go hang around Coco's. See if he shows."

The kid sighed in relief. "You got darn strange for a minute. Like this." He hung his jaw open and let his neck wobble.

"So let me sleep. Get moving."

When the kid left, Hickey gobbled one sack of peanuts, then sprawled on the couch and pulled his hat over his eyes, figuring Metzger's curse, wishing Hickey to hell, must've been fright and liquor talking, no message. Unless there was a connection between Zarp and the ricos, Zarp and the Lomas. Between Zarp and Cárdenas?

He mused, could Lázaro Cárdenas, called the greatest, least corruptible presidente, a reformer, the guy who axed gangs of crooks from office and shut down the Agua Caliente Casino, calling for an upright Mexico—could the same man be tight with these Germans and del Montes? "Yeah, sure," he muttered. Anything was possible in TJ.

Arriba con los ricos, he thought. There must be a nightclub up in the Lomas, where the *ricos* lived. The big shots always get the best of everything, liquor, music, all the luxuries, women. Wendy Rose had to be there.

At last Hickey faded, slept for a second, it felt like, then snapped awake. He checked his watch. 4:10. Clifford stood over him. Hickey rubbed his eyes and sat up. "What's new?"

Clifford said, "That cabbie's waiting for us. They beat the tarnation out of him, Pop."

"Who did?"

"Some guys at that Hell place."

Hickey shook his leg that'd stayed asleep, straightened his clothes. He got out a comb and ran it straight through his patches of hair. He went to the bathroom and washed his face and hands. As he stepped back into the office he took a key from his pocket and opened the cabinet where he'd left the guns they'd snatched off del Monte's thugs. He and Clifford each grabbed an extra gun. They stepped outside and marched to the gate. Lefty and Boyle stood watching their approach. When Hickey glared, the fink looked nervously both ways then turned his back. Hickey pulled Lefty aside.

"Forget it, Pop. I'm not going down there anymore."

"Sure, I know. You got my note?"

"Yeah. I'll do that stuff. But I ain't going to TJ anymore. When do you give me the twenty for last night?"

Hickey passed the money over. "There's a couple more things."

"Nope."

"Just cover for me. Anybody shows up, calls, asks why I'm not on duty, tell'em I got the runs, locked myself in the john, or something. And keep an eye on this creep for me." He pointed a hidden finger toward Boyle. "He's ratting on us to the Mexicans. I saw the payoff. Just let me know if he asks you anything, who he talks to, if he makes any phone calls."

Lefty gave him a surly okay. Then Hickey and the kid crossed the line, through Boyle's lane. They walked up the cracking mud road to the coffee and taco stand where the limo waited and Tito sat on the fender with his head folded into his hands. As they neared, he didn't move but his single eye glanced up and he said sorrowfully, "You should give me a few dollars, man. Maybe then I feel better."

Finally he showed his face. The whole right side was bluish and swollen, the socket of the good eye puffed out in a ring. A bloody wound showed through the torn front of his Hawaiian shirt. He took the sunglasses from his pocket and slipped them on.

Hickey got out a ten. "Look, amigo, I can't do right by you now. But I will. That's a promise."

"No, man, I don't go crazy no more. Not here in TJ. I got enough money I'm going to see my uncle in Matamoros."

Hickey peeled a few bills from his wallet, counted them. "Thirty-five bucks," he said. "All you gotta do is show us a nightclub in La Lomas, someplace they got dancers and Wendy might be. I'm looking for some joint Zarp might own, where the *ricos* hang out?"

Tito stared at the money for a long time, then grabbed it. "Sure. I know that place. Casa de Oro. Señor Zarp, he's not the owner, but I think he lives there. Hey, the girls cost a thousand pesos, that's the cheapest. Indios can't go there, don't matter how much money you got, what kind of suit you wear. Gambling too, they got. Good idea, boss. You bet that's where she's gonna be."

"Take us there?"

"I can drive by, show you where it is. After that, no more."

The kid rode in back, Hickey up front, staring across the river through an open window. The warm breeze had picked up. A boy in the shantytown was flying a kite and a hundred children stared into the sky. Down near the bridge pilings, some Indians were building a statue out of mud. It looked like a horse or cow.

Hickey decided to take the road to Las Playas, bypassing downtown so they weren't as likely to be seen, to approach the Lomas from the west, maybe visit Juan Metzger on the way. He kept watch for police cars, for the Model A the cowboy drove and the red Chevy of the slick German. And he asked Tito to say all he knew about Señor Zarp.

Driving slowly, leaning forward to squint with his swollen eye, the cabbie said, "He comes up from the Capital, maybe about last year. He buys that bar and calls it Hell. You tell me, why does somebody go in a place called Hell, man? I don't know that. And I think it's him owns the jewelry store at Las Playas. They are buying jewels cheap from the refugees. I hear a lot of talk, but one thing sure—anybody wants peyote, I take him to that Zarp. He can get you the hard stuff too, if you want plenty, but peyote, what makes the Indios talk to el Diablo, he's the man."

By now, they had crossed Revolución and started bouncing up Calle Tres to the west mesa and the sea. On their left was a cemetery, the front gate guarded by a giant bronze Virgin with arms opened wide.

Then something made Hickey look behind them and he saw the red Chevy, with the German driving and another fellow he knew leaning out the window. El Mofeto. He saw the pistol rise. He yelled at Clifford, lunged for Tito, and the shot zinged through two rolled-down windows and shattered the glass front of a hardware store.

Through a riot of shouts and noises, Hickey felt sure he heard the car speed away. He waited for another shot that didn't come, then raised up slowly and looked, first behind, and out front. The Chevy screeched a U turn at the end of the block.

"*Ya vamonos?*" Tito yelped.

"You know it!" The big motor roared, and the limo wheeled out, hard left. "Other way," Hickey shouted, throwing his arm up the hill, from where the Chevy came speeding at them. "*Derecho, derecho!*"

But the cabbie shouted, "Ay, this road don't go noplace." He cranked the wheels full left and gunned the motor—the limo headed straight for the cemetery, and crunched into the giant bronze Virgin. She toppled partway onto the hood, one of her hands pointing through the windshield. Tito muttered a frantic prayer, let go the wheel, and crossed himself with one hand while he slammed into reverse. He backed up a few feet. The Virgin fell onto her face. And the Chevy, which had veered left toward the hardware, crashed their rear hard enough to jar Hickey's brain loose and throw Clifford over the middle seat onto the floor. At the same time, two more shots cracked. Tito banged into first. Leaned on the wheel. He stomped the gas, and ran over the Virgin's higher arm. Then they went blazing down the hill.

Hickey and the kid looked back, and Clifford shouted, "They broke down—whoa—here they come."

At least the Chevy had fallen a block behind, and Tito kept pulling farther ahead as he neared the intersection of Revolución—where straight in front of them, like bowling pins, waited a jam of cars, taxis, two busses. So Tito gripped tight, pushed his swollen eye open wide as a cyclops', and zoomed into the maze. In a flash, he swerved right, left, right, bounced off a green Plymouth, cut a corner on the sidewalk, took out a road sign and the pushcart of a taco vendor.

Clifford lay on the floor, facedown, hands folded across the back of his head. Over the noise of horns, motors, smashing metal, Hickey's pulse beat on his ear drums. They zoomed past the bus station, down to the plain. When they made the bridge, Tito yelled, "Are they coming, man?"

"They must've got stuck back there!"

They flew over one last rut and the brakes ground and screeched as the limo slowed to sixty mph and made the bridge. They kept slowing as they climbed, until at the top Hickey spotted the red Chevy. It had gone a different route. Now it sped toward the bridge on the high river road above the shantytown.

"Step on it! All the way over the line!"

The limo roared, and Tito snarled, "Maybe tonight I kill that pinche Mofeto." He crossed himself once more, as they zoomed off the bridge. Squealing the turn past Coco's Licores, they saw the lines—a dozen cars stacked at each gate. Hickey groaned, the cabbie yelled a curse, and the kid sprang up from the floor, yelping, "What's wrong?"

"Go that way," Hickey shouted.

Tito wheeled a quick left. They crashed into a field and flew over rocks and rivulets alongside the line of cars, up to the gate, and pulled in tight, diagonal to the line, roadblocked by tourists.

Clifford wailed, "Here they come."

The red Chevy bounded past Coco's and onto the field, hitting puddles and mud, spraying a red tail behind.

At the gate stood Lefty and Boyle with hands in the air. Even when the limo knocked the fat green Olds that blocked their way, it wouldn't budge. The man in a white Lincoln convertible, next in line, stood up, shouting, "C'mon, monkey, wait your turn."

Hickey pointed at the car in the gateway and hollered, "Ram it through."

When Tito smashed the Olds' left rear fender and half the trunk into its backseat, and raced his motor, in low gear, the limo's back left wheel spun, broke the hard crust, and stuck deep in mud.

69

The Chevy came burning at them. El Mofeto fired three times before the German wheeled a U turn, showering the gate with red mud, and sped back toward the bridge.

One shot just missed Tito, slammed through the dash and firewall into the motor. Another slug spent itself in the air. The last one got Lefty.

11

Hickey got up from where he knelt beside Lefty. For a while he stood glaring at the sky over Tijuana. Every half-minute or so he kicked the limousine's tire or rear fender. Then he looked down at Lefty, where he lay making the damndest sounds, sucks and gargles through the bullet hole in his throat.

He was a wise guy, but a decent kid. And Hickey stood there in a cool rage—vowing to beat Mofeto and the German and whoever had Wendy Rose. He bent and snatched up the gun beside Lefty, and stuck it into his own empty holster. Then he picked up Lefty's coat that had got thrown aside. In an outside pocket he found the Jeep key.

The slug had split Lefty's windpipe and passed out the back of his neck. Sometimes he couldn't get enough air, and he thrashed around as if he was having a seizure. If not for the nurse who ran from the clinic shack and cleared the pool of blood from Lefty's windpipe, and put his head on her lap to calm him, he might've died from thrashing and gulping. One time Hickey needed to hold him down, until Boyle showed with a stretcher and they belted Lefty to it.

An ambulance came from Ream Field. A minute later it was

gone. Hickey watched it speed away, then he walked straight for Coco's Licores.

He bought a liter of Mescal Carlos, crossed the road to the riverbank, and sat on the ground staring at the whitest part of the sky. He took a long pull on the bottle, caught some deep breaths, and downed a few more swallows, thinking how their lieutenant would show before long, see Hickey was gone, AWOL. Not likely they'd hang him. Probably toss him into the brig. Anyway, he wasn't going to stand there rousting drunks while Nazis and Mexican goons were holding the girl and shooting his partners.

Finally he capped the bottle, stuck it into his pocket, and looked around. Tito and Clifford watched him from a hundred yards away, over beside the limo parked next to the coffee and taco stand.

The kid still appeared in shock, pale and dreamy, a lot like his sister when she danced at the Club de Paris.

Tito's old Stetson was on backward. He puffed on a brown cigaret. His free hand couldn't find a place to rest. It touched his hair, his shirt, scratched his ear.

As he neared them, Hickey asked the cabbie, "You still gonna skip town?"

"I don' know boss. Maybe I leave now, but maybe too I go see Mofeto first. I got to think."

"You better forget El Mofeto."

Tito leaned back against his car. "A long time I been watching that one. I can tell you what dogs he's fucking and how many times he spits every day."

"Well," Hickey said, "if you're figuring to take him on, you might want this." He pulled off his jacket, unhitched the holster with the .45 Colt he'd swiped from Lefty, passed the holster and gun to Tito, who grinned like somebody proud of his teeth. He pulled the gun and stared awhile before he shoved it back into the holster and strapped it around his waist. He turned and caught a picture of himself in the window of his limo, and cocked his hat straight.

"Think you could catch him alive, if you took along some help?"

Tito pulled out a smoke and a match he torched with his fingernail. "Maybe. Say for two hundred I think about it."

Hickey nodded, took a business card and a hundred dollars from his wallet and passed them over. "Call this number, let me know what's up. And whatever happens, we meet at midnight. You know Las Brisas?"

"Sure."

Then Hickey told the cabbie where else he'd be tonight, at Luz's place, and how to get there. Finally he clapped Tito's shoulder, motioned for Clifford to follow him, and started toward the limo. As they walked, the kid drawled, "I think he's gonna die."

Hickey didn't know if the kid was talking about Lefty or Tito. Either way, he said, "Naw," then lightly, trying to lift Clifford's spirits, he asked, "How'd you like getting shot at? Starts the blood pumping, no?"

The kid looked off into space for a while, walking crookedly. "Where we going, Pop?"

"Find Leo. And if he wants to sock you back, don't look at me to stop him."

Boyle stood alone at the one open drive-through gate, and Hickey stepped that way with homicide on his mind. Sure Boyle had alerted the Mexicans when they crossed the line, he pictured his fist mashing the double-crosser's nose. But he just glared, for now. Looking everyplace except at Hickey, Boyle said, "There's a lieutenant at the office wants to see you. Wants to know what all the shooting was about."

"You tell him," Hickey snarled, and poked a finger into Boyle's chest. "See you later, pal."

He and Clifford walked behind some cars, keeping out of view of the office shack, and hustled past the clinic shack to the gravel parking lot, where they found the Jeep. Hickey took out the key that he'd snatched off Lefty. They hopped in, sped out of there. It was 5:20. Hickey had plenty to do before midnight.

At the office building on Broadway, the three flights of stairs made him feel the sleep he'd missed, the mescal he'd drunk, the faint spell he'd had, and his thirty-seven years.

Leo Weiss lay in the desk chair puffing on a smoke, with his big argyle feet on the desk. "Say," he droned, "you're the guys I been waiting for." He killed his cigaret on the side of his desk, then tossed the butt about ten feet, dead center into a trash can. "Mr. Rose, you and me are gonna have a talk."

Clifford looked away at the window that glowed twilight red. "Sorry," he mumbled.

"Save it awhile," Hickey said. "We got gunned. Lefty's pretty bad. He'll make it, though."

Leo sat up at attention, while he listened to the story in brief, and Hickey said, "You with us?"

"Hell, Tom, why should I be? You gonna pay?"

"Yeah."

"With what?"

"You'll see."

"And you think the kid'll pay you back someday, right? Well, forget it. Look, Tom, you got a whole town full of Mexicans, and then you got Germans and cops. On the other side, your side . . ." He scowled at Hickey and Clifford.

"Point is," Hickey said, "I'm the kind of guy who gets nightmares, and I don't want to have 'em because I got spooked and left this little girl down there. You wanta know the truth, losing Elizabeth and Madeline took a big notch outa me. If I lose another hunk of pride, what'll be left, I don't know. Besides, these del Montes, skunks and Germans, cops, they got me pissed. I'm declaring war."

"Lord, how many times will this guy throw me to the wolves?" Leo implored, gazing above then at Hickey. "Okay, Tom. I'll do some legwork. Snatching the girl's all yours."

"Swell," Hickey said. "Here's the plan. I've gotta talk to some guys. Clifford'll stay here by the phone, like a dispatcher, see."

"No. Darn, Pop, that's no—"

"*Because* they're gunning for us in TJ, but they don't know Leo. So he's going down to snoop that joint in the Lomas, Casa de Oro, while you and me keep out of sight."

74

The kid stood with his mouth open, one hand poised in the air, and Hickey turned to Leo. "How about it?"

"I got no previous engagements, except with the kid here."

Hickey told him dress rich, splash with cologne, after his bath, and take some gambling money. He could spend a few hours at the Casa de Oro, then meet Hickey and the cabbie at midnight at Las Brisas on the cliffs at Playas de Tijuana. And meanwhile, to lend him some cash.

Leo dug out three twenties. Then Hickey called his old home phone, told Captain Curtis the bayside cottage was his if he'd bring a down payment to Hickey's attorney by tomorrow.

Finally, he told Clifford, "You stay here by the phone all night, understand? Leo's gonna call and maybe Tito, and me." He gave the kid a chuck on the arm. "Keep your guard up, and don't worry. Old men can't hit so hard."

At 6:40, after a stop at the barracks, a change into his uniform, phone calls to his lawyer and to Al Smythe, Hickey raced the Jeep up Harbor Drive to Laurel Street and turned east up the pretty green mesa they called "Pill Hill," where the doctors presided.

The Naval Hospital might've been a medieval city during the Black Plague. Bigger than a mile square, it took up dozens of buildings that used to be gyms, recital halls, cafés. The Navy had commandeered Balboa Park from the zoo down to the eucalyptus groves, and filled it with half-dead boys. The wounded lay stacked three floors deep on beds that encircled the bones of dinosaurs, or beneath paintings of beautiful women. Still more boys lay in garages, in tents large as football fields, in dressing rooms behind the Shakespearian stage.

If Lefty wasn't in the quonset near the gate where they usually kept the poor chumps who got knifed by pimps or pachucos, it could take hours to find him in all this mess.

The MP armband took him through the gate fast. He pulled up beside the quonset, jumped down. For a minute he listened to

75

faraway screams and guttural shouts of outrage, then he got hit by the smells—blood, lye, burned skin, guts—which made his desires seem pointless and his intrigues small. He walked into the quonset, talked to a nurse who checked a list and sent him two quonsets farther down, from where he got sent to a tin bus garage near the zoo, where he finally caught up with his partner.

They had Lefty's neck wrapped in a blood-soaked bandage. A tube ran through the middle of it, and hooked into a gadget beside the bed. He lay still with his eyes closed. Hickey looked at the weary, freckled nurse. Suddenly a bell clanged and she ran off. A hyena brayed above the human cries. Hickey tapped the boy's arm, watched the eyes, until they finally blinked open and drifted up.

"Yeah, I know. I owe you a big one. For starts I'm going after those gunmen. But you gotta tell me—Boyle set us up?"

Lefty's mouth opened but stuck there, and Hickey said, "Try this—did he phone anybody just after we left?"

The boy's chin moved slightly down. A gibbon screamed, and Hickey sighed. "Thanks, partner. I'll come back tomorrow. Bring you a pinup girl."

As Hickey drove out of the park and off Pill Hill, the last quarter of sun dropped into the Pacific. Beyond the sprawl of Consolidated Aircraft draped in its camouflage net, the harbor flashed and glittered. Palms along shore bent in a gust of warm breeze. On a trolley car chugging up 5th Street, an old black woman leaned out the window, singing loudly. But Hickey missed it all, with his mind at the border, on Boyle, and back at the park with Lefty, and out searching for Wendy Rose. He forgot to speed. He arrived late at the warehouse alongside the Broadway pier. Lieutenant Smythe, a sweaty little man, glanced up as if peering around a corner, then turned back to nibbling the rim of his coffee mug. Without a word, Hickey stepped over, poured himself a cup. Smythe gave Hickey a wicked little smile. "Where's my salute?"

Hickey sneered, sat on the desk and swallowed his coffee. Then he got out his checkbook and wrote one for $200. He slapped it into Smythe's waiting paw. "That's for the Jeep. Now, how many Colts will twenty bucks get me?"

"How many you need?"

"A dozen, at least, the way things been going. But I'll settle for three."

Smythe nodded, got up and waddled away down a row of shelves. "Shells too," Hickey yelled after him, "and throw in a skein of rope."

Hickey downed another cup of thick coffee, took a shopping bag from Smythe, muttered thanks, and walked out.

He sped south and reached the highway just as honest dark fell. In the clear air under a moon that'd be full in a couple days, he could see pretty well, even with the browned headlights. Sidewinding Mexican produce trucks ran him onto the shoulder. He made the border at 8:15. He hitched the skein of rope onto his belt, loaded a .45 revolver, strapped on his shoulder holster and stuffed the gun into it.

He took out his briar. Fired up a bowl of Sir Raleigh. Told himself that of all the stupid acts he'd done, this next one might be tops. His lips felt parched. He took a sip of mescal, washed it around his mouth and swallowed. Finally he climbed out of the Jeep, heaved the duffel bag over his shoulder, and moved toward the line.

Just the one drive-through gate was open, manned by Lefty's replacement, a new MP called Alvarez who'd gone through boot camp with Hickey and Clifford, and by Mr. Chee, a civilian. He was the oldest guard and a friend of Hickey since the night a couple drunk Marines called Mr. Chee a Jap, and one guy shoved him—Hickey caught that guy blindside with a right jab.

"What say, Pop?" Alvarez called out. "Decide to work for a while?"

"Naw. I gotta look for the stiff who shot Lefty. They send anybody down there to investigate yet?"

"No sirree," Mr. Chee said. "They put the sign up again." He pointed overhead between the gates to a canvas banner that read, TIJUANA AND VICINITY OFF LIMITS TO U.S. MILITARY PERSONNEL—the same one they posted for a few days about every other week, when another gringo got killed or disappeared over the border.

77

"What about Mexican cops? Anybody call 'em in?"

"No siree," Mr. Chee said.

"Well, then, I hope you boys can cover for me. And Boyle. He's coming too. I figure the shooters are friends of his. See, I've been working on a case down in TJ, a missing girl, and Boyle's got these friends that pay so he tips them off when I'm going down. Then they have fun chasing me."

Mr. Chee folded his hands on his chin and nodded. "Boyle has unfortunate friends."

"I'm gonna treat him to a vacation," Hickey said, and turned to the walk-through gate. He stepped halfway, paused for a second, glaring at Boyle who'd been watching him close and now squared off, yet tried to look casual, even with a hand on the butt of his gun. In the dim light he hadn't seen Hickey already draw his Colt. It pointed straight out from his chest, at Boyle's nose.

"Slow night, huh, partner?"

Boyle's eyes locked on the pistol. "Yeah, Tom. You got a beef with me?"

"Sure do." Hickey reached out, brushed the fink's hand off the gun butt, snatched the customized police .38—polished to a gleam, the barrell engraved "for my darling," teak and cherry wood laminated grip—out of the holster and stuck it under his own belt. "Let's have a stroll by the river."

When Boyle hollered, "The nut's gonna kill me," old Mr. Chee scrunched his face and shook his head.

Alvarez said, *"Vaya con Dios."*

With Hickey a few steps behind, the gun beside his stomach where people couldn't spot it in the dark, they crossed the port of entry road toward Coco's.

"You get brought up religious?"

Boyle twitched and kept walking. "Yeah. Presbyterian."

"Ever think about the Commandments and feel slimy?" Hickey caught the fink's neck, wrenched his face around to look at it. "Wanta pray?"

With bulging eyes, Boyle whined, "What'd I do?"

"I just can't figure guys like you, is all."

Outside Coco's stood workers from the upholstery shop across the bridge and two bus drivers with their caps on. Hickey gave them a nod, over his shoulder to be sure they wouldn't see the gun. Then he led Boyle up the sidewalk of the bridge. "Think anybody'll come to your funeral? Your kids? You buy 'em lots of stuff with the blood money? Buy the wife minks and all? I bet they'll miss you—folks love a winner, huh?"

Boyle walked stiff and slow as they neared the crest of the bridge. "Better'n a bright-eyed chump like you."

"Yeah," Hickey muttered. "What you suppose makes one guy get stuck with a conscience the next guy doesn't have?"

"You got a conscience? So take that gun off me."

"Naw."

"You oughta wise up, Tom."

As they stepped off the bridge, Hickey said, "Yeah, I am, and you oughta go to hell. So let's both do what we oughta. What you say?"

He gave the fink a nudge with the gun, made him turn left toward the river and the shantytown. About thirty feet ahead, near the bank, a gang of Indian men stood around a campfire just big enough to give light to their game, throwing sticks and bones at a spot in the dirt. At once they all looked up.

"*Buenas noches,*" Hickey said.

There were two grandfathers. A middle-aged guy. Three grown boys. All thin, but with round, passive faces even while they stared at Hickey's gun. From the lively eyes and shiny hair you could see they hadn't been starving at the border as long as most.

Hickey tried his poor Spanish. The others turned to the middle-aged guy, who offered his hand and bowed slightly. They shook, made introductions, and the one named Crispín told Hickey that the others only spoke Olmec. The gentle tenor voice and small bright eyes got Hickey trusting this fellow.

Nodding toward Boyle, Hickey said, "*Hombre malo. Bandito. Asesino.*" That about exhausted his Spanish. "*Necesito ayuda,*" he said. "You help me?"

The Indians stared while he pulled the rope off his belt, and

79

gave it to Crispín along with a five-dollar bill. The others moved closer and gawked at the bill. Hickey pointed to Boyle's hands and feet, mimed tying him up.

"God, no, Tom," the fink yelped, "they got diseases down here."

Hickey got out more bills, passed them to the other Indians, who thanked him and chattered with glee. Then he gave Crispín Boyle's police .38. The Indians leaned in close, sighing as if they'd seen diamonds hanging between a princess's breasts. Turning to Hickey, Crispín muttered something and bowed solemnly. Hickey told him to keep the gringo hidden until tomorrow.

He walked up close and winked at Boyle. The fink squirmed and strange little toots came out of him. Hickey turned to the Indians. *"Alguno problema, tirar los cojones."*

As he walked back to the bridge and up, Hickey gazed out across the dozens of little fires flickering in the gray light of the shantytown and out over the brown and reddish lights spaced around the lowland of Tijuana, up the west mesa, and the far hills called Las Lomas. As he looked at the moon, something moved inside him. He suddenly felt content for the first time this year. Maybe he needed the kind of power you get from pushing creeps around. Maybe he needed to feel a grip on things.

12

Sunset cooled the dust and gilded the air, as El Mofeto swung the red Chevy coupe off Calle Seis and onto a dirt road that angled across the red dirt slope of the west mesa. Beside him sat a big mestizo with a smashed nose, and an Indian from Guatemala.

They bumped over dips and rivulets. As they neared the shack where Tito lived, El Mofeto gunned the motor, flew the last fifty yards, whipped around behind the limousine, and skidded broadside to a stop a couple feet from Tito's door. The two big thugs leaped out. The mestizo fired twice at the door before they crashed through it.

The place was only one small room, with no place to hide. El Mofeto stepped in past his men. He kicked a blanket on the pallet bed. A cat screeched, shot out, and dove through a window. From a shelf, the runt picked up two sun-blued glass jars and smashed them on the brick floor. He kicked in the side of a dresser, knocked over a kerosene lamp. He spat on the retablo, a painting on tin of the Virgin and Child that hung above Tito's pallet.

Finally the thugs trooped outside, El Mofeto in the lead. He checked both ways down the street. His hand with the pistol lifted high, and he squawked, *"Ven a fuera, Tito, putón."* He waited a minute, shouted again, chuckled and walked to the Chevy, unlocked the trunk, and got out crowbars and a heavy chain. The mestizo grabbed the chain. The Guatemalan picked up a crowbar. Each took one side, smashing the limo's windows and lights. The Guatemalan wedged his crowbar and kicked until a door fell off. Both of them pulled another door and the hood loose. The Guatemalan jumped on a fender, leaned toward the motor and golfed with his crowbar, knocking the carburetor twenty yards. He ripped hoses. Gouged the radiator. Then he climbed on the roof with the mestizo. They trampolined until the roof became a deep bowl.

All that time, El Mofeto stood cackling. As his grin soured he yelled his men down, then raised his pistol, blasted tires. Finally he shouted, *"Estas un muerto, Albertito!"*

He walked cooly to the Chevy. The thugs climbed in and they drove away back to Calle Seis. At the corner they passed a police car with two cops. The Chevy turned down the mesa. The cops sat gazing where the limo had got smashed and neighbors were starting to gather.

Three shacks north of the demolished limo, Tito stood beside his friend Enrique Peña, a Yaqui with gray flecked bushy hair. They'd been staring through cracks in the walls, and Tito knew better than to go outside yet, with the cops down there. They'd arrest him for owning a junk car, or something else, and sell him to El Mofeto. He cursed and smacked his head with his palms but couldn't think of any curses foul enough. Finally he turned to Enrique and his teeth started clacking. He felt his bladder loosen then spill down his leg. When he moaned, his friend reached out to hold him, but Tito didn't move. He couldn't see, as tears flooded his eye. He fell to his knees, bowed lower, and socked his head on the dirt floor. After a minute he straightened. Stood up. Embraced his compadre. Then stepped back and asked Enrique why it could be that he hadn't killed El Mofeto already, before.

13

Hickey bought a pint of mescal at Coco's, and a liter of anís for Luz. She liked that stuff and it made her breath smell good. He caught a cab, then lounged in the backseat, uncorked his bottle, nursed it, and thought about Luz's sweet breath, her breasts that he could burrow between, and the thick black hair cascading over his face when she got on top, so all he could see was the shadow of her face, and that swell hair, and soon the rest of the world was beyond the moon somewhere. Then he'd forget the sorrows, dangers, dreams he needed to give up on. He'd forget to long for Madeline and kick himself in the heart for loving somebody who'd betrayed him, somebody he tried every day to hate for stealing his daughter. Leaving him wasn't so bad. For that she had plenty of reasons. But she could've run to some officer out of the hundreds prowling uptown looking for a classy dame like her, and stayed in town where Hickey could visit Elizabeth and take her riding horses up in the mountains, sailing on the bay.

Crossing the east mesa on the border road, as you started down the grade, the first thing you saw was the Pacific. Bigger than the sky, it glowed dark emerald with streaks of red in the moonlight. There were tiny ships, dark currents, clouds like puffs of smoke passing in front of the moon. Straight below on the coastal plain lay the marshland and sloughs of the river, and just south of the border, the town of Las Playas, a thicket of rundown hotels, bars, derelict mansions.

Luz's place was up sandy roads about two blocks back from the seacliffs. It was built of scrap wood and tar paper, with chicken wire instead of glass for windows.

Hickey paid the cabbie, got out, stood for a minute listening to the crash of waves and shouts from the Casino de Lux. He stepped to the door, gave a holler and waited, then reached through a disguised hole and unhooked the latch. He went in and tossed his duffel bag beside the mattress. He looked around, grumbled, walked back out and turned down the road toward the cliffs, suddenly thinking about Leo, Tito, Wendy Rose. Any of them could be in a jam, while he was coming to get laid, when he ought to be visiting Juan Metzger, trying to figure things like who El Mofeto and the slick German worked for. He should walk down to the Hotel Esperanza where the wealthier refugees stayed, ask about Zarp. Or he could walk on the beach to clear his head. But he turned into the Casino de Lux.

It was an old barn next to a bull ring that had been part of a rancho before the war. Now there were afternoon bull fights, roosters jousted at night, and Sundays they brought in pit bulls since the pariah dogs they tried would just lie down and make peace. You couldn't rile dead spirits.

The air was thick with fishy smells and mildew from straw on the dirt floor. Around the ring stood a couple dozen gringo troops, half that many girls, a few Mexican caballeros, and a platoon or so of Mex soldiers from their fort just south of the Playas. They wore fatigues, and kept their rifles beside them—a couple weeks before, Cárdenas had placed the coastline on twenty-four-hour alert, suspecting a Jap invasion. Mixed through the crowd you saw refugees of the kind who wouldn't grieve too much for the homeland, since they'd escaped Antwerp or Prague with a bankroll. The men and the whores yelled for blood and money. The cocks ripped each other's feet off. They flew, screeched, beat their wings like they'd gone berserk from wanting to become real birds and fly. As Hickey pushed through the crowd, he paused to watch the banty lunge at the Polish cock's gizzard.

For a minute, as he stood beside Mexican soldiers, Hickey thought again of going to their general. But it seemed like the girl was enslaved at a brothel and casino where, on Tuesdays, Cárdenas played cards with old del Monte. Cárdenas, as presidente, had shut down gambling in TJ, six years ago. Now maybe he was part of the crowd who ran this Casa de Oro, which made Hickey wonder how great a fraud the old Presidente could be. Hell, you might trace the whole deal to him. Down here you never knew where things could lead. The worst stench might be on top of the heap. Like in ancient Rome. Maybe like most times, everywhere.

Finally he caught sight of Luz's thick, shiny hair. She was holding the arm of a Marine. Hickey scowled and started that way. He'd been giving Luz twenty dollars every week or so, plenty enough to live on down here, to keep her clean, to make him feel less like a John. He pushed his way through, getting cussed by the sailors he bumped. Then he grabbed her shoulder. She turned fast, panting.

"Ay, Tomas."

The Marine spun around. A corporal with battle scars, as though he'd caught a fist or two with his lips. He bared his teeth, then sighted Hickey's MP armband and turned back to the roosters. Luz slid past Hickey and started tugging him out through the crowd. On the way she got pinched and goosed, and she tongue-lashed one sailor until his chin quivered and eyes misted, but outside, she gently laid her head on Hickey's shoulder as they strolled up the sandy road.

"Where you are for eleven days? I think you don' love me, no?"

"I got you a present."

"Aw, *mi amorcito.*" She hugged tighter against him.

When they got to her place, she stepped to the table that was an old crate and lit a votive candle. Above the candle on the wall, a crucifix hung and beside it a picture of Jesus with flat black eyes that followed you everywhere.

Hickey got the anís from his duffel bag, and Luz took it with

85

a flourish, blowing him a kiss and dancing a spin around the room. Then she leaned toward him and whisked off her blouse and skirt as if they were bandages that itched. Hickey liked that way that Luz had. Only now it made him think of Wendy Rose.

A vision came to him. The girl kneeling down, crying, head on her knees. A gang of Germans, soldiers, Mexicans surrounded her, hooting at her, nudging and jabbing her with their feet.

Suddenly he wanted to get to a phone, talk to Clifford, see if anybody had called in. He checked his watch. 10:12. Before long he'd meet Leo and maybe the cabbie. So he flopped on the mattress, the only furniture except the crates and a low table with a small gas cookstove, some canned food, a bottle of water. He got out his pipe, loaded, fired it up, and watched Luz as she stood naked brushing out her hair and gazing down at him. He smiled at her pendulous knockers, flat belly, slender hips, all that black wavy hair, and those heart-shaped lips blowing kisses at him, making his brain steam.

"Don' you lay down?"

"Yeah," he said, and sat there smoking. She came and sat beside him. She took off the MP armband, the tie and shirt. With one hand she fingered his hair in back where it still was thick. Her other hand rubbed his chest. She kissed his forehead lovingly now, lingering, not a whore job like the first couple times.

He took a swallow of mescal. "Tell me something—you know a guy, Señor Zarp?"

She looked away and huffed, "Why you talk about him?"

"Tell me."

She pulled her hands off him, squeezed them between her thighs. "I know he kills a girl, Carmencita, up there."

"Whoa—up where?"

"The bar called Hell, hombre. For the goddamn men!"

"Like a show, you mean."

"For the goddamn *pinche cabrones ricos!*" She put a hand across her mouth and muttered, "And those goddamn Nazis."

"Wait now, doll. I been there, and it looks tame compared to stinkholes like the Blue Fox and the Club Paris."

"You don' go upstairs." She reached for her bottle and took a long pull, swished it around in her mouth, spit it out on the dirt floor.

And Hickey sat thinking, upstairs, upstairs, *arriba*, the *ricos*, the Nazis.

He jumped up, grabbed his shirt, threw it on, and strapped on a .45 and holster, while Luz watched him savagely, shaking her fist in front of her. Finally she gnashed her teeth and screamed, "You don' go there."

"I'm going after that Kraut."

Luz dropped her hands and stared, her lip curled into sneer. "You don' go watching the show?"

"Yeah, I don't. And I'll be back after midnight. Wait up for me, huh?"

Slowly, she got up and hugged him. She was trembling. Hickey rubbed her back and squeezed her for a minute or so. Then he said, "If I don't show up by midnight, go to Las Brisas and find an old gringo named Leo. You and him wait for me there."

He eased away from her, grabbed and pocketed his mescal, then walked out and hurried down the road toward the Casino de Lux.

He picked the newest, fastest-looking cab and told the driver to race downtown, but the driver shook his head, didn't move even when Hickey flashed a ten. Hickey didn't find a taker until the fourth cab. Either the cabbie had missed hearing the threats El Mofeto sent around, to stay clear of Hickey, or he was some daredevil the skunk couldn't scare. Or he was a snitch.

As they started up the sandy road, puttering along, lights out, Hickey squinted at his watch. 10:35. This way, just getting there could take halfway to midnight. "Hey, forget the Japs. Turn the damn lights on and speed." The driver shrugged, so Hickey got out another bill and slapped it on the dashboard. "*Luces. Ándale. Rápido.*"

The cab went hurdling over the sandy ruts. And Hickey figured, no matter about the meeting at Las Brisas, he only had until midnight. Because three nights ago at the Club Paris, somebody said La Rosa never came on until midnight. He was betting they'd worked her two shifts. The swing shift in Hell. Where they preferred blondes, like the Dutch girl and her pal who'd talked to Clifford.

Sure enough, he thought, the real enemy wasn't del Monte, the police chief and his gang, El Mofeto, the slick German. Zarp, it was.

He grabbed for his bottle and took a gulp, then smoked his pipe while they roared up the grade and across the east mesa. The few cars on the border road, all with lights out, pulled over to let the beaming cab flash by, while Hickey sat digesting fear. The rest of these punks didn't spook him much. But Zarp did. He didn't know how to fight the man. He'd met guys like Mofeto and the Tijuana cops. You look in a man's eyes and read a little of his mind—like he'd read Zarp as a deep looney you couldn't predict, a man who's threatened by peace because when everything else is quiet, he hears his own screams. So he goes out seeking chaos. Like Hitler. A guy turned inside out. The kind who might punch when you know he's got to feint, or hit you with a bomb when you're watching for a knife, or kill a girl with pure joy.

When they made the stoplight at Revolución, Hickey told the driver to cut the lights, drive slow down Calle Siete, and circle the block around Hell.

On the bright yellow building, the upstairs windows were shaded but from alongside one shade came a strip of flickering reddish light and running down from that same window a fire-escape ladder hung. They turned right on Avenida Cinco de Mayo, the cross-street just west of the Club de Paris, and cut back up Calle Ocho. Hickey told the driver to park and wait on Revolución.

He got out, straightened the coat over his gun, walked around the corner, and stopped. He waited a minute then peered back around the corner, to see what the cabbie was up to. Sitting on the fender, the cabbie took in the balmy air.

At 11:05, Hickey stepped carefully down the hill, looking out for cops and other dangers. Ahead on the narrow street lit only by the moon, he couldn't see anybody except a gang of drunk sailors climbing the hill and trying to whoop like Mexicans. Then, as he crossed the street a block up from Hell, he spotted the doorman out front and the cop resting on a porch across the street.

Hickey stepped back into the dark by the door to a medical clinic where poor gringos got their teeth pulled and their offspring aborted. He waited while the sailors stumbled up the hill and met a whore and her Marine coming out of an alley. They all walked into a tattoo parlor. Finally the doorman went back inside Hell. The cop sat gazing downhill. Hickey eased out to the dirt sidewalk and crept, staying close to the buildings until he reached the passway between Hell and the bakery next door. It was a stinking passway about eight feet wide. His feet slipped on moldy trash. Three cats and a gang of smaller creatures scattered out of his way just as he reached the base of the fire-escape ladder.

When he grabbed hold it rattled loudly. He stepped back, looked around, up, stood listening for a minute. Then he held the ladder gently and started to climb, his right hand pulling while his left stayed on the gun. He got five rungs up and saw that the next three were missing.

He cussed in a whisper, shimmied down, stood a minute with his ears keened, finally turned to the bakery next door, a one-story place with a flat roof. After sloshing through the crud to the rear of the buildings near the corner of the bakery, he found an oil drum full to the top with ashes packed down hard by the rain. He muscled it over next to the wall, inches at a time—it must've weighed three hundred pounds—then he climbed onto the drum and grabbed the eaves of the roof. When they started to crack he let go and caught hold of a sturdier place. Then pulled, strained, and got up. The roof was too rickety to walk on. So he crawled along the edge on the wall line, about thirty feet before he reached the spot across from the upstairs window toward the front of Hell. Now he had to stand and focus through the flickering light on the space down the side of the windowshade. What he saw looked so weird, he reached for his glasses.

A naked man lay on his back on a long wooden table. A red mask covered his face. His hair was slick and blond like the German's in the red Chevrolet. His chest stuck out. The arms lay flat alongside his slim waist and hips. He might've been dead, except for the giant erection. Behind him stood another, higher table, and on it a cactus in a gold pot, and a golden cross entwined by a serpent, about three feet high. Beside that stood a crystal pitcher full of red.

Hickey felt knocked off balance, as if the building shook. His legs kept tipping but he held still, waiting for the man to rise or do something. Then came the sound like a chant, low and muffled through the walls and windows of Hell. Eerie, dense, harsh words, maybe Latin. Hickey's mind wound tighter, higher until he pulled his gun and sighted on the blond man's erection. A tremor ran down his neck and arm to his trigger finger. He stood like that for a couple minutes while his hand twitched and he conjured pictures of the stiff's rod exploding. He made himself chuckle at the sight, trying to release some pressure from inside him. Until the girl appeared.

With steps as slow as a wedding march she crossed in front of the window, her head bowed. You couldn't see her features from where Hickey stood, only the ivory skin. She wore a shiny scarlet-and-rose–colored dressing gown.

Hickey's gun dropped to his side and the girl passed out of sight. A few seconds later she stepped behind the table, moved in front of the cross, slowly reached up to the crystal pitcher. She took it in both hands and stood a moment facing the cross. Then she turned toward the body on the table.

She poured a little of the red stuff on his chest. The body quivered. She replaced the pitcher on the high table, and turned once more to the body. Lightly, with her fingertips, she traced the red stuff into lines on the German stiff's belly. He quivered again, shuddering harder this time as if he'd start having a fit. Wendy stepped back out of sight. A few seconds later she passed the window, head down, walking slowly back the way she'd come.

Soon a big man in purple robes, his rear to the window, came and threw a white robe over the blond stiff, who slowly quit shaking, got up, and left the scene, led by the big man. Zarp.

Hickey watched a few more minutes, but nothing passed, and the chanting stopped. The arm at his side began trembling, as if the gun had grown ten times heavier. He shoved it into the holster. He squatted and looked at the sky. Stars pulsed yellow and red. Soon he got a passion to run through the front door of Hell, charge up the stairs, burst in, and commence shooting.

He laughed, quietly, fiercely. Then he crept back along the roof, hoisted himself down, and walked through the stinking crud. He looked out for the doorman, slipped from the passway back to the sidewalk of Calle Siete. He stepped up the hill slapping dirt, cobwebs, and the smell of wet soot off his clothes.

Hickey told the cabbie to drive lights-out back to the Playas. What he needed now was a tangle with Luz, to get that black mass off his mind. Then a little mescal, and sleep. Maybe he'd get the dream of Elizabeth. Something innocent, to help him lose this picture of Wendy Rose smearing blood on that quivering German stiff.

When they pulled up in front of Las Brisas, the bar of a small, rundown beachfront hotel, it was almost 12:30, and Leo's Packard Phaeton waited out front, looking like a beached whale. There was no red-and-pink limo.

The bar was a huge cabaña tacked to the side of the old stucco hotel. Some of the patrons were Mexican, but most were refugees who looked bitter, confounded. A couple of them stared longingly out to sea. Hickey stepped into the cabaña, drifted across the floor, whiffing the scents of coconut, pineapple, whiskey, and rum. Luz called to him from a table overlooking the beach. He went and sat down between her and Leo, and warmly kissed her hand.

"You shoot that cabrón?" she whispered.

He shook his head and turned to Leo. "I found the girl."

Leo rolled his hand, asking for more. Luz clutched her man's arm, and he said, "Upstairs in Hell. Playing witch."

Hickey ordered a round, then told them what he saw. The mass and the same slick German who drove the red Chevy, naked on the table, like a corpse bound for hell with its prick aloft. His mouth kept tasting more foul. When the drinks came he swished his mescal around and took a mouthful of the gin and grenadine mess Luz was slurping. She petted and kissed Hickey's arm. Leo wadded bits of paper and tossed them three feet, into a mug. He told Hickey about the Casa de Oro, a mansion big and rich enough for Napoleon, at the crest of Las Lomas. A private club with the valet and doormen armed and costumed like soldiers. They'd turned Leo away at the door. But earlier he'd phoned Ruiz, his contact with the Federales, and gotten some background on Zarp.

"Some crackpot. Part German. Other parts might be Hungarian, Gypsy, who knows? His family's been around awhile. Coffee planters down by Guatemala. Sells dope, big time, and Ruiz says the nut thinks he's a witch—a *brujo*. I got a name on that other Kraut—the naked joker. Franz Metzger. Could be a Nazi agent."

"Metzger," Hickey muttered.

The moon, the wind beginning to rise, the waiting for Tito, and Luz's worried eyes were dragging Hickey down, sapping his courage. He checked his watch. "Where's Tito?"

They all looked toward the front for a minute.

"You phone the kid?"

"Yeah," Leo said. "Couple hours ago. He's okay. Didn't hear from the cabbie, though."

Hickey stared out to sea. The foamy waves glowed darkly. Leo ordered a round. Luz put her head on Hickey's shoulder and rested, while he sipped mescal and Leo drank coffee with Scotch and kept one eye out front, the other on Luz's knockers.

They spent a few minutes talking over plans. Then at 3:00, Leo got up to leave. He said he'd return in twelve hours.

Hickey and Luz moved to a bench near the seacliff. She lay with her head on his lap. Reaching a hand beneath her blouse, rubbing gently, Hickey gazed out to sea. His eyes fogged. He heard a strange wail from the ocean, and let himself moan along with it. He felt sure Tito was dead.

14

The breeze had shifted. You could hardly smell the sea. A whirlwind crossed the east mesa and skipped downhill past the house Juan Metzger had rented, at the western foot of Las Lomas.

Metzger lay trying to sleep, but his mind reeled with worries and when those began to fade, Consuelo started groaning and tossing. Probably a nightmare about his cousin Franz, since Franz had stopped at their house that evening, drunk, boasting he'd shot a gringo and terrifying the children. When the little one cried, Franz whirled his arm and would've knocked their baby senseless except Consuelo ran between them and ordered the brute out of their house. With a mad laugh, Franz shoved her into a wall. He threw himself toward her, made a kiss in the air, turned and howled a laugh at Juan. Then he stomped outside. His car squealed and roared away.

Consuelo was used to Franz's meanness, the way he'd burst in giving orders and gloating over women who loved him and whom he scorned. He'd stare at her breasts, his eyes aglow, licking his lips, and mutter obscenities. Last visit, when his cousin stepped out of the room, Franz grabbed her face in both hands and kissed her viciously. Only tonight, after the visit, had Juan learned of that. His wife hadn't spoken before, out of fear the cousins would fight and Juan would be killed. She still believed her husband had courage.

Consuelo invited Juan to hold her. She massaged his neck and, while he mourned for Tom Hickey, if that was the gringo Franz boasted he'd killed, she rocked him to sleep in her arms. After midnight they were startled awake to a pounding out front. Consuelo followed Juan. From the closet he grabbed his shotgun. He went to the front door, stood a minute praying the noise would become footsteps walking away. At last he flung open the door.

There stood Franz wearing only trousers, his eyes and mouth gleaming hideously. Down from the neck to his belly ran thick streaks of blood. He laughed coldly, for a long time, then strolled to his Chevy and roared off. Toward the Playas.

Hickey and Luz humped and moaned like souls in limbo. Afterward she put him to sleep with a long massage, and he dreamed of Elizabeth. He woke up and lay reading until Luz woke and they made love again. He read a little more. Dreamed again.

The next time he woke, at 10:30, he dressed in just trousers and his undershirt, washed in cool water from a clay pot, and walked to the phone office a few blocks down on the cliff road, between the grocery and a panaderia. It was already hotter than yesterday.

He phoned Clifford and the kid shouted, "You find her?"

"Yeah. We're gonna bust her out tonight."

Clifford fell silent. Praying or something, Hickey figured. He got a warm feeling, like things suddenly turned right in the world. It lasted a second. "You hear from the cabbie?"

"No. Where is she?"

Hickey let out his breath and sighed. "Well, if Tito calls, tell him to meet us at Las Brisas at three and bring along a couple other guys. Tough guys. Got it."

"Yeah."

"Leo's coming for you at one or so. You hungry?"

"Naw."

"Sure you are. Call down to the Pier Five Diner. They'll bring you anything and bill it to Leo."

"Where's Wendy, Pop?"

"Later."

"Are they . . ."

"Hush. She's doing great and I got business."

Next he phoned Groceria El Portal and asked the woman to get a message up the street to Juan Metzger—*"Las Brisas a las doce y media de la tarde."*

He paid for the calls and walked back fast, scuffing his feet through the sand and trying to convince himself the cabbie was safe, maybe on the road to Matamoros. Before he reached Luz's, his head started aching and his legs got heavy as though he hadn't slept at all. He crept inside, took a snort of mescal, and rested beside Luz. Soon he picked up the dream about where he'd left it.

In Hickey's dream there lay a harbor in this place where he slept, between the Playas and the border. The people were like the ones he'd seen out walking. Farmers from Poland. German watchmakers. Chinese merchants. Gamblers. Forgers. Dealers in passports. Anarchists. Japanese spies. German spies. Good people, bandits, schemers. All of them milled around the small harbor of Hickey's dream, like Sunday on Hollywood Boulevard.

He led his daughter through crowds that spoke weird languages, bought and sold everything, made bets on some battle around Tripoli. They walked out on a pier and looked down in the harbor at water thick as oil, mossy green and swarming with fish—fat groupers with doglike teeth. Long thin mackeral. Eel fish. Fish with golden hair like mermaids'. Then came the sharks with mouths like swinging doors and black steel teeth. They swam gracefully, and fed on everything, so the eels and mackeral got swallowed whole, the groupers ripped in half, until you couldn't see through the bloody water.

Elizabeth wrapped him in her arms and cried, "I want to go home, Daddy."

He woke up shivering. Luz stood beside the mattress pulling on her panties. Hickey's watch said 12:20. But he lay still, knocked in the head by that dream. He stayed there, trying to blame it on the mescal, and vowed to give the poison up, if it was going to treat him that way. Finally he rose, went to the hotplate and put some water on to heat. Luz gave him a sponge. He washed his armpits, between his legs, his feet. She loaned him her straight razor and he shaved. He combed his hair and mustache.

When he reached for his trousers, she came over and kissed him. "You have bad dreams, Tomasito. We go one more time, you forget them, okay?"

He shook his head, stepped into his shoes and laced them, strapped on his shoulder holster with the .45 and pulled his coat over it. Only telling her he had to meet somebody, he kissed her and walked out.

A block before Las Brisas, he cut down, on a footpath, to the trail that led along the cliffside from where he could see into the patio but could hardly be seen, against the sun glaring off the ocean.

Metzger had showed. At a corner table, he sat staring at a double shot of mescal next to a beer bottle. Hickey circled the place twice, looking out for Franz, El Mofeto, or cops. Then he got his own beer and joined Metzger. The man's face looked bloated, pinker than before, with bloodshot, deeply frowning eyes.

"Cheer up," Hickey said. "Talk to me, pal. I want to know more about your cousin Franz, the one that raised hell in Chiapas. He's in TJ, right?" The German nodded. "You think he's crazy?"

Metzger wouldn't raise his eyes to talk, and he muttered lowly. "Yes. In Chiapas, I thought Franz was a little mad. But here—at times he acts like a rabid dog."

"Why, do you think?"

Metzger shrugged. His jaw wrinkled and jutted out, as if he might weep bitterly. "I can't tell you. Why has mankind gone mad, Mr. Hickey? Why have we all come to hate each other?"

"Some guy wants something, bad. He doesn't get it. He blames somebody. From there it snowballs."

The German gave a little hiss.

"Who'd Franz work for?" Hickey asked, waited. "Okay, who's he pals with?"

Between each question he gave Metzger a minute or so. He asked what drugs Franz took, where he hung out. The German said nothing, only wagged his head and kept drinking, first the beer then the mescal. When he finally lifted his eyes from the table it was to call for another of each.

"Hey, let's not just sit here moping," Hickey said. "Why'd you tell me to go to hell?"

"I was drunk."

"No kidding."

Metzger glanced at Hickey and turned his gaze north across the border, over the brown sun-baked hills and glassy, still water. "Over there, in your country," he asked, "do they hate Germans? Will they soon dispossess the Germans and send them to camps like the Japanese?"

"Could be."

Metzger stared out to sea, silent and paralyzed, afraid to breathe.

Hickey saw the German had drifted. The eyes had moistened, jaw gone slack, shoulders hunched to his ears. His hands lay fisted on the table. He only broke the trance long enough to swallow liquor. Hickey tried asking the man what he knew about Zarp, Lázaro Cárdenas, del Monte, what connections those fellows might have with each other, or with Franz. But the German was gone.

Hickey found Luz painting her nails. When she finished she lay on the pallet, beside where Hickey rested, wishing he'd gotten anything out of Metzger that would clue him better to what they'd find in Hell tonight, to who and what the enemy was. Luz peeled his clothes off slowly, kissing him all over, and Hickey began to shiver. He shivered all the time they held each other, until he rummaged through a pile of old slips and sweaters and red skirts on the floor, gathering his uniform, and dressed. He didn't wear the tie, coat, or black MP armband. He strapped on his side holster with the gun and checked through his duffel bag to take stock. Luz sat watching.

At 2:50 he was on the mattress beside her, with her head on his shoulder. He reached for his wallet and said, "After tonight I better stay out of TJ."

She stiffened and bared her teeth. He put fifty dollars into her hand. She took it but her face didn't change. Her teeth still gnashed as if she'd chomp his arm off. So he stood, mumbled adiós, picked up the duffel bag, and walked. As he stepped through the doorway she screamed, "*Cabrón que chingas las chicas.* You wanting the little girl for you, *pinche* sonabeech."

Maybe so, he thought. Who the hell knows what I want anymore? Except to get time back, and try again. Sure—he wanted the same as everybody, another chance.

Luz was in the doorway hollering, "I gonna pray you don' get her, goddamn Heeckey, I gonna pray you don' get nothing."

15

He stomped along raising dust, until he got hit by the idea that Luz might rat on him. He thought, man, what a sucker. You tell her your plans, then dump her and leave a scorned broad to get rich selling you out to the bad guys. He ought to tie her up and stick her down there with Boyle for a day or two. But he kind of loved her.

Up ahead was Leo's Packard. Then Clifford ran out of Las Brisas and hustled down the road. When he reached Hickey he yapped, "We got the guns and everything."

"Hush."

"Sorry." The kid's voice sounded scratchier and a little mean. He wore a tight leather civilian jacket, and you could see the lump of a gun over his heart. It pulsed out with his heartbeats. "What's the plan?"

"When we're all here. I don't wanta say it five times. Did you hear from the cabbie?"

"Sure did," Clifford said, and Hickey felt like a clamp had loosed off his chest. "He wanted to talk to you," the kid said. "Sounded awful funny, like he was sick or lying bad. I told him what you said."

"And what'd he say?"

"Nothing. Hung up on me."

"Least he's alive," Hickey muttered. "Okay, what'd Leo tell you?"

"Just that Zarp guy's got her. I wanta stab him in the heart, Pop, I reckon the devil's got me good."

Hickey draped his arm over Clifford's shoulder and walked him toward the cabaña. "Maybe he's got us all."

"Devils fighting devils," Clifford mumbled. "It don't make no sense."

"Might if we were smarter."

Hickey saw Leo at the corner table, same as last night. Beside him sat a giant, a young guy with a face all cheeks and a high tuft of wheat-colored hair. He was twice as wide across the shoulders as Leo. Hickey went over, dropped his duffel bag, and shook both their hands at once. He sat down beside McColgin, the giant. He knew the guy, a pool hustler, a maniac who'd got kicked out of the Marines. He was in a tank battalion, a driver, until on manuevers he chased a Drill Sergeant over the hills, trying to squash him with the tank.

"Thanks for joining up," Hickey said.

The giant drawled, "My pleasure."

Hickey asked Leo if he'd gotten the money from their lawyer. The old guy nodded. "Only the flyboy won't cough up fifteen hundred till you sign papers, and the pencil pushers can't draw the papers for a couple days. I got eight bills, though."

"Swell." Hickey turned to McColgin. "I hear you brought an arsenal."

The giant grinned and chanted, "M-1, pistols, silencers, a fifty-round Thompson, a buncha tear gas cannisters."

"Masks too?"

"Yeah, yeah, and Smythe gouged me," Leo grumbled. "Four hundred. Didn't come down a nickel when I told him my kid's applying for Stanford."

"We'll meet that guy in hell someday," Hickey said. "Then let's beat the crap out of him."

Leo raised his beer in a toast. Then he pointed at McColgin.

"Burly here says he can get a couple more pool hall loafers to join you."

"Just take a phone call," McColgin said.

"No, Pop," the kid said. "Can't just the three of us fight 'em?"

Hickey stared him down. "You like to run this show?"

Clifford's eyes turned down and in, as if to glare at the tip of his nose, and his lips squeezed tight in a surly way. Finally he looked up and away, over the cliffs. The beach was crowded. Toward the shoreline, heatwaves rippled up from the darker sand, and scores of people walked, mostly refugees, men in dark suits they'd been wearing for months, girls with skirts that billowed, fluttered, making them look angelic and free. Children built castles and dredged rivers. Refugees with broken hearts stared out at the water.

Hickey signaled the waitress, ordered beers. The four of them sat waiting, watching the beach and eyeing the waitress when she swished by. Clifford would glower for a while, then shut his eyes, and you could see his breaths get shallow, as he slipped in and out between fright and rage. He wanted to carry the Tommy gun. He told that to Hickey.

Hickey said nothing. He finished the beer and ordered black coffee. He smoked his pipe and watched the door for Tito. About 3:40 McColgin said, "I figure the Mex don't plan to show."

Leo growled, "Cut it out. You start figuring, you'll want to charge more money."

"We should get some more white guys anyway," McColgin said. "I don't trust no greasers."

"Sure you don't," Hickey snapped. "Well, Tito's good as they come."

"You oughta go along," the giant said to Leo. "Ain't too old for a little shoot 'em up, are you?"

"Hell, yes I am."

A two-tone, green-and-brown cab skidded to a halt out front, throwing up a tail of sand. Tito jumped out of the passenger side and bounded into the cabaña, wearing a maroon Hawaiian shirt with yellow palm trees. He spotted them and rushed over. The patch on his eye was new, dark green. He was shaved, his hair oiled. Even his

101

teeth looked whiter. When he saw the giant, his eyes swelled with awe, then he looked brightly at Hickey and said, "Man, you going to love what I bringing you. I got all what the kid tells me you say. I got four hombres *con muchos cojones*. And they don't need too much money. What you want them to do? Maybe you found La Rosa?"

"Yeah," Hickey said. "Tonight she'll be dancing upstairs in Hell, and we're gonna take her. These guys you brought can shoot, to kill?"

"Sure, I don't bring you no *putos*, man." He threw back his shoulders, puffed his chest out. "Only thing, you better pay my amigos before they going to fight, so they believe you. And me, I'm going too, for only one hundred, just for I catch a bus to Matamoros, and a little extra. These *pendejos* turn my limo to a junk." He bowed his head, snuffed, rubbed his eye. Then he straightened up and said, "Now you come see what else I got."

He led them out to the green-and-brown cab, where five Mexicans waited. In the backseat were twin brothers, about thirty years old, stocky Indians with squarish faces. Yaquis. Teodoro and Isidoro Peña. Between them sat their older brother, Tito's pal Enrique. They appeared tough, serious, the way Tito had told them to look. The driver was Enrique's son Rafael, a sweet-faced kid about Clifford's age. And beside him, roped to the seat, gagged, wearing a cake of blood where his mustache used to be, sat the little thug called El Mofeto.

When Hickey saw that, he croaked a great laugh, and Tito bowed deeply.

Hickey looked closer at the man. Besides a smashed lip, there was a gash an inch wide up the side of his head, and small red welts around his right eye. "Who knows you got him?"

The cabbie frowned and rubbed his neck. "Could be a lot of people. Hey, you want to know what he tells me about the girl?" Tito looked at Clifford, took a long breath, turned back to Hickey and led him away a few steps. "That part I think you don't like so good." He shuffled his feet. "What you believe in, boss? You Catolico, or what?"

"Just what'd he say?"

"Okay, he's saying you don't want La Rosa no more, no more she's anything, only a killer and a whore of the Nazis."

"A killer?"

"Yeah, she kills this gringo junkie."

"George."

"Maybe that's the one."

A sick feeling caught Hickey's brain. He cast it out fiercely. "Who're these Nazis she's the whore of? Zarp? That shooter, Franz?"

"Sure. Maybe other ones too. Lots of them coming here, when Cárdenas don't send all the Germans to the Capital like he is supposed to."

Hickey grabbed the cabbie's shoulders and squeezed. "Don't tell the kid any of it. What else'd the skunk say?"

"Nothing. I ask him plenty, I kick him, but he don't talk much."

They walked back over to the cab. The kid looked pale enough to collapse, but savagely he demanded, "What'd he say?"

"Nothing about your sister."

"Then how come it's secret?"

Hickey backstepped a few paces, rubbed his eyes and stared at the faces, Clifford with the surly mouth and ferocious eyes. McColgin's impudent sneer. The Mexicans relaxing in the cab. He told the twins and Clifford to ride with Leo and the giant, then he got into the cab, in back, and ordered Rafael to head for the border station.

Tito climbed in beside his prisoner.

A couple minutes later while they still bounced along the sandy road, Hickey said, "Ask him if they got guards there in Hell. If he's lying we'll put scorpions in his shorts."

They turned onto the main road and started up the mesa. Tito lit a cigaret, took a drag, blew smoke at the runt, then moved the cigaret up to an inch from El Mofeto's right eye.

"Alla en Hell. Cuantos pendejos con armas?"

It looked like the runt tried to spit, but drooled. With a grin, Tito touched his cigaret's coal to the prisoner's eye lid. Through the

103

dusty heat you could smell flesh cooking. El Mofeto yelped, didn't say a word.

Tito leaned over the seat. "First time I burn him, kind of makes me sick, you know. Every time gets easier."

They were halfway up the grade. Hickey leaned out the window for air, then looked back and saw a Chevy, like Franz Metzger drove, pulling out of the Playas, about a half-mile behind. He kept one eye on the Chevy. "Ask him again, how many guys are gonna be upstairs in Hell tonight. And which of 'em pack guns. Or, we feed him to the rattlesnakes down by the river. When the poison hits, he'll get crazy and talk. That'll be more fun." As the Chevy drew a little closer, Hickey put on his glasses, and decided the driver could be blond, though he wore a hat.

Tito lit another smoke, puffed awhile and lay a hand on El Mofeto's forehead. With a thumb, he reached down and pulled back the right eyelid, then he moved the cigaret close and hissed, "We push the rattlesnake up his ass."

Rafael the driver laughed gayly. His father, in the backseat, nodded and smiled as the cigaret eased closer. And Hickey sat wondering what kind of men they were. The Peñas. The cabbie. Himself. Last night he almost blew off somebody's prick. Today he walked out on Luz, who'd treated him fine. Now he was helping the cabbie torture a guy. Finally he reached and tapped Tito's arm. "Save it." He told the driver to wait until they crested the hill and then speed, turn off somewhere, and lose the Chevy before it came back into view. When they crossed the hilltop, Rafael jumped on the gas and burned rubber.

Tito, innocently as though he never could dream of blinding a guy, said, "This is one hot rod, no?"

They cut right on a dirt street that led to Calle Tres, and bounded over the ruts downhill past the cemetery where the Virgin stood guard, on her feet once more. Another block and the traffic got heavy. Rafael had to bump a Studebaker to make it hurry, and when they made the intersection at Revolución they zoomed diagonally through a dirt parking lot, went flying off the sidewalk, just missing a taco vendor's cart, then chopped into the wrong lane, and Rafael had to slam the binders and skid to miss front-ending a bus. He backed up and nicked a long blue sedan, but finally got straight and flew down Calle Quatro toward the river.

Hickey gave an order, and they pulled into an alley. He opened the door, stood on the running board, where he could see across traffic all the way down to Calle Uno, the border road, where a minute later, Leo's Packard rolled by. They waited a couple minutes longer and no red Chevy appeared, so they drove on down along the river road, swung right and crossed the bridge, then cut back on the dirt trail to the riverbank across from the shantytown.

They had hardly stopped when the Indians began crossing the river, wading in groups of three or four. First came the men, then a few women and some older kids, until about thirty of them circled the car, just watching. A hundred more stared from the far shore. Hickey leaned against the taxi, his heart turning mushy at the sight of gaunt faces, bony ribs, legs like ostriches', filthy rebosos that once had been colored like rainbows, old muslin rags twice too big for bodies they used to fit. Not one of the them put out a hand or asked for a dime, but most of their eyes were begging.

The Olmecs, Crispín and two of his sons, stepped through the circle and up to Hickey. Crispín zestfully shook hands.

"Ask him if the bandito's making trouble."

After Tito translated, the Olmec smiled and said everything was fine, except the bandito had caught a fever.

Hickey pulled some bills from his pocket, held them out. "Tell him we got this other cabrón. Same deal."

When Tito dragged El Mofeto rigid from the cab, a few Indians made crosses and backed away. Tito grabbed the runt's hair and threw him hard to the ground, kicked him in the back, and told the Indians what to do. Finally he rolled the skunk over and stomped on his balls. El Mofeto just groaned a little. Tito got into the cab and slammed the door behind him.

Hickey told Rafael to park at Coco's Licores. His nerves wanted a bottle, but his brain made him tell the Mexicans to wait there, and stay sober, while he went over the line to meet Leo and the kid, wait for Smythe to show with the rest of their arsenal, and decide for the final time if he ought to risk lives for the sake of some Nazi's whore.

He crossed the road, walked past Leo's Packard that was parked a hundred yards south of the line, saluted the Peña twins who sat in the car guarding its trunkful of weapons. When he reached fifty feet from the drive-through gate, Alvarez shouted, "You're a goner, Pop."

Hickey kept walking. "Yeah. What's new?"

"Colonel's been calling me up every hour, in person, using bad words, like deserter. Asked if I'd be on the firing squad. I'm s'posed to cuff you and call him on the double."

"Good luck," Hickey snapped. "Who's out looking for the creeps that shot Lefty?"

"I guess nobody 'cept you."

"Sure. They got their own problems, right? Japs. Nazis. Covering their own butts. Getting rich. Nobody's gonna fix this Mex bunch unless it's me."

"Whew. Watch the blood pressure, Pop. Your face looks like a plum."

As Hickey turned and walked his way, old Mr. Chee asked, "You okay, Tom? There's been a very lot of people come for you."

"Oh, yeah? Tell me about 'em."

"Well, first two Mex cops—didn't introduce themselves, but one in uniform. Other was made up like a cowpoke."

"The uniform guy was tall? Light-skinned?"

"Yes siree. A big Mex that talks good English."

"Cowpoke wear a straw hat or Stetson?"

"Not straw. Maybe a Stetson. What they want with you, Tom?"

"My neck. The police chief. He's the one in the Stetson. If he comes back, break his legs for me, will you?"

"Sure, okay. Say, that kid, your chum, and a couple other guys are waiting for you in the shack. One's big as a truck. Oh, and one guy came asking for Boyle or you, either is okay, he said. From the south. A tough Kraut."

"Drove a red Chevy."

Mr. Chee nodded. "And he's very mad. A Nazi?"

"A psycho," Hickey said.

"Well, he left one package for you. I put it in the shack. It's a little thing, couldn't be a bomb."

"Thanks. Look, about Boyle. If something goes haywire, if I get wasted or anything, in a few days you should go down by the bridge, ask for an Indian named Crispín. Boyle's lodging at his place."

"Don't you get hurt."

Hickey patted the old guy's shoulder, made him a promise, turned and walked to the office shack. When he opened the door a whirlwind of smoke gushed out. Leo and the giant sat beside the desk, drinking coffee, puffing cigarets, and gazing at the package. Clifford was on the couch, one fist pounding lightly on his knee, the other hand holding a cigaret, the first he'd ever smoked.

Hickey left the door open and cracked a window farther. Then he sat on the desk and stared at the small package. He lit his pipe, held the smoke until it reached his brain. Then he picked up the package, a small white box. Something in his gut said to run the thing out to the incinerator. Don't even look. As Clifford got up from the couch, and came over, the other men followed with their eyes. Finally Leo said, "A diamond ring, from some rich broad."

Hickey shook the package. Something no bigger than a ring but even lighter. He broke the twine, lifted the boxtop slowly. He and the kid stared into the box at a little pyramid less than a half-inch high. Pink or salmon-colored. Suddenly Hickey knew. He closed his eyes, ground his teeth. Leo and McColgin stood up to look, while Clifford pulled the thing out of the box. Spongelike, slightly moist. Flesh and skin. The kid moaned, "Awwww . . ."

Hickey looked at the others. "God damn those . . ."

"A hunk of her lip," Leo mumbled.

Her brother squeezed the thing tightly into his fist. He stepped to a corner of the room, put his left hand over his eyes. His body started jerking with spasms. At the same time, Hickey kicked the oak desk so hard a toe bone cracked, and he roared at the giant, "Go get the Mexicans. Tito should be over at the Licores. Bring 'em through the walking gate. I'll meet you there, talk to Mr. Chee, and

107

we'll get 'em across. I gotta pay everybody. Then we're all getting a nice dinner. Relax awhile, before we go slaughter the dirty fuckers."

"Yeah," McColgin snarled, and ran out.

Leo flopped onto the couch. A minute later he sprang up. For once he looked awake. He lit a smoke and growled, "I'm going with you, Tom, get my shot at the Nazi bastards."

Hickey stood watching the kid, thinking he should go stand by him. But he couldn't touch a sorrow that deep. So he thought about the rifles, the machine gun, the grenades. In his clearest vision they blew that place called Hell into rocks and splinters. Like a whole air raid got it.

16

The Santa Ana blew in that night. It began with hints. A warm gust now and then. A few stars flickered hotly. Moonbeams danced around.

Out over the Pacific, it looked like you could see a thousand miles, so you felt pretty sure no Japs were flying that way. And except for the rare gusts, silence prettier than music hung in the air.

At 8:30, in the office shack, Tito got the phone call from Teodoro Peña. From the corner of Revolución and Calle Siete, he'd watched two uniformed men escort a girl in red, with a hood and her face covered, out of a Cadillac limo and into Hell.

Just past 8:45, Leo Weiss's Packard eased around the corner, off Revolución to Calle Siete. It pulled to a stop just where the sidewalk turned to dirt in front of the dental and abortion clinic that was closed for the night. The only places open for a long block either way were Hell on the south side a hundred yards downhill from the Packard and the tattoo parlor on the north side a half-block up the hill. The parlor wasn't busy yet. That would be later, after midnight when the sailors got blind and stupid.

Hickey jumped out from the shotgun side of the Packard and loped across the street, to the dark beneath an apartment balcony. From there he had a straight view to Hell. Upstairs, some lights burned. In the window toward the rear of the building, a reddish glow bled through the shades and down their edges.

On that block only five cars were parked. Two old Ford jalopies. A white, spit-shined Cadillac limo with its chauffeur inside. A green British touring car. And the red Chevy.

There were only a few pedestrians. A couple strolling toward the river. A few sailors wandering up from the Club de Paris. A beggar woman with a gang of kids tagging behind, snooping in trash cans and gutters. The cop on the porch across the street from Hell looked awake, but just barely. And there was the doorman.

Hickey waited until the doorman glanced away down the hill, then he hustled back across the street.

Clifford hung out the Packard's rear window. "Is she there?"

"Sshh!" Hickey leaned on the car, got an inch from the kid's sorry face. "Yeah, she's there. Let me in."

He looked up the hill for the giant to come around the corner and give him a wave, telling him the Jeep was parked and ready, on Revolución. But McColgin didn't show yet. Hickey slid into the Packard. The kid moved over. He sat with both hands under his coat, one hand on the pistol, the other on the gas mask. Whenever he glanced at Hickey, a grimace tightened his face. When he turned away, it became a vicious snarl, and his hands squeezed the mask and pistol brutally. In the front seat, Tito sat puffing on a brown cigaret. The smoke seeped out between his clenched teeth. Enrique kept busy popping his knuckles and watching out the back window.

"You gonna take orders, now," Hickey asked the kid, "or do just like you want in the battle?"

Clifford wagged his head sullenly.

"Hey. Hey." Tito slapped the seat. "There he is."

Blood gushed to Hickey's brain. He waited for the ebb, then checked his guns, the pistol at his chest and the M-1 rifle on the seat beside him. He checked his mask and the tear gas canister. "Let's move. *Ándale.*"

He started out and waved up the hill. McColgin disappeared behind the corner and Hickey came around the back of the car to Tito. He motioned toward the driver and said, "Tell him one more time—he doesn't move from here till after we go in. When the shooting starts, he gets down there fast." Tito gave a nod, then leaned into the car and talked to the driver, while Hickey turned to Clifford. "Got it straight? Keep your head?"

"I think so, Pop."

Hickey grabbed the kid's shoulders and stared at his misty blue eyes. "Say, 'yes sir. Damn right'!"

"Yes sir."

"Yes sir what?"

"I can do it. Damn right. I can."

By now the sailors had walked out of sight up the hill and the beggar with her kids had passed Hell and turned into an alley. Tito opened the trunk. Hickey and the kid stepped back there. Each of the three men took out an M-1 and stuck it under his coat with the butt hitched into a loop roped around his belt and the barrel pointed high. Hickey eyed the kid one last time and chucked him on the arm. Then Tito shut the trunk quietly. He looked at the others and smiled, but a gust of hot air blew uphill—his face jerked toward the wind and his teeth started chattering.

On the far sidewalk, Leo came edging down the hill close to the buildings. About when he got to the tattoo parlor, McColgin stepped around the corner, ran across the road, and followed Leo, fifty or so yards behind. Hickey gave a last encouraging look at the kid and ran over to Leo. They raised their eyebrows at each other and stood there a few seconds while Hickey keened his eyes down the hill and saw nobody except the cop who slouched on the porch gazing toward the moon, the Cadillac's chauffeur, and the doorman who was fussing with something in his hands.

Hickey and Leo walked side by side down the hill, stiffly because of all the weapons, off the concrete where it ended, along the shoulder, and across the dirt side street. About fifty feet past the intersection, Hickey stopped. They reached into their coats. Looked around once more. Still no innocent folks came walking and the only car that moved was down past the Club de Paris near the river.

Hickey raised one arm high. A moment later, McColgin cut diagonally across the road toward Hell, stumbling to act like a drunk, as the Jeep wheeled around the corner from Revolución, full of Mexicans and with two high ladders sticking up—it bounded down the hill and came alongside Hell about the same time McColgin staggered up to the doorman. At the same moment, Leo and Hickey moved on the cop.

As the cop's face turned, he looked robust and friendly, until he saw the gringos, one with a rifle aimed at his gut, the other with a silenced Colt .45. The cigaret fell from his mouth, and he made his last mistake—he reached for his gun. Hickey shot him twice. You heard only *pfft* sounds like wine bottles opening—then a deadpan moan as the cop rolled onto his side, one hand grabbing his chest where the bullets sucked in, the other hand flying from the butt of his pistol up toward the sky. Then Leo was on top of him, throwing a gag on the man's mouth and rolling him over to tie it. But the man was gone. His back looked like a squashed dog in the road.

Hickey stood there, a little dizzy as he stared at the cop. Somebody zipped past him—Tito running to the Cadillac. Somebody else came sprinting by. Clifford Rose.

The Japanese chauffeur had seen the cop go down at about the same moment he glimpsed the giant dragging the guy from the doorway of Hell out toward the Jeep. Frightened, baffled, he froze for a second, then grabbed for the door lock and the window crank. The window got halfway up before Clifford's rifle barrel knocked the chauffeur's cap off and put a gash in his skull. He threw his arms in front of him, fists under his chin, while Tito jumped in on the passenger side and rammed the silencer of a .45 to his ear. Tito pulled the chauffeur out and to the ground. In a minute, the bound and gagged chauffeur and the knocked-out doorman lay piled in the rear of the Jeep. And by now the Peña twins had set up the ladders.

The street was quiet. The loudest sounds were drunken gringos hollering a few blocks away, drums from a boulevard nightclub, and a mariachi whooping in falsetto. The Jeep took off with the captives, down the hill toward the river where Rafael would make sure they got tied well enough and dropped out on the riverbank.

Hickey crossed the road on a diagonal toward the uphill side of the bakery. The whole gang except Rafael gathered around him. He rubbed his eyes, which still saw the bloody cop. Then he looked at the kid, winced, and snapped, "Where's your rifle?"

Clifford stared, deranged for a second, panting through his nose. Finally he spun around and ran across the street to the Cadillac, grabbed his M-1 off the hood, and ran back to the others.

Hickey told them to stay put. He crept down past the bakery and stood at the corner of Hell, listening. An African rhythm came out of the place, a conga and a tom-tom, along with the noise of chattering, laughter, and harsh, shouted words. All from downstairs. He moved to beneath the side upstairs window toward the front, and stood beside the ladder. After a minute he started to make out a deep voice in Spanish, like the railing of a preacher. Next he vaguely heard several hands clapping.

He stepped to the sidewalk, waved, moved back into the passway. When the others got there, he snarled, "Let's go get her," and moved toward the street. Clifford jumped out and followed. His eyes had grown big and enchanted, wandering. Hickey pushed him back toward the ladder. "You climb up there, remember?" he snapped. "And don't make a move till I fire. Then smash the window, jump in, run for Wendy and grab her and get out the door. Fast. Understand?"

The kid nodded dreamily. Yet Hickey couldn't wait another second. He moved to the corner of the building and waved McColgin ahead as they'd planned. Hickey came next, then Tito. Leo held the rear. They paused for a second, single file at the door. Then McColgin burst in, bellowing, waving the machine gun, and Tito ran past him, jumped on the bar, and stuck his rifle on the bartender's nose before that one could hit the alarm bell to upstairs.

The room was full of blond whores, sharply dressed, wiry Mexicans, Okie stevedores, Marines who'd sneaked over the border dressed like civilians, a few of Cárdenas's army, Indian waiters, and three bouncers—yet nobody argued with the giant who waved a machine gun, whooping as he jumped up and down.

Hickey ran over and grabbed the giant's arm. "Cut out the damned yodeling!"

Then he caught up to Leo, passed the old man, and stopped

before the stairs. From a scabbard on his belt, Hickey pulled a bayonet. He snapped it onto his rifle. He stabbed through the curtain and jumped to the stairs with the bayonet out, ready to stick the guard he imagined would be on the landing. But there was no guard. Hickey charged up the stairs, and Leo trudged behind. When Leo reached the landing, Hickey kicked the door, yelling, "Freeze, cabrones!"

As he fired into the room, high so the bullets powdered the ceiling, Clifford and Isidoro burst through the windows. The kid's M-1 jerked spastically and his face looked purplish through the incensed light.

A long, mahogany table stretched the length of the room. Around it in padded chairs of soft, tucked leather, sat a dozen men in military officer uniforms. Scarlet campaign hats with gold braided bands. Suits of dark, velvety blue with gold clusters on the shoulder, golden stripes around the sleeves, and large gold buttons everywhere. Not one man had dark skin. Half of them were blond. They aged from around thirty up to one ancient man. Santiago del Monte, Hickey suspected—the patriarch, the entrepreneur who'd given soda pop to Mexico. The way his hat perched showed his pointed head. He looked shrunken except in the long neck, the gray bush mustache and bulging hazel eyes. In a rage he lunged forward and jabbered commands as if nobody held guns on them. Nearest the patriarch sat Leon del Monte of the Club de Paris. He'd frozen with a golden chalice at his lips. About halfway down the right side of the table Franz Metzger hissed curses in German. At the far end, at the head of the table, wearing a big golden star on his hat, Zarp stood flanked by a tall, husky blonde with naked breasts. She held a gold tray of golden cups, until they dropped.

With a strange grin and a pitch like joy in his voice, Clifford cried out, "Where is she?" and wheeled his rifle at Zarp, who stood just a few feet away.

"No!" Hickey yelled.

In a flash from a holster at his side Zarp drew a big automatic and fired three rapid shots. The right side of Clifford Rose's head

114

flew off. It splattered on the wall beside the window he'd jumped through ten seconds before.

The next shots, from Hickey's M-1, launched Zarp's big carcass flying backward. His chair toppled, and flipped on its side. He rolled out onto the floor. Then quiet fell. All you cold hear was Zarp's growling and a thunk as Franz Metzger heaved forward onto the table. Isidoro Peña had cut the slick German down from behind. Yet Franz began to rise, pushing with his arms on the table. His head angled upward, eyes gleaming, he loosed a howl so miserable, loud and deep it might've cracked windows and terrified neighbors—except Isidoro Peña finished the psycho with two slugs in the neck.

"Whoa!" Hickey shouted. "Jesus!"

Leo gulped a deep, rasping breath and pounded the floor with his heel as he stared at the kid, who never uttered a sound. Clifford jerked a few times, and then gave in.

"Guns on the table," Hickey yelled. Only some of them reached to their sides. Hickey slapped Leon del Monte in the head and shouted, "Tell 'em in Spanish." Soon the table was covered with pistols, and Hickey prodded del Monte's neck with his bayonet. "Where's the damned girl?" he roared.

Nobody spoke except old Santiago who kept squawking volleys of curses. But a few eyes turned toward the northwest corner of the room as though to watch the servant girl, who had backed against the wall when the guns fired, and now squatted, huddled in a ball between an icebox and a closet.

As Hickey looked at her, she squirmed a little and leaned against the closet door. Stepping over, he eyed the girl closer, backstepped, and motioned for Isidoro to gather the weapons, then he nudged the servant away from the closet door. He grabbed the handle, turned and pulled it open a crack. He raised his M-1 and used his foot to throw the door open wide.

She was dressed as before in the red velvet robe. Her head was bound in a pouch of leather with draw strings tied around her neck, only a small hole to breathe through. She was on a chair. Gasping. Her hands folded tightly on her waist.

115

Hickey leaned his rifle against the wall by the closet door. He reached in and touched the girl's hands. They gripped tighter together against his touch but loosened after a moment, and she whispered, "An angel."

She rubbed his hand and then squeezed it, tight as she'd held her own, and when he raised her arm she stood. With his left hand he untied the pouch's leather string and lifted it off her head.

There was her face, bright as ever, glowing a little in the reddish light. Her eyes drifted and sparkled. Her lips quivered. For a minute, Hickey shed his meanness and fury. All the terror left him. He put his left arm around her shoulders and she fell tightly against his side. As he turned her toward the table and the doorway, he picked up his rifle. Then he spotted Clifford lying there. He pushed the girls' head down a little and turned it so her eyes were against his chest. Too late.

"My Clifford," she whispered.

"Don't look. C'mon, we're getting outa here."

"My Clifford too."

Hickey shut his eyes and tried to think. Finally he hollered, "Leo, you guys get the kid outa here. Then come back for the girl."

"No use, Tom. He's dead as they come."

"Do it anyway!"

"Well, who's gonna watch 'em?"

"Me!" Still holding the girl, Hickey moved back his coat, hitched the rifle to his side, pulled his .45 and leveled it around the table. So Isidoro, and finally Leo, hitched their rifles too and came around to the kid. For a minute they gazed down at Clifford. Then the Mexican hoisted the feet, Leo the shoulders. Blood poured down Leo's right leg from where the kid's ear and temple used to be. Leo began moaning, "Aw Lord, no," and kept on every time he looked at the kid, as they dragged him out and down the stairs. He cussed while they passed through the bar and all the way outside. They threw Clifford into the Jeep, parked across the street by the Cadillac. Then they ran back upstairs.

The girl cinched both arms around Hickey as he watched the table, the pistol following his eyes, which kept drifting to where

116

Zarp lay a couple yards from his feet, still except when he made little grunts of breath. Hickey wished any of the rats would twitch, give him an excuse to blast somebody. If not for the girl, he sure would've made Zarp's head like Clifford's. But she clung to him so tightly that he trembled with her. With each of her breaths, a little shudder and moan escaped. She squeezed so hard he could feel her cool skin through the velvet robe. It made him wild with tenderness—like years ago when he first held his newborn daughter—but now at the same time a part of him kept raging. And another part of him looked at the gold. The chalices and urn. It seemed he remembered them from sometime long past. He stared at the golden cross with its twined serpent, at the men's coat buttons and shoulder bars. For a moment he got so lost in Wendy and the gold, that when he heard noise on the stairs, he wheeled enough to get off shots at the door.

Leo yelled, "Hey, spare me, you goddamn boob." He and Isidoro stood in the doorway. "Okay, whatta we do now?"

"Take her down," Hickey said.

The Mexican slipped by and ran around the table. Old Leo dragged behind, panting. He finally got there and hooked the girl's arm but couldn't peel her off Hickey, the way she had fastened like a noose around his waist. And her little moans came higher, faster.

"I'll take her then. You hold these guys." Hickey glared around the table. "Waste 'em all, if you feel like. I don't give a damn."

Leo made a grim smile, and raised his M-1 and swept it back and forth along the table, as Hickey led the girl to the door.

On the first few stairs, her feet kept missing. So he lifted her into his arms. She felt light as a spirit. He carried her the rest of the way down and out through the saloon, where the people sat frozen at the bar, around the stage, and at the tables. Some of the men looked ready to cheer. A few whores sat beaming. Nobody spoke—except one blond whore, her bottom lip bandaged. *"Andale,"* she hollered, and stiffened in pain. *"Hombres, bravo."*

When he got through the front door, Hickey saw the Jeep waiting across the street and the Packard with Enrique set to drive, parked a few feet away from him. "Where'd they put Clifford?" he yelled. Enrique pointed at the Jeep.

He shoved the girl into the backseat of the Packard, and had to get tough and shake her to make her let loose of his side. Then he stood on the curb and yelled, full loud, "Now, Leo!"

A few seconds later came screams from upstairs as Leo let go the tear gas. In another few seconds when the tear gas blew downstairs, the screams became a legion. Then Leo hobbled out and nose-dived through the open rear door of the Packard. He pushed Wendy to the middle. Hickey jumped in on the left side, while Tito sprinted past the Packard and across the street and sprang into the Jeep, with Isidoro following. McColgin, the last of them, spun around and beat his chest, gave a cowboy whoop, and piled into the front of the Packard.

Hickey shouted, *"Vamonos!"*

The Packard rumbled down the hill.

They had reached the first cross-street, three long blocks from the river, when they heard sirens. Nobody had sense enough to figure which way they were coming from. Hickey was far gone, sitting still as granite, feeling as though parasites gnawed his insides from the skull down, thinking that Clifford lay dead in the Jeep, and how the kid had asked to die.

"Make a left!" Leo yelled.

The police car sped out of the cross-street just uphill from the Club de Paris. Another one followed, zoomed out from behind the Packard, in front of the Jeep, which leaned one way, then the other, and swerved and crashed through the wall of an upholstery shop. Gunfire rattled, fading as they sped on toward the river. Leo rested his face in his hands and groaned.

"Wait, look, somebody's running," McColgin hollered. "Maybe it's Tito. There goes the boy. They're getting away."

The Packard slowed down almost to a stop, with Enrique Peña's head out the window. Leo pointed and said, "This guy's kid's back there."

"So's every cop in Tijuana," McColgin said. "But, I bet they ain't got one of these." He lifted the Thompson gun, aimed it through the window, and fired a burst at the sky. "C'mon, you old farts, let's take 'em!"

Everybody stared at Hickey. Leo. Enrique, with a hand over most of his face. Even the girl, her eyes sparked with fear.

Hickey didn't know—given a hundred years and a clear head he still wouldn't know the answer. What finally came out of his mouth wasn't from his brain. Maybe from his heart.

"We're taking the girl to the border!"

The driver bowed his head, crossed himself, turned around and drove. He slid left onto the river road and gunned it while McColgin leaned out the window blasting the moon and stars. They swerved through deep sand, then Enrique bent forward and slugged his head on the steering wheel.

Leo reached over, touched the driver's arm. "So they take 'em to jail, we'll get 'em out. That's a promise."

Enrique just sped faster over the craggy dirt, ruts, and washboard. By now the girl had quit moaning, yet she pressed Hickey as though rooted there with her cheek hard against the front of his shoulder. Her face lifted up. In a voice gentle as a Brahms tune, she asked, "Where is my Clifford?"

Hickey couldn't say it. He just stared, at her face, like none he'd ever seen but closest, in his eyes, to Elizabeth's, when she was a child who got hurt and needed him.

The girl's lips parted and crooked into a smile. "Is he—in—Heaven?"

Hickey shaded his eyes. "Yeah."

She drew back her arms from around him, put her hands on his chest, and beamed. "Oh—it's pretty. Clifford likes the big—fish—he can catch them and—can we go there tomorrow?"

They were nearing the bridge. Sirens wailed again. You couldn't tell from where. There might be a roadblock. Hickey didn't give a damn, not about anything except holding Wendy Rose. He squeezed her tight as a lover.

119

17

Suddenly, about 3 A.M., a gust of wind came howling as though frantic to reach the sea. At Mission Beach, along the sea wall and back on the walkways between the little houses and courts, the wind bent the palms, knocking dead fronds loose. One of them banged on the roof above where Wendy Rose lay.

She snapped awake and looked frantically around for the Devil. When she didn't see him, or Mofeto or Franz, she caught her breath and closed her eyes for a second. Then they shot open wide. "Oh, oh," she wailed.

She was lost again. The war and the angels must've all been a dream.

The room had big windows. You could see stars behind the curtains. A piano, a mirror, and a chest with many drawers. Two beds and pink blankets. And somebody asleep. Getting up, Wendy noticed the soft pajamas she wore. She ran her hands down her sides, picked up the hem of her shirt and rubbed it against her cheek. Then she tiptoed close to the other bed. A pretty girl lay sleeping there.

Wendy's chest heaved, fluttered, and she got sad, thinking that somebody else had come to Hell tonight. "Poor girl, poor girl," she whispered, and touched the long black hair. She'd thought the black-haired girls stayed in Paris and never came to Hell. This one must've done something horrid. Wendy kissed her on the cheek. She wanted to climb in bed with her and touch the milky skin.

But she stopped still, thinking of the dream and the angel Tom Hickey who Clifford had brought to carry her out of Hell. She remembered his big, warm hands, his mustache and big nose and kind, pretty eyes. She sat on the edge of her bed and moaned very low. To quiet her heart, she prayed. After a while she saw an image of God. Far away, in a cloud, wearing a dark suit and hat, he didn't speak or move but watched over her until she got a little warmer, then she heard noises. They sounded like nothing she knew. She tried to say them in a whisper. *Whssh, kalump, shoosh, kaloomb.* Finally she got up and went to the window.

Outside, beyond the sea wall and white sand, red glowing water crashed down. A brand new sight for Wendy. Once, in the Presidente's house, she'd gotten to look through a window and see, far away, what she guessed was an ocean. It was bigger than the lake in Heaven. But the water so close was a new marvel that gave her a pleasant chill, and she wanted to see it even closer. Beside the window was a door, unlatched, that opened as she touched it. She stepped out, anxious about what she'd find and wondering if she was allowed out here. She stared at the singing, crashing water full of stars, and finally tiptoed across the brick patio and boardwalk and stood at the sea wall. Off to her left little fires burned, crackling on the sand near the tent city. From beyond the tents music began, a swing band in the ballroom where factory workers danced all night.

A man snorted and Wendy gasped. She whirled and saw Tom Hickey asleep in a redwood chair with his hat pulled down over his eyes. Too joyful to hold back, she ran to him and touched his face. The hat lifted and his eyes popped open. "Don't sleep here," she whispered.

She helped him up and led him inside. She took off his coat and shirt, trousers, shoes, laid them all across a chair.

Hickey watched her dreamily. Like Clifford used to do. She nudged him toward the bed, and when he'd slid under the covers and moved toward the wall, Wendy climbed in beside him. With a grateful sigh, she reached out and held him the way she had before in the car. He laid an arm around her back, his hand came snug on her waist. Same as the first time he touched her, in Hell. Wendy thought his touch felt like Clifford's long ago, before he got scared of her. Nobody else ever touched her like Ma and her Clifford used to. Nothing like George, or the Devil or his captains. Or Pa. She closed her eyes, kissed Tom Hickey's shoulder, and prayed he was like a prince in Ma's story who would come and take care of her and sleep beside her every night forever. Angels could be princes and they lived forever. In Heaven, with Clifford.

She put a finger to her lips, kissed it, and pressed it lightly on Hickey's eye. She tightened her arm around him and gripped him tightly with her fingers, as she started remembering too much. It made her breathe hard and moan in little gasps because she couldn't scream, or the Devil would hear, and tie the bag on her head. But the big hand squeezed gently on her waist and she thought how Clifford had brought Tom Hickey to rescue her. Tomorrow they could drive to Heaven. She saw the emerald water and rocky shore where birds swooped between rustling pines and aspens. She breathed more quietly and soon the wind stopped. She slept without a single bad dream.

Hickey lay still. All he wanted and all it seemed he could do was to feel the heat of her fingers, the press of her knee against his side. Feel the sweet air that breathed out of her onto his cheek. The brush of fine hair against him. Her toes wiggling just down from his knee. He didn't want anything else, and it felt like bliss, that relief from wanting things.

At 10 AM, Leo sent his daughter Magda in to rouse them for breakfast.

Magda, the pretty girl with black hair, showed Wendy Rose her closet and said she could wear any of the dresses. Wendy picked out a white pleated skirt and a shiny blouse, with puffy shoulders, colored like balloons in a white sky. She pulled down the clothes, laid them on the bed, unsnapped her pajamas and stepped out of them. With a giggle, Magda turned and ran to the kitchen. Wendy finished taking off her blouse, then she looked at Hickey to see how

122

he'd watch her—because people acted different when they saw her skin. Happy. Or scared, like she was ugly. Or mean.

On the bed with his head propped up by an elbow, Hickey smiled a little and his eyes clouded. He wiped one of them. "Get dressed," he said.

She backed up slowly and dressed, watching Hickey slip on his white shirt and dark gray suit, remembering that last night he'd worn a uniform. Maybe the war got over last night, she hoped, maybe the fighting in Hell ended the war.

Smells of hotcakes and bacon floated in from the kitchen. She thought, This sure mustn't be Hell, in Hell the food stings, even your nose. She smiled way up to her cheekbones. "Oh, I love this place."

Hickey led her out to the kitchen, a big yellow room with a white table, flowers, sunny windows. He pulled out a chair for her and Magda brought her a plate of hotcakes dripping with butter and syrup. When Violet brought them coffee and bacon, Wendy started for the bacon with her fingers, but remembered her manners and picked up her fork, and hooked a piece of bacon with it. She ate and looked at Violet, a blond, smiley lady with glasses who finally came over, put a hand on Wendy's arm and called her Honey, and asked her to feel at home here as long as she pleased. Wendy said thank you. She nibbled the hotcakes so they'd last longer. She was still nibbling after Hickey, Violet, Leo, and Magda had all finished. After Leo went out on business, Violet washed most of the dishes and left to go shopping, and Magda went to answer the phone. Hickey sat near an open window, smoking and watching her. Finally she chewed her last bite, licked her fingers, and said, "Your family is nice and pretty, Tom Hickey."

"They're Leo's family. They like you too."

"Oh yes. I can cook. Rabbits and fish—and potatoes—and corn. And bread. I'll do everything like that for you—oh, does she have horses?"

"Nope."

"Then I can wash all—the clothes. And make pillows. And quilts. They'll be glad we can stay here."

123

Wendy had to turn away, because his eyes got like bullets, the way the Devil's captains' eyed did. Her chest gripped tight, a cramp shot to her brain—she threw her hands to her face and started to cry. Then Hickey stood above her. He touched her face and she grabbed and clutched his hand. When he asked what was wrong, she said, "Do you have to go to the war like my Clifford?"

"Not much chance. I've gotta work for the army, but I'll be staying here in town."

"Oh," she cried, and kissed him lusciously, high on the cheek, which stirred him too much. He backed away a step, patted her hair, and stared at her eyes until they made him dizzy. Then he walked her out to the sea wall. It was Thursday. The tent city people were gone to cut, weld, run machines, building ships and airplanes at Consolidated and Rohr or down the coast at National Steel. Their kids were in school. On a mile of beach, that perfect, breezy summer day in April, you might've only found a dozen humans. Palms that lined the sea wall swayed back and forth in the errant wind. The waves arched back like stallions. Wendy stood barefoot, her toes wiggling in the hot sand. She gripped Hickey's hand and kept smiling. She brushed Hickey's arm with a kiss. "What is this place?"

"Mission Beach. Swell place, huh?"

"Oh yes. Is Mission Beach far from Heaven?"

Hickey grinned. "An awful long way."

She hugged herself tightly. A deep frown took her face and her eyes wandered. "Oh look," she said, and stared at a gliding pelican. After a minute her body uncoiled and she reached up a hand to brush back her hair. Hickey looked out to sea where even in daylight the foam seemed reddish, from billions of plankton drawn to the warm tidewater.

The last thing he wanted was to break this spell, when the world looked harmless and full of bright moments, people and things. But there were questions he couldn't hold back, the need to find out who she was, and he couldn't wait. Since last night he'd felt jerked around on puppet strings by his feelings for the girl. As if she'd been split in two. One side was pure as anything he'd touched.

124

The other side, the one that probably killed George and poured blood on Franz Metzger, must be crazy, living in a different world with strange and dangerous rules. He'd known enough crazy people so they spooked him. You couldn't get peace around them, not knowing any second what they'd do.

He said, "Maybe you can tell me what happened down there."

She started blinking rapidly and turned away, toward a gust that blew sand at her eyes. "No."

"Sure, okay. You want to forget it."

"Yes, and I'm scared."

He made his voice softer. "Yeah, anybody'd be scared. But you know all that's over, right?"

"I don't know," she said fervidly. "They can hurt me. Mofeto and Franz and the captains can find me—in Mission Beach."

"Mofeto's a prisoner. We've got him, and Franz is dead."

Her mouth widened, her eyes pinched closed and then shot open wide. "The captains can find me. Or the Devil. He will. Oh, he told me—the first time my Clifford came to Hell. After three years I can leave. He promised. Before three years is over—if Clifford takes me away, the Devil promised he'd even make a war to take me back there."

"The Devil, that's Zarp?"

"Yes. But the Devil or the captains can't go to Heaven. Can they? And we can drive to Heaven? See my Clifford and be safe there."

She grinned. Hickey wanted to lie, convince her there was no chance Zarp's men could jump the border after her, when in truth those Mexicans and Nazis had a better chance of taking her back than he'd had of freeing her. They had soldiers, brains, they were ruthless. He wanted to say he'd drive her to Heaven in a few days, find Clifford. He wished he could say any lie, to keep her happy. But lies didn't work that way. He muttered, "I can't take you to Heaven."

Facing him squarely, hands at her sides, she stared a long moment. Her eyelashes batted erratically and her jaw began to quiver. She raised a hand, ready to cover her eyes. "Why?" she

125

moaned. "You are an angel. They go to Heaven. My Clifford's there."

He gripped her shoulders gently, looked so deep into her eyes it seemed he found the source of their light. It looked like a star, miles away yet inside her. He stared a minute, entranced, puzzled, feeling his will to speak slip away.

"I'm not an angel," he said. A pain shot up from his belly through his heart. Wendy's shoulders tightened hard as bone. Her lips stiffened and closed. She turned just enough to let her eyes scan the beach and sea.

18

Twelve hours after Franz Metzger died in Hell, his cousin Juan got summoned to the Casa de Oro. Metzger had sat up drinking all that night, even after Consuelo threatened to send the children to her sister in Morelia. Each day he drank more, slept less. He hadn't been sober in a week. But when the message arrived that Franz had been murdered, the despair that trapped him included such a wicked nausea, he couldn't drink anymore. Consuelo had gone with the children for a walk to the ocean. Metzger lay on the floor, his head propped against the wall.

Tom Hickey was the murderer, Metzger believed. He couldn't remember what he'd told the gringo, but he must've betrayed his cousin, and the Bund. He breathed shallowly, listening, tormented by the kitten scratching at the door, a neighbor's hens clucking, footsteps crunching on the gravel road, turning into his yard.

A boy from the grocery wedged a note into the screen door. It took Metzger five minutes to cross the room and read his summons to the Casa de Oro. They would pick him up in an hour.

He staggered into the bathroom, filled the tub with cold water and fell into it. He didn't wash or shave, just lay there wondering how they'd kill him. When his shivering got violent, he stepped out, dressed in his sergeant major's uniform, and paced until they came for him.

The white limo drove Metzger and four other officers around the hill, through the gateway to Las Lomas. The officers finished expressing their grief about Franz and sympathy for Juan. They turned to speaking of plans for revenge, while they sped past the race track and past meadows alongside the country club where thorough-breds grazed, and up, winding between the orchards, the gardens, the high block walls.

The Casa de Oro was a Spanish colonial mansion the size of a football field, three stories high. White and square, with arching windows of inlaid tile, wrought iron window bars and balcony railings. The gate and front door guards presented their rifles and saluted. The officers passed through the entryway and ballroom, across the mosaic floor, beneath the golden chandelier, beside the rare paintings in gilded frames.

They climbed the stairs and waited in a parlor near a long hallway of bedrooms and offices. With them waited four captains and a lieutenant general. Sipping brandy, munching fruit and nuts, the officers talked of how Field Marshal Zarp was on his feet already, in spite of the dangerous gunshot wound in his side. A captain raised a toast to Zarp's courage. Metzger didn't toast. It was too late to pretend. All he could choose was to die with honor or shame. He wouldn't have to beg for his family. Consuelo would escape, take the children to Baltimore, find a brave gringo like Tom Hickey.

The Presidente's office door opened, let out an old German captain who marched down the hall and sat with the others. Raising his swollen, brown-spotted hands, he proclaimed the gringos would die today or tomorrow. He gathered the officers closer and whispered that Zarp had commanded three soldiers, three Federales and the police chief to bring back La Rosa.

On the drive downtown, Hickey said, "The girl's a treasure, Leo. I watch her and think, nobody's this honest, everybody's a little phony, nobody's got this much heart."

Leo said, "Looks to me like you're stuck on her. Control yourself, Tom. Don't go getting sympathy confused with love. 'Course, she's some cutie, real nymph-like . . . "

"Whoa."

"The faerie kind, I mean. Free spirit, until this coma or whatever the hell. She's a kid, though, a moron kid, and you never been the kind's gotta take any skirt he can get."

"I'm not too sure she's a moron."

"Yeah? What is she then?"

"Don't know. Seems like her brain dreams off. Not stupid. Punchy though. Maybe she's gotten socked too many times." Punchy, the way he felt right now, with his brain zinging off to visions of Clifford's bloody head, Zarp writhing on the floor of Hell. Hickey's conscience filled with the noise of gunshots, sirens, screams. Suddenly all went quiet and he saw Wendy running across the beach in white and polka dots, kicking up sand, jumping and clapping as the shorebreak got her in the knees. Soon that vision blurred to a room full of gold. One he'd seen almost twenty years ago. The memory that had flashed last night in Hell, of a room in the old Agua Caliente Casino. Madeline had shown him the place, one night when she was singing there. A salon full of golden statues, candlesticks, plates and bowls, two golden chandeliers, displays of jewelry and knicknacks, all polished to shine like noonday.

As they cruised down Harbor Drive past the wharves and ferry landing, Hickey lamented that he hadn't stolen the gold in Hell. The chalices, the candlesticks, gold buttons off the uniform coats of the high officers. If he'd been thinking straight, he could've been a rich guy. Sailed off to Cuba and found a place where mountains ran down to the sea. Bought a nightclub resort where bigshots gathered and Elizabeth could stay with him every summer, to swim and dance and ride horses through the forests. A finer place than Paul Castillo could give her. A place that would prove to Madeline and everybody that Tom Hickey'd made a dent in this world. That he was a dad to make any kid proud.

Just as they reached the door to their office, the phone quit ringing. Leo thought it might've been his contact with the Federales.

So he got on the phone to a Mexican operator, repeated the number four times, swatted his hat on the desk.

Hickey stood by the window that looked out over Broadway. He watched a pack of salesgirls stepping out of Marston's, across the street and three stories down, laughing, their hair flung back, and skirts clinging tight in the wind. A couple sailors, enlisted guys, ran across the street, dodging traffic as they raced after the girls. They must've been new in town—didn't know yet that girls like those could pick from a hundred officers and flyboys. Lookers like that didn't need any lowly swab.

He turned and listened to Leo on the phone. "What's up? . . . Yeah, sure . . . Who says?" Hickey sat in the wooden roller chair and took out his pipe. For a minute, Leo sat mutely, ear to the phone, his free hand wadding paper from a note pad and shooting baskets into the far trash can. "What's the story on those guys? . . . Which del Monte? . . . That's all you got. . . . Yeah. Sure. Thanks, Ruiz."

Leo hung up, sat on the desk, and leaned close to his partner, then closer. His mouth pulled back grimly. "Four new stiffs down there."

Hickey muttered, "Four," and looked at his pipe a long time as if he expected a genie to come out and fix everything. Then he stuffed it full of Walter Raleigh. Slowly. Took a match out. Sat still for a minute. And without meaning to, he started to bite his tongue—just hard enough to feel some pain. Make it real.

"One kraut," Leo said. "That'd be Franz Metzger. One gringo." He sighed and looked at the door, as if Clifford might suddenly appear. "Two Mex fellas. No names yet."

"Four dead men."

"Yeah and nobody in jail. That means two of our guys got away. Maybe."

Hickey lit a match and sat watching the flame. When it touched his fingers he shook it out. "Either of the Mexicans have an eye missing?"

"Shit, Tom, any of 'em might've had a lot more than that missing, taking on all those cops. But, yeah—I bet Tito got it. Else he probably would've called by now."

"Maybe he did."

"Naw, he's got my home phone, too."

"Call Vi."

Leo's cheeks puffed out. He glowered down at Hickey. "You been acting too damn bossy for my taste."

When he reached for the phone, Hickey went back to the window, trying to shift his mind off the dead guys for now, telling himself, You got years to think about them, if you live so long.

Even at 3:30, before the rush, hundreds of pedestrians scurried below. Stockbrokers heading toward the Grant Grille for a shot of pedigree Scotch. Navy wives pouring off the busses, streaming into Woolworths. Pretty girls from Visalia, Barstow, Cucamonga, running in their wobbly high heels out of the YWCA where they shared little closet-size rooms. In this last year and some, since Pearl Harbor, San Diego had grown to be the most crowded city on earth. You couldn't get a hotel room without bribing a desk clerk, and the Chamber of Commerce had declared, "Don't come here until after the war."

Yet among all the people down there, Hickey thought, you might not find a gem like Wendy Rose. Even if her brain *was* split in two.

"He didn't call," Leo said. "So we got nothing left to do but pray for the dead and figure how to pay back your money."

"What else did the Federale tell you?"

"Nothing. Just four dead men and not a damned word in the paper."

Hickey let that sink in for a minute. "What's he make of all those officers up there last night, and Zarp in the general getup?"

"Aw, what the hell's it matter? The kid's dead. His sister's okay. And you gotta speed your ass back to the army. And I gotta go to the john."

As Leo trudged out, Hickey stepped back to the window. Four dead men, he thought, and started seeing them fall. Clifford's brains flying. Franz Metzger screaming goodbye. A wave of nausea flooded him. He looked out, focused on the corner of C Street at the sign that said THE GOLDEN LION, where it used to say RUBIO'S STEAKHOUSE.

131

Less than four months ago. Until Hickey wised up, found out his partner Paul Castillo had bribed a guy on the rationing board, put some kind of heat on the boss at Central Supplies, the biggest meat packing house, and that was why they were getting half of the grade-A prime beef in town. So Hickey, the loser, who thought you didn't need to cheat to make your mark, told Castillo to get straight or get lost. And Castillo got lost, all right.

Less than four months it took for Hickey to study the collapse of his world and realize he was a fool—not a shred of doubt anymore. Not when four dead men lay on his heart, and there was no Elizabeth to cheer him, to make him feel big and generous. In less than four rotten months, his life collapses like Europe, and he can't even volunteer for a suicide mission or else who'd take care of the girl—this ignorant nineteen-year-old beauty he'd knocked into some crazy spell by confessing he wasn't any angel? In a second she turns to a dummy, can't hear you anymore, picks up handfuls of sand, tosses them up and lets them rain down on herself, starts humming one tune and changes to another every measure or so. What the hell could you do with somebody like that?

He gave the wall a light kick, smiled darkly and turned to meet Leo coming back from the john.

"Now," Hickey said. "What'd the Federale tell you about Zarp and those creeps?"

"To forget the whole mess, keep it out of the papers. They're gonna take care of everything. We're supposed to bury our heads in the sand."

"Yeah. Swell," Hickey muttered, and went to the phone. He scowled through the bad connections and requests he had to repeat three or four times to the Mexican operator before she understood him. Finally he reached Groceria El Portal, told the clerk to run a message to Juan Metzger. He hung up, looked at Leo and shrugged.

"What'd you say, Tom?"

"I gave Metzger a choice. Either he can meet us at the border tonight at six, or I'm coming down to his place at seven."

"You crazy? Go down there, you probably won't get ten feet before some cop blasts you. Even if you got to Metzger, all you'll find is the Gestapo waiting to boil you in oil and gnaw your bones."

"Yeah," Hickey said. "I know. I'm betting on Metzger. He was already spooked bad. You couldn't reason with the guy. I'm betting a threat's all he can hear."

With a couple of free hours, Leo decided to drive up to La Jolla, talk to a lady about another case he had, trying to refute evidence against a rich shoplifter. Hickey caught a ride back to Leo's house, to check on the girl.

She was on the beach with Magda, still in the white dress with bright balloons. Since morning her hair had gotten frizzed by the sun and breeze, her face had turned pink, her lips paled. Even when Hickey got close and said her name, she didn't look up. He stood silently watching. Now and then she would smile and toss her head. Other times her brows furled, she drew her chin down to her throat and moaned softly, kneeling on the sand, rocking back and forth on her knees, in the same rhythm as when she'd danced at the Club de Paris. All the while, she picked up sand and let it pour through her fingers. Magda said she'd been like that all day.

Nearly three hours, until the tide had gone down and kids from the tent city were running home toward supper, Hickey sat beside the girl.

Four dead men, he thought. Maybe Tito. Clifford. His gut cramped just to think the name. A sweet kid gone to hell for his sister, and Hickey let him die, let him go down there playing soldier when any dope could see he was too heartsick and nuts with worry to know what he was doing. Clifford should've been standing guard outside or downstairs holding a gun on the drinkers. Better, he should've been waiting at the border.

And Tito. Three days ago the poor chump was just out looking for a fare. Then Hickey steps in with a deal he can't turn down, on account of all his life hustling in TJ he's learned you've got to go where the dollar is. And he makes this fatal mistake—thinking Hickey knows how to run a battle. Thinks Hickey's a sharp guy.

Sparks flew up from Hickey's pipe in the hot breeze gusting from the east. The wind hissed through the tops of palm trees, blew against the waves and made the whitecaps shudder. Wendy Rose gazed out to sea where sailboats glided, miles away but looking far closer. Cormorants swooped, pelicans sat on the breakers, trios of dolphin bobbed past. Kids rode the waves. Hickey watched the girl, ransacking his brain for what to do, how to fix her.

19

= = =

At 5:50, Leo dozed behind the wheel of his Packard, at the curb a block north of the San Ysidro border. Hickey stood about twenty yards from the walk-through gate with his back to the MP, talking to Mr. Chee whom he'd called to and motioned over while the MP harrassed a Marine.

"Yes siree," Mr. Chee said. "They all got your vital statistics and orders to grab you. For AWOL and accessory to homicide, both. But the corporal here don't care. I squared you with him. So maybe you tell me about last night?"

While Hickey talked, each of them kept an eye on the border. Then Mr. Chee pointed. "Okay. Look at this guy. Could be he's German."

Hickey sneaked a glance and spotted Juan Metzger approaching the line. He dragged two large suitcases. A few steps behind, Consuelo followed, wearing a topcoat, probably to keep men from leering. She was tugging each of their kids by a hand.

"Let'em all in, pal," Hickey said. "Point'em straight up the road." He patted Mr. Chee's shoulder and headed for the Packard, keeping his face turned away from the drive-through gate and the two MPs. He sat on the Packard's front bumper, watched the Metzgers cross the line and walk his way, thinking he should act tough with this German, keep him afraid until he spilled everything. But the whole family looked so timid and spooked, he got up and walked a few steps to meet them, shook Juan and Consuelo's hands. Metzger's felt like raw beef. Consuelo's was warm. He took their bags, stashed them in the Packard trunk.

The trunk door slamming woke Leo. After a minute he followed the others into Sally's Cafe, a two-table, four-booth place with yellowed walls and tablecloths. Consuelo and the kids took a booth of their own. Leo and Hickey sat across from Juan Metzger. The German snatched a pint of tequila from a coat pocket and offered the other men a drink before gulping his own. Hickey studied the man and thought, Metzger's changed. Now he could look you in the eye, for a second at least. His face didn't sag or twitch.

"We are not going back," Metzger vowed. Even his voice had deepened. It was gruff now, more German.

"Swell. Then you're gonna need papers, contacts. You want that stuff?" Metzger nodded, and Hickey said, "You got it. All you gotta do is tell me what in Christ is brewing down there. These Nazis, Zarp, the del Montes—are they playing games or for real?"

"Not games." The German's voice cracked with outrage. "I'll tell you." He gulped a few breaths, rubbed his brow and started over. "Today Santiago del Monte called me into his office at the Casa de Oro. There is a very large desk. In front of it are two golden crosses, at least three feet high. On one of them is Jesus, nailed to the cross. On the other is a cobra. And Señor Zarp lies on a couch staring at me. His eyes are red like the devil's, and he tells me they know I am the gringo-loving coward. The one who sends you to Hell."

"Yeah," Hickey muttered. "Thanks."

Metzger shut his eyes, wiped his brow and finally looked over at Consuelo. She nodded. Her husband took a swallow of tequila, folded his hands.

He said, "Santiago screeches, 'Ha!' and thumps on the desk with his fist. Then Señor Zarp commands me to remove my clothes, and my crucifix and my wedding ring. The door is locked, the

136

window is barred, the guard points a rifle at me. I can do nothing except cross myself and pray to die bravely. I undress . . . " He drew a long breath and squeezed his eyes closed. "My golden crucifix and wedding ring, del Monte orders me to place on the desk. He steals them. He stares at me, and laughs." Metzger's boyish face had reddened and swelled with impotent fury. He reached for his bottle, gulped twice and hissed, "Señor Zarp orders me to kneel in front of the two golden crosses and repeat after him a terrible blasphemy. To the Christ, I am to say, 'Weak and miserable Jew, God of servants, old woman, beggar, poor lamb, I give you up to slaughter.'" Metzger whispered something more in German, then translated, "'I serve the lord of victory, the destroyer of the meek with his sword of burning light and . . . '" He covered his face with his hands and sat rigid.

"Whew," Leo said. "The hell. . . . Say, I'll bet you folks are hungry."

"First I wanta know what those guys are up to," Hickey demanded.

Throwing his hands out as though in surrender, the German groaned, "They are to help the Reich. For this purpose, I hear, somebody close to the Bund will try to overthrow the government of Baja California." His voice had cracked into a screech. The two gringos, Consuelo and her children, an old couple drinking cafe con leche, Sally the cook—everyone stared at Metzger.

"I'll be damned," Leo said.

"Which somebody?" Hickey growled. "Zarp?"

The German shrugged.

"Cárdenas?"

He shrugged again, miserably, and reached out, called for Consuelo, who left the children drinking sodas and came to sit beside her husband and hold his arm. She sat straight and gazed pensively from one man to the other. With Consuelo at his side, Metzger looked taller, younger, proud. Hope appeared in his widening eyes. He asked something in German and she answered, her voice making German sound almost pleasant. He folded his hands on the table and gave Consuelo a nod, allowing her to speak.

137

"We don't wish to believe Lázaro Cárdenas is a friend of the devil." She paused, watching Hickey and Leo as if to make sure they understood her English. "Franz boasted he dined with Cárdenas, but Franz would say any lie. That is why we don't believe that Baja will be in German hands by the middle day of April, as Franz boasted. We trust in General Cárdenas."

Hickey calculated and mumbled, "This Sunday." He sat pondering until Consuelo touched his arm. When he looked up, they met eye to eye.

"It was you killed Franz?"

A few seconds was all he could hold her stare. His throat got stiff and dry. "Yeah."

"Franz was a demon," Metzger whispered, and Consuelo nodded fiercely.

Hickey asked for the tequila, sipped a few times and passed it to Leo who'd nudged him. "Last night. Upstairs in Hell. Tell me about the gold up there. Chalices. Buttons on the officers' costumes. Gold bars where stripes ought to be. Who's passing out the gold?"

Consuelo said, "Santiago del Monte. Do you know of the Casa de Oro?"

"Whore house for the ricos. In the Lomas."

Metzger nodded. "Being there, one thinks of Heaven, El Dorado, the legend of Cibola. Del Monte believes gold contains elemental power that comes from the underworld. So Franz told us."

"How about Cárdenas? If he's on the level, why's he hang out with the del Montes and why doesn't he round up the Japs and Germans like he's supposed to?"

"Whoever his friends are," Consuelo said hotly, "the General is too humane to imprison innocent people."

His next question, Hickey didn't want to ask—from hearing the truth about Wendy Rose, he might wrestle Metzger for the tequila, swill it then stagger to Coco's for mescal. "What'd they do to the girl? Why'd they want to keep her so bad?"

Metzger shook his head a long time. "She is beautiful. I don't know any more. Only what Franz told me. I didn't see her. I can tell you Señor Zarp has sent people to steal her back."

Hickey bolted up with Leo right behind him. They bumped into each other, then Hickey fell over a chair, racing to grab the wall phone.

≡

The Metzgers wanted a ride to the Santa Fe depot, to catch a train for Baltimore and Consuelo's sister. As far as they could get from TJ. But Hickey drove them to a motel in East San Diego that Leo's nephew owned. He warned them to stay put. They'd be watched. He'd track them all the way back east, or anywhere, if they tried to ditch before he gave the okay. Whereas, if they stuck around, told the whole unembroidered truth, he promised to call in a favor, get their immigration papers.

Downtown, Leo dropped Hickey off in front of their office and went hunting a parking spot, while Hickey ran up the stairs to make a phone call. He dialed the Surf and Sand Motel, where they'd sent Vi, Magda and Wendy Rose. From Sally's Cafe, Leo had told Vi to take the pistol out of the nightstand, sneak herself and the girls across the court to a neighbor's, cut through there to the alley, back along the footpath to the seawalk, and hustle the three blocks to the Surf and Sand. To take a couple rooms and wait by the phone.

"Vi," Hickey said. "Everything quiet? . . . Nobody tailed you . . . How's Wendy? She say anything yet? . . . Okay. Now we're sending a couple fellows, lookouts. They won't bother you, just hang around outside. Okay? . . . Sure. Call you later."

Leo walked in, panting. "You oughta remember to shut the door. Looks more professional." He flipped his hat about six feet onto the rack. "All right, what've we got, Tom? A bunch of fruitcakes thinking they can take over Baja. That's all."

Hickey sat on the desk. He laughed bitterly. "Oh. That's all."

"Sure, just crazy talk. Look, there's nothing to it. Old Santiago del Monte's at the root of it, and he's about fifty yards out of his mind. You heard him squawking. He's sure too senile to run anything."

"How many sons are there?"

"Six, seven, I don't know. Look, suppose—what's gonna happen—if they really got the nerve to try and aren't just talking through their hats—if they got some weight in the Federales, the Rurales, the Army, and everyplace else, like they do with the cops. What's gonna happen is, if they got all that, they'll raise a little fuss and get blown to China and that'll be the end of it."

"Wait," Hickey said. "Who's this gonna blow 'em to China?"

"The Mex Army, Tom. Lázaro Cárdenas."

"Makes sense. Nothing to worry about. As long as Cárdenas is on the level."

"Sure."

"Yeah, and even if he's not, when the whole human race is blasting each other, who cares about some nuts in Tijuana, even if some of 'em are Nazis? And heck, what good is Baja anyway, even if they grabbed the place—a lotta rocks, sand, cactus. Right?"

"Yeah," Leo mumbled warily.

"Course it'd give the Nazi's a place to cremate San Diego from."

"Hold it, Tom. First German troops set foot there, we'd blitz the joint. Wouldn't be a thing but dust left on the whole peninsula."

"That'd be swell."

Leo got up, paced a few times around the desk and sat down again. With a pout, he said, "Sure, it'd be lousy. A lot of poor saps'd get massacred. But you know it won't happen. That bunch, the del Montes, Zarp, and them—they're not such dopes, except the old man. What you're talking about'd be like spitting at a tidal wave. Nobody's that cockeyed."

Hickey slugged the ash from his pipe into the trash can. "Whatta you figure that meeting last night was about, all those gold-braided monkey suits? Maybe planning a boy scout troop?"

Leo reached into the desk for a letter knife and started cleaning his fingernails, looking down at his hands. "Hell, Tom, there's Nazi meetings every day in Des Moines, Pittsburgh, Denver, right here in town. It don't mean we're in grave danger." He gazed over Hickey's head at a pinup calendar on the wall. "I'm hungry. You coming?"

"Naw. Bring me something back. I don't want to go out, the fresh air might wreck my black mood."

After Leo left, Hickey moved to the easy chair, and thought that no matter how he'd argued, this rumor of a coup seemed nonsense.

But just suppose. Then would the creeps try to take over in the open, or put a gun to the governor's head and run things that way? He wondered how close an eye the Mexican government kept on Baja. Two thousand miles from the Capital, less than ten thousand people, and half of those were outcasts, refugees, foreigners, Indians, religious sects hiding out in the desert. The only great wealth was the seacoast. And Mexico had five thousand miles of that on the mainland. Anyway, if some honchos in the Capital got wise—Hickey'd never heard of a Mexican official who didn't have his price. On his side of the border, he guessed, maybe one out of three was crooked. Mexico was almost twice as corrupt, with mordida being as great and honored a tradition as cuthroat free enterprise in the States. Hell, Cárdenas himself might be part of the scheme, wanting to run things like when he was President of Mexico. Suppose the Nazis offered a trade, a little something to help the Feds look the other way for a while. Like Texas. A hundred years later, revenge for the Alamo.

One thing Hickey felt sure of—you never could tell what craziness would come to pass, what the world would be like four months from now.

Four months ago, Hickey was a PI and partner in a restaurant looking to finally make the loot his wife had always craved. With Madeline and their precious daughter, he lived in a swell place on the bay. Every Sunday morning, he and Elizabeth walked four miles around the bay, or rode the waves on an inner tube, or found the best coffee cakes to take home for breakfast. Four months ago, Tito was driving his limousine. Enrique Peña had two sons. Stalingrad was German. Now the Germans were on the run, backtracking toward the Russian border, freezing in winter camps, getting buried under the snow. Four months ago, Clifford lived with his sister on a farm.

Hickey got up and went to Leo's holster, where it hung across the back of a chair. He grabbed the gun, stared at it a second, then threw it across the room. It crashed a hole a yard around in the plaster. "Sorry kid," he muttered.

You believe in a guy and he gets you killed. That was the worst, the one that drove Hickey down so far he might've taken a dive out the window, made a big splash on Broadway. If he'd had the guts. Or if Wendy Rose and the scent of gold hadn't piqued his will to live.

He sat on the desk, head in his hands, trying to figure how he'd messed up so bad. He knew better than to go at something big without more scouting and concern for details. If mescal had rotted his brain, still he was the one who drank the poison. Nobody poured it down his throat. Sure, he started drinking hard when Madeline ran off with Castillo and took Elizabeth away. So maybe he could shove some blame onto Madeline.

Except she'd held on for sixteen years before she dumped him. What he did was to take an eighteen-year-old beauty headed for the stars, promise her the moon and give her the crumbs left over after the big rats ate their share. When he could've struck it rich, easy. There'd been plenty of chances. He just didn't take them. Always trying to act like a swell guy. Probably, like she said, so he'd feel more noble than the next fellow.

And what did all that honorable living make him, after thirty-seven years? A killer.

Leo came in and Hickey motioned to the smashed wall. "Funniest thing happened. Wall just caved in."

"Uh huh," Leo said. "Make you feel better?"

"Oh, yeah. I'm brightened up considerably. Now I want to hear how you figure some things. How all those creeps fit together. Like Zarp with the del Montes. You expect he was running the show?"

"No reason to think so. I figure the big guy would be a Mex.

Anyway, nobody with sense is gonna get led by some witch doctor, and, sure, old Santiago's lost his marbles, but there's smarts in the family. Ruiz says the old fart went to university in Europe, way back, and his first couple wives were Russian countesses. He came up this way with Francisco Magón, during the revolution, and made a killing, with plunder and all. Ruiz says he's got ships, fishers out of Mazatlan and Vera Cruz, a couple gold mines, ranchos here and there, who knows what else. Now, whoever runs all that's gotta have sense. You know what they say about a fool and his money."

"They say a lotta crap. You don't need sense. It's like in the movie, that old guy tells Orson Welles, 'All you need to make money is to want it more than anything else.'"

"Aw, Tom, you got all the answers," Leo scoffed. "You think Zarp's the kingpin?"

"Is or was. Last night he was giving a speech, right at the head of the table."

"Sure. In his own joint, with his drinks, his rosy-titted waitress. He puts out the loot, he gets to make the speech."

"Yeah. His gold."

"Huh?"

"You didn't see maybe ten grand of gold, with the cups, the urn on the table, about two hundred buttons?"

"I figured it was real shiny brass."

"You're going blind, Dad."

Leo harrumphed, got a toothpick from his desk and started chewing. "Other stuff was on my mind, Tom." They locked eyes for a moment. Then Leo went to the hat rack, put his hat on the desk and started sailing cards into it. "So this coup—maybe it's a silent kind. Hell, Tom, there could be Krauts landing in Ensenada right now. Or Japs. See, one night, the Krauts roll over the border while the Japs invade by air. Wouldn't be much crazier than Pearl Harbor."

"They could stop at the Rosarito Beach Casino and capture most of our brass and flyboys."

"Jesus," Leo groaned.

143

"You bet." Hickey stepped to the window, looked out over hundreds of people crossing Broadway, waiting for the trolley, shouting at cabs, stalled in traffic though it was 10 P.M. He wondered how many'd get snuffed the night the Japs finally showed.

The phone rang. Leo answered. "Yeah, Vi. . . . Whatta you mean she's gone?"

20

≡ ≡ ≡

No one had seen Wendy leave. Vi was bathing, Magda had dozed. The bodyguards, McColgin on the boulevard side, his pal Nels on the seawalk, blamed each other. She'd disappeared about 11 P.M. By midnight McColgin and Leo were searching on the boulevard and bayside, while Nels took the beach south toward the jetty and Hickey combed the beach northward.

Tide was low, going out, the moon half-full, giving the water and beach a greenish color. Sand flurried up in the gusty breeze. Waves, instead of rolling, rose against the breeze to their full height before they crashed. Their noise sounded distant and ghostly. Hickey tromped the wet sand at the tideline, sweeping his gaze out to sea, then back across the beach to the seawall. Every time he'd spot a body and look closer, it was either a hobo sleeping against the wall, out of the sandy breeze, or a lonely nightwalker. Only the miserable came here at night, or men with bad dreams and nothing to lose.

A few miles up, as Hickey neared La Jolla, the cliffs began and each house got larger than the last. Some had walled yards with tropical gardens and pools. Pathways and wooden steps led down the cliffs and the moon shined on NO TRESSPASSING signs. Nobody except Hickey walked the beach here. Guard dogs pulled on the ends of their chains, sometimes halfway down the cliffs, and barked in frenzy or howled.

About 2 A.M., Hickey found a trail up the cliff, through a vacant lot to the residential street that wound past walled villas up to the coast highway, where he knew of an all-night gas station. The attendant, a bearded guy who smelled like fish, took a quarter and gave him the phone. He called Vi.

"You got her?"

Leo had checked with Vi and gone out again, driving the bayside alleys. McColgin and his pal, deciding the Mexicans had nabbed her, had given up and were dozing on the couch. Hickey told Vi to wake the bums. He got McColgin on the line. "Hear this, Palooka. Nobody rests until she's safe." He slammed down the phone and hustled back to the cliffs, kicking rocks on the way.

The tide began rising, the sandy beach narrowed, and rocky points jutted out from the cliffs. Where the points met the breakers, sea lions lay barking softly in their sleep and pelicans napped on the highest rocks. Crossing the mossy boulders, Hickey stumbled and slipped. The third time he cussed out loud, somebody yelped, "Who goes there?"

On the cliff stood a tower, long and triangular, like a life guard station, with a large air raid siren on top that blasted a rehearsal at noon every day. The man stood in the moonshadow of the tower.

"What's your business?" he shouted.

It was too dark and far to notice much about the guy except that he held a rifle, aimed. "Say, buddy," Hickey shouted. "You seen a girl pass by? Last couple hours?"

"Maybe. What's she to you?"

"My kid. Help me out, pal. She's in trouble."

"Okay. Sure. A blonde, in white. Didn't seem to hear me shouting. Got about twenty minutes on you."

Hickey yelled thanks, jumped to the next rock, racked his feet trying to jog across a hundred yards of beach covered with baseball-sized stones. He ran and walked another hour, knee deep around the point at Bird Rock, down Wind and Sea's mile-long sandy beach where the rollers curled under and out again without touching shore. He finally had to rest before climbing across the next point and wading through the inlet just south of La Jolla Cove. The tide had turned. It roared in close, slapped and thundered against the thirty-foot cliffs, began flooding the rock ledges where tidepools had been. It swept around huge boulders that partitioned the beach, invaded grottos and caves. The tide rolled a foot deep into the narrow, dark gorge between the cliff and boulders, where Hickey needed to pass to reach the next sandy beach. Where he stumbled over Wendy Rose.

She sat as though wedged into the tunnel-like gorge, lying back against the cliff, arms to her sides, eyes blindly open. The ebb tide covered her legs and waist, touched her ribs. She hadn't moved, until Hickey tried to pick her up, to drag her out of there. Then as quick as though she'd been poised to sprint, she bolted out the far side of the gorge.

It was so narrow, Hickey had to squeeze through sideways, which cost him a half-minute. He came out on a beach the locals called "Boomer," where the steep drop from shore doubled the breakers' force. Wendy was already caught in a wave. It flipped her over backwards, shot her up again.

Throwing off his coat, kicking off his shoes, Hickey raced into the water. But the girl had disappeared. An hour ago, wet and exhausted, he'd lost the feeling of cold and thought he'd gone numb. Now he learned better. The water burned. In some places it felt like a razor slashing him. He dove through a wave, surfaced and tried to hold still, treading water. Finally he spotted her hair floating about ten feet away.

When he grabbed her, she writhed for a moment, then went limp. He got her head above the water, holding her by the waist and under one arm, and towed her in. About halfway to shore he heard her breathing. He slung her gently over his shoulder, carried her south a hundred feet to a trail and lugged her up the cliffside. He laid her on grass in front of a tearoom.

He took her pulse, waited until her breathing got steady, then left her and crossed the road to the nearest house, where an ancient fellow who'd been fetching his newspaper let him use a telephone.

When he got back to Wendy, she was shivering wildly. Her eyes seemed all white, as if the blue in them had frozen. He tried to hold her but she pushed him away. The man from across the road came hobbling, carrying a blanket for her. Hickey laid it across her shoulders. She thrashed it off. Her mouth kept opening, but only a few words and sounds came out. She wailed, "Clifford?" Any second, Hickey thought, she was going to die or dream off too far, out wherever it is that crazy people go and never return from. When Leo's Packard pulled to the curb she was saying, "Fish. Come here fish. Over here, please."

It took some muscle to get her into the Packard. Hickey climbed in back with her. She slid to the far side, pressed against the door, braced her arms against the front seat and stayed that way the whole three miles.

At the motel, Vi and Magda got her into a hot bath. After a few minutes the girl asked for Hickey. Vi stopped him at the bathroom door. "God sake, Tom, don't look at her. It's not decent."

"Yeah." He stepped around Vi and sat on the edge of the tub. For a couple minutes, he managed not to look. Then he gave up and turned her way. Her graceful arms and long fingers floated on the water. One of her nipples kept surfacing. Everytime heat rushed through him, he winced in shame, especially when Vi stepped in, gave him a glare and doused the water with bubblebath. She ran the tap and swished suds around until they covered the girl.

For an hour, Hickey sat there, staring at her face. Every few minutes, Hickey ran the tap, heating the water. It was all he could think of to do. He was digging for ideas that might fix her, cursing himself because he never found a good one. After she stopped shivering, Wendy lay as if she were asleep except that her eyes stayed open, looking at the ceiling.

Finally Vi came in, chased Hickey off, and coaxed the girl out of the tub and into pajamas. Vi led her to the bedroom, tucked her into bed and turned off the overhead light, leaving on a dim lamp in the corner. Wendy tossed a little, then closed her eyes. From a chair by the lamp, Hickey watched her.

It looked as if she'd fallen asleep, but suddenly she raised herself onto one elbow. Her eyes, which since yesterday had seemed not to fix on anything real, widened and settled on Hickey.

"Sit here," she whispered, and patted the bed beside her.

He moved over there. She took his hand. In a minute she'd fallen asleep. Hickey leaned back against the headboard, determined not to move, not if she slept ten hours. He wouldn't risk letting her dream off any further without trying to coax her back. Anyway, he was happy there. Like a hiker in a thunderstorm who'd discovered a cave to hide in. Dozing on and off for a couple hours, every time he woke he felt warm and content.

Early the next afternoon, Hickey pocketed Leo's snub nosed .45 and led Wendy out to the beach. She'd talked a little over breakfast, to ask Vi what the jam was made of. He wanted to keep her talking. He needed to learn more about her. For both their sakes, he told himself, he should know everything—before he figured the next move. The more he knew, the better chance he'd have to think of a right answer. For her. Or himself.

If the Metzgers weren't lying, some folks in TJ ought to be disabled, by him or somebody, before Sunday. Folks who had plenty of gold.

He decided to risk a question, see how she acted. "Down there in Hell," he said gently, "besides dancing, what'd those guys make you do?"

Wendy seized her head in both hands, she could hardly breathe, and she stumbled but held her legs stiff, the way she'd learned from dancing, and made herself talk, because Tom Hickey wanted to hear.

"At church—when they are *penitentes*—they go to the altar so I will annoint them."

"Yeah. I guess I saw that." He noticed her legs trembling, led her back across the beach, thirty yards to the sea wall. They sat down. "You don't have to tell me anymore. Not now."

"Not about George?" she whispered.

"George—he's the guy that brought you to Tijuana, right? And George is dead?"

She kept nodding harder. "I saw him burning."

149

She moaned long and deep. Tom Hickey didn't know that she was bad. When he knew he'd lock her in a tiny dark room, she feared. But if she lied to him, even God would hate her. With a moan as though she'd been kicked in her belly, she confessed, "I stabbed George, Tom Hickey. It's why the Devil—made me stay in Hell. Two years, he said, and you know—if I ran away with my Clifford, the Devil would bring me back forever. Oh," she cried, "it's not two years. He will take me back there now."

Hickey stood up and walked out across the sand. "Nobody's taking you," he growled. He turned and stared, with his head cocked and his body twisted sideways, as if he'd yell at her, but the next words came softly. "Why'd you stab him?"

Already she'd fallen off the sea wall to her knees, and now she crawled to him across the hot sand and burrowed her knees into the sand at his feet with her head bowed.

"In church. The Devil—he says George will die. Because George tries to stab Mofeto. The Devil says when a body dies he has to save the blood—for annointing the *penitentes*."

She glanced up. Tom Hickey was a big shadow across the sky. Frantically, she said, "He was the meanest person in the world—George—meaner than Mofeto or Franz. Or the Devil. And he didn't feel. He didn't. I stabbed him fast like Mr. Meyers killed the horse. Honest . . . " She started pounding her thighs with her fists, hard as though trying to drive her feet into the sand. "If I lie, Tom Hickey, God will hate me—but if I tell you, truly, you will take me back to Hell."

She thrashed her head violently. Hair fell over her eyes, and she had to throw an arm down to brace herself, to keep her from tumbling onto Hickey's feet. He kneeled in front of her. "Nobody's taking you back to Hell."

"Promise," she whispered.

"Promise."

"I thought you were an angel. I'm silly."

"No, you're . . . " Hickey couldn't think of a word.

She threw her hands up, gripped her shoulders, squeezed her elbows and forearms tight in front of her breasts. "I stabbed and stabbed," she whispered. "He bled on me. Like a—fountain. In my mouth. My hair got full of blood."

Hickey started to reach for her hands but drew back, worried he'd spook her—it looked like she only wanted to touch somebody she thought was an angel. Now she knew he was a man like the rest, like George, like the Devil, all those guys who pawed her at the Paris Club. Or maybe he was worse, the guy who got her brother killed. He couldn't figure anything to do except curse himself for making her talk. She rocked to both sides, stiffly, and her lips started trembling. He couldn't just watch. Maybe, he thought, if he kept her talking until she spilled everything—maybe she could go through hell and come out the other side.

He asked, "George was on the altar? You were gonna annoint him?"

"No. It weren't time for annointing. It was time to eat the green balls. The red light. The captains got so big and red, when they stepped the building shook—we were in the sky. Please—the Devil told me—and promised—George was already gone, from his body."

"Peyote," Hickey said. "The green balls. They taste awful?"

"Oh yes. Awful weeds."

"And Zarp, the devil, he told you to stab George, right?"

She nodded, and then she was tugging her hair. "I'm sorry," she whispered, again and again, until finally she sprang up and walked, dragging her toes in the sand. Hickey followed. Fifty yards down the beach, three Mexicans sat, facing the sea but glancing at him and the girl. They wore khaki trousers, sport shirts and hats. Hickey reached into his pocket, gripped Leo's .45, and kept one eye on the Mexicans until they strolled off beyond the sea wall.

Wendy looked calmer now. She tossed her hair in the wind, walking more loosely, before she turned and stopped square in front of Hickey, nailing him to the spot with her eyes. "I was good to the Devil," she cried. "He whipped me. And he annointed me—every day—I annointed him too."

She grimaced ferociously, then turned and marched along the tideline, swinging her rigid arms. Hickey stood a moment reeling

151

from the image of her smeared with blood beneath that bloody monster. He looked around for the Mexicans and then caught up with her, socking his fist into his other palm and aching to go back over the line. This time he'd kill the devil.

"You know where he lives? The Devil."

"In Hell," she murmured.

"No place else?"

"Oh yes. In the gold room."

"What gold room? Where?"

"Oh, after you go through the great room, and the dining room, where the pretty ladies—they ate ducks and fish eggs. They wouldn't give me any. I asked but they hate me, Tom Hickey."

"Just Tom."

"Tom," she said, and walked faster.

"Why'd these ladies hate you?"

"My hair. It's not black. They like black hair."

"These ladies, they eat in the gold room?"

"Oh no. They aren't allowed. Only soldiers are, and the Devil and me."

"Where's the gold room, then?"

"You go up the round stairs and down the tunnel."

"Tunnel? Like a cave? That bar down the street from Hell?"

She stopped, exasperated, shaking her head. "In the Presidente's house."

"Presidente? Who's he? Cárdenas?"

"I don't know." She covered her face, blew out a couple shivering breaths.

He stepped so close his cheek touched her hair and he whispered, "It's okay, doesn't matter. Just tell me a little about the gold room."

"It's full of gold things, that's all."

"Lots of gold things?"

"Oh, so much."

He stepped back and with his heel lined a square in the sand, drew his hand across the square, waist high. "It'd fit in a box this big?"

Wendy laughed, the first time Hickey had seen. "Silly." She dragged one bare foot through the sand, marking a square about ten feet wide, then reached above her head, high as her fingers would go.

"Whoa. Okay, what kind of gold? Rocks? Bars?"

"Not rocks. Swords. Plates. Dollars. Coins. Many things I don't know what they are. Candle holders. The bed is gold."

"Even the bed," Hickey muttered.

They stared at each other until both at once turned north and started off along the tideline again. Ever since she'd laughed, Hickey's mood had kept brightening. Already he'd forgotten about killing the devil.

People they walked close to gazed in awe at the girl with her pretty dress fluttering as she stepped so graceful like on her toes, pressing her face against the sunlight, her back to the offshore wind. They walked with Wendy on the sea side, where the tide ran in over her feet. Out past the foamy waves, the water had turned cobalt blue.

21

When Hickey walked into the office, a few minutes after 6 P.M., Leo was on the phone to the Army. That morning, after dialing information and getting chased from one number to the next three times, he'd connected with an aide to General Finnegan and told him there was something brewing down in TJ, a gang of Krauts and high-up Mex guys plotting to shoot the governor or some such. He offered names and places to start. The aide claimed he'd talk to the general and call back. Before an hour, he said when Leo pressed him. Since then, Leo had called the aide twice and left messages.

He told Hickey what was said, got out a deck of cards, and dealt a solitaire hand. After a minute he asked, "Rummy?"

"The girl says there's a whole cache of gold, at some house that belongs to a guy they call the Presidente."

"Presidente," Leo muttered. "Who do you figure?"

"I got a few ideas. You hear me say there was gold?"

"Yeah, and the girl told you. Trouble is, she's not exactly Solomon. Maybe she don't know gold from frijoles."

Hickey wadded the paper from his sandwich, aimed it at the trash can across the room, missed by a yard. "Maybe she does. Listen, I saw those gold chalices and placed them somewhere. Then

Wendy said there was a gold room, and I remembered—the old casino at Agua Caliente. I played dances there, Leo, Madeline sang. And there was a banquet room where nobody got in except stars. Chaplin, the Pickfords, Buster Keaton. Called it Salon de Oro. You never saw that much loot. Enough to make King Midas soil his trousers."

"Sure, I heard about it."

"And when they shut the joint down what happened to the gold?"

"Beats me."

"Beats everybody, pal. It disappeared. And maybe you remember who gave the order to shut down that casino."

"Tell me."

"Lázaro Cárdenas. The Presidente."

"Hold it," Leo said, and drew a bead on Hickey with his finger. "Everybody says that guy's a square dealer. Tom, they got more presidentes than civilians down there. Municipal presidentes. Union presidentes. Old del Monte's presidente of a slew of companies. She could be talking about the presidente of the sewer department."

"I'll give you that," Hickey said.

"Anyway, it might not matter so much. To this conspiracy business, I mean. Could be, say, the Presidente's not the top dog. Down there, real movers don't want the heat, so they make their junior partners politicos, put them where they can make enough loot to keep up with the del Montes."

"Yeah," Hickey said. "Remember when we first got into this mess, you said one of the del Monte boys was an adviser to the governor?"

"Sure. I follow you. The governor might be on del Monte's payroll."

"Anyway, the 'Presidente's' the one with the gold. I make him to be a del Monte, probably Santiago. Old del Monte's the hoarder of the gold, Metzger says. It looks like this—Santiago's got a real home a couple miles away, but he never goes there. These days he spends all his time at the Casa de Oro. Where I'm saying the gambling and gold showed up after Cárdenas shut down Agua Caliente."

Leo flipped his hat onto the desk, upside down, shuffled his deck of cards and began sailing them into the hat. "So, where's the girl fit in?"

Hickey mused a while. "Leo, you ever seen a beauty like that?"

"Watch it, Tom."

"I mean, besides she's a swell looker, she's blond. Blond as they come. A lot of Danish in her. Now, maybe Zarp set her up like a symbol. The backside of the Holy Virgin—you know how the Spanish crawl for that dame. I don't know just what—maybe they were keeping her for some conjuration they learned from Indians, like an Aztec sacrifice. Wouldn't be the first of those."

"Now what are you talking about?"

So Hickey told what he'd gathered about how the girl got stuck down there, how this rat George had crossed the border, found Zarp to sell him heroin, but he tried to cheat the Devil and wound up stomped by El Mofeto and Franz Metzger. Then Zarp got a bunch of them stiff on peyote. And they made George the star of a snuff ritual, with Wendy on dagger and Zarp conducting. Afterward, he convinced her she needed to get punished by two years of slavery down there.

Leo glared incredulously, a cigaret hanging from his mouth, and Hickey went on, "Maybe Zarp played her up like a Celtic mother-fertility goddess. You know, witchery jive the Inquisition found displeasing. I read where lots of it grew out of the same old tradition. German. Where Faust came from."

"Huh?"

"Dr. Faustus, the one that traded his soul for knowledge, power . . ."

"Stop right there. I'm not buying, Tom. But if . . . when we snatched the girl, could be we foiled 'em by accident. Say, without the girl, without the sacrifice, they gotta change their plans."

"Yeah, I'll sit here a minute and try to believe that. I hope to Christ we foiled something, with four dead men."

"Couldn't be helped, Tom."

"Yeah, it could. If I'd been thinking better."

Leo blind-shot a few more cards into the hat. "It could've been worse."

Hickey snarled. "I don't imagine the kid would think so, or those dead—Mexicans."

"Lay off the hindsight, Tom."

"Yeah. Okay. Tell me something. Suppose we didn't wreck 'em. And Finnegan doesn't buy your story. And suppose there's this Presidente sitting on a ton of gold and it keeps looking like these guys might be holding hands with the Krauts. Then what do we do?"

"You mean, ought we risk our necks trying to stop 'em?"

"Yeah." Hickey nodded. "And ought we swipe the gold?" He filled his pipe but didn't light it. First he noticed Leo staring hard at him. The old man took out a piece of gum and started chomping while he sneered and Hickey picked up the cards and sailed a few at the hat. Every one missed.

When the phone rang, Hickey's pulse quickened. Still, even after two days, at every call he hoped for Tito. But this one was Vi.

"Yeah," Leo said. "Pick us up a few sandwiches and beers. . . . Okay. Get her sweets or something. Keep her busy. Don't let her out of your sight. Sure. Bye."

"How's Wendy?"

"She's got weepy, Tom. Keeps asking for you. Magda's trying to keep her busy. Gave her a shampoo and wave. Now she's prissing up her toenails."

Hickey got weepy too, for about a second. Then he looked at his watch. After seven. Still no word from Tito, and no general had phoned. He said they should call Finnegan's aide back, and Leo rolled around to the phone. He dialed, waited, grinding his teeth, "Yeah, Lieutenant, this is . . . come back here, you louse." He whacked the phone on the desk, waited long enough to smoke a whole cigaret and sail at least ten cards into the hat before the lieutenant returned. "Weiss. . . . Spell it however you want, chum. What'd the general say? . . . About what I told you eight

157

hours ago. The Mexicans. A coup. Nazis. Look, pinhead, I don't think you told him . . . Been apprised, huh? So what's he gonna do about it? . . . Yeah, well if it's not my affair, how do I know they got mischief planned for day after tomorrow? By Sunday you might be eating schnitzels. Tell the man if he wants details to call Belmont four-seven-two-five, leave a message where I can reach him tonight."

Finally he dropped the receiver into the cradle. "Talking to the Army can wreck your whole day."

Hickey smiled as best he could with his mind on the girl, four dead men, and a room full of gold. It stayed longest on the gold. A big suitcase full of dishes, medallions, candlesticks, was all he wanted. Plenty to cover what he'd spent and the dozen times more he might spend tomorrow, to void the sale of his bayside cottage if he wanted it back, enough to purchase a swank resort in Cuba. Buy Elizabeth diamonds, gowns, a fancy car if she wanted one in a couple of years. With a fortune left over.

"Tom, you hear me? Maybe the Army knows all about it, I said. Maybe they got it under control."

"Sure."

Leo rolled his chair back, hoisted his feet onto the desk. "Yeah. Maybe not'd be my guess."

They sat quietly fidgeting, smoking, gazing around, mostly at the phone. Until Hickey leaned on the desk, looked Leo in the eye. "I'm going back down there. After the gold."

Leo held his gaze for a minute, rolled in his chair to the window, stared at his reflection, turned, and rolled back partway. "Naw, Tom. I figure you're only about half that crazy."

"You got me wrong," Hickey muttered. "I'm gonna need plenty help."

"You bet. Who's that gonna be?"

Hickey's mind shot off to questions of its own. "We get Smythe to lend us credit. Then we gotta train a bunch of guys. You think two days are enough?"

With a groan, Leo sat up tall and knocked his fists together.

158

"Hell, no. I'm still praying Finnegan calls. And even if he don't, Tom, I'm not fighting anymore. It'd be the end of me."

"Sure," Hickey said. "I figure you'd help with the arrangements, though."

"Oh you do?" Old Leo looked into a desk drawer, then shut it. "Got any poison on you?"

"Nope. And I'll bet fifty bucks Finnegan won't call."

"Find your suckers elsewhere," Leo grumbled.

"Let's get back to the girl," Hickey said.

22

It was a bitch knocking himself out of bed from lying next to Wendy Rose. But he managed, about ten minutes or so after Leo rapped on the door. The girl didn't wake up—he thought that was a good sign. Maybe she wouldn't have nightmares.

Hickey washed, and dressed in his uniform. Lightly, he stroked the girl's hair, threw things into a duffel bag and went out to meet Leo.

They walked down Mission Boulevard, past the tourist cafés, motor courts, alleys where bums slept, stands where you rented bikes and inner tubes. At Leo's place, they made coffee, heated rolls. Hickey checked over the list—what Smythe would deliver for half cash, half credit. Two crates of Springfield rifles. Two thousand rounds of ammunition. A half-case of grenades. A couple of Browning or Thompson machine guns and a dozen clips. Three two-way radios.

"Maybe he'll get us a tank."

"Say you're joking," Leo grumbled. "If you get snuffed and run out on the tab, he'll chase after me to pay it."

"You know, we could make Symthe a partner, cut him in. Then he'd finance the whole deal."

"Cut him in—Tom, the gold's all in your head. All you gotta

look forward to is getting outa there alive, and bankruptcy." Leo tapped a Lucky on the table, sipped coffee. "I oughta get fined just for not lassoing you into a straitjacket. Say, I might do that any minute. Thinking you can steal a mountain of treasure out of Mexico. Acting like Ponce de Leon, that guy that went hunting for the seven cities of gold that never were."

"Wrong guy," Hickey said. "De Leon was after the fountain of youth."

"Same damn thing," Leo mumbled.

Hickey looked out at the brightening sky. He told Leo to meet him at Sally's Café in San Ysidro at noon.

In the garage, he took a leather sack full of pistols from the Packard, carried the sack and his duffel bag out to the Jeep.

He drove carefully in his vehicle, which the Army and the law might have their antennas out for—down the boulevard, across the Ocean Beach bridge, then keeping to the side roads a mile east of the Navy and Marine bases, and finally to the coast highway. Before the Navy docks, he cut east behind the Santa Fe depot and Lane Field where the Pacific Coast League played baseball, then took A Street all the way up to 10th so he wouldn't pass near the YMCA, the Greyhound depot, or Horton Plaza where the city bus lines connected. You'd always find MPs loitering around those places.

In National City by the shipyards he met the coast highway again. And, since they'd be watching for him at the border gate, just before San Ysidro he turned east and took a dirt road up onto Otay Mesa. From there he used the smuggler's road. Dope, guns, refugees, refrigerators, hot cars, even stuff like onions when the import tariffs got raised. Both armies patrolled the line up here, but Jeeps were scarce enough so that the patrols mostly used horses, and they rode in squads. You could spot one a mile away.

Somewhere, Hickey crossed the line. Then he made a right turn down a creek bed that ran off the mesa and finally met the river a couple miles east of the shantytown. He pulled up on the outskirts, a wrecking yard and housing project of old, stripped cars, their shells made into family homes. Five small Indians could sleep under the body of a Chrysler. He parked there so the Jeep would be

161

less conspicuous, in case there were cops around. As he jumped down, a gang of ragged, spook-eyed kids charged to surround him and stare. Hickey grabbed his luggage and walked toward the shacks. Up ahead, a green Ford sat near the riverbank, not far from the scrapwood hovel where Crispín and his Olmecs lived. Hickey ducked behind a shelter, crept around, and got close enough to see inside the Ford. Where Tito slumped at the wheel. Alive. Snoring.

Hickey dashed over, reached in, and shook the cabbie until he snapped awake and gave him a dopey smile. Tito looked pale and weak as he dragged out of the car.

"Where you been two days, boss? You taking La Rosa to Hollywood?"

Hickey wasn't apt to hug guys. But he thought, When you're in Mexico and somebody rises from the dead—he gave the cabbie a rib-cracking squeeze. "We figured they got you, else you would've phoned."

"Hey, I been hiding. Maybe there's a phone in TJ I can use without nobody sees me, only thing I don't know where it is. Mostly I'm waiting here with my amigo El Mofeto. You got to come back for the gringo, no?"

Hickey backed off a step and muttered, "Who'd they kill?"

"The *mellizos*. How you say?"

"Twins?"

"Yeah. They are shot in the back while they running." He pointed east. "Right there by the river. Somebody puts a cross there already. But Rafael and Enrique, they got away. Yesterday, they are gone already, driving like crazy. Maybe they got to Hidalgo by now."

Hickey stared at the hills and saw the Peña twins, brave, handsome guys, about thirty, no older. Probably had kids. He leaned on the hood of the Ford, watched some Indians walking toward the river, and wondered what kind of louse he was, come down here to risk more lives. You could say life was cheap these days but he knew better. Yet he picked up his bags and led the cabbie toward the river. They sat on the bank and stared across, past Coco's, over the border gate. Spots of light glared off a tank and a troop

162

carrier that crawled up the gray-brown hills. The sun was low but already burning like coals on Hickey's brow.

"I guess you oughta leave town, huh?"

"*Puta madre,* you bet," Tito groaned. "Why do I go fighting with these del Montes? I make a hundred dollars, but my taxi's junk and I got to go some damn place like Matamoros, pay maybe three hundred for a taxi license there and two hundred more for a cab, some jalopy. Man, I think I was a smart guy. Now I don't be too sure. I could go with Rafael yesterday, but I think no, better wait and talk to the boss. Maybe you will be happy about La Rosa, and want to pay me what else I need."

"So I oughta give you about four hundred bucks?"

"Five or six, I think."

"How about seven? You give me a couple days to raise it. Or, maybe instead you'd want to go partners. Stealing gold."

Tito lifted his sunglasses and squinted his weary red eye. "Tell me."

"The girl says there's a big cache of gold, somewhere. She says it's at the house of a guy she calls the 'Presidente.' I think it's del Monte, old Santiago, and the gold's at his Casa de Oro. So tomorrow night, I'm going to snatch it."

The cabbie put his chin on his fists, and asked to hear more. So Hickey told him: a lot of what the girl said; his own idea that plenty of the gold might've been swiped, say by del Monte, in the revolution when he rode with Magón, and six years ago when Cárdenas shut down the Agua Caliente Casino; how Zarp could be a Nazi agent; about Metzger and the rumors of a coup.

Tito knocked himself on the brow, folded his hands on top of his head, and stared at the dirt. "I want this gold, *de veras.* But you going to need a little army. Where you getting one?" When Hickey stood up, motioned with a hand around the shantytown, the cabbie groaned, "These *gallinas?* Man, they don't know nothing. What they going to fight with? Machetes. They got a gun, maybe they shooting their balls off."

"Maybe. So, in a couple days I'll bring you seven hundred at the gate."

163

"Sure boss," the cabbie hissed. "Some trick. You going to be dead two days before then."

"Think it'll be a massacre?"

"You know that one. It won't be like Hell was. They got to have guards and maybe some of the Army is there with General Cárdenas."

"Yeah? Well, how about I give you fifty today, if you help me find some cars and send a guy to scout Las Lomas. Get all the dope we can on the place."

"Fifty," Tito snarled. From his green Hawaiian shirt he pulled out a Hershey bar, ripped off the paper, and chomped fiercely. "How much gold you say?"

"Millions, anyway."

Tito pushed on his head with his hands and spun like he'd corkscrew into the ground. Then he leaned close to Hickey. "I tell you something, about I used to be *muy guapo*, and I got this limo. Women are loving me, boss. Used to be. And I tell you, of everything there is, it's maybe only women that making me happy. Drinking, dancing, fútbol, I don't care about them no more. Only women. So I'm happy, until this brother of a bitch I know, he calls me names and I call him back. I win, you know. I call him the best name. And he makes me look like this. Now, don't nobody love me till I'm paying her. I tell you, if I had one woman, maybe three or four niños and a good taxi, I don't go with you for ten million pesos. Even dollars. That's because it's too crazy and I think we going to die. But goddamn, I got nobody, so maybe anyway I going with you and steal this *pinche* gold."

Hickey stood, lifted his bags, and turned toward the hut made of reeds from a swampy place downriver, the jacal where Crispín and his Olmecs kept the prisoners. The cabbie walked along, kicking his sharp-toed boot at the ground.

"Mofeto still alive?"

"Sure. You think I better kill him?" Tito frowned deeper and said, "I don't know if then I feel more good or no."

Four Olmecs stood waiting outside the jacal. Then women holding babies and a gang of dirt-caked children appeared. They

164

watched Hickey close, waiting for money to fly out of his pockets.

Hickey saluted. The Olmecs saluted. One of them laughed and they all turned shyly away. Then Crispín stepped out of the jacal, chewing on a brown root, and Hickey asked to see the gringo. A few Olmec words got passed around. The men at the door stood aside and Hickey passed through the doorway. He had to stoop so low he strained his back.

The dark inside was striped with bars of sunlight angling through the walls of reeds. The place smelled like chiles and rot. Along each of two side walls lay a body on the dirt. On the left, El Mofeto, turned to the wall. Boyle on the right, his eyes vaguely on Hickey, his face muddy and gagged. He jerked with little tremors. Hickey squatted in the dirt, put a hand on the fink's head—it felt like his hand would melt. By tomorrow, the fink would be dust. Making five dead men. But, Hickey thought, a dead guy buried in Mexico couldn't accuse him of kidnapping. On the other hand, if Alvarez or Mr. Chee snitched, it'd be murder. Mr. Chee wouldn't talk, but Alvarez might. Still, if Boyle got loose, he'd be the one to talk, and kidnapping, easy as murder, could win Hickey the noose.

So finally he said, "Bob, when you get home, tell 'em you been in the TJ jail, and I'll dig you up a grand for the favor and the inconvenience. Or else you could tell the truth for once and start running from me for the rest of your short life."

Boyle hardly blinked. Hickey untied his ankles and thighs and watched his legs squirm and shake until it seemed the fink could use them a little.

Then Hickey stepped outside. He asked Tito to find a cabbie who'd run the gringo to some doctor in Tecate, thirty miles east—he said promise the doctor fifty or so to keep Boyle away from the border for a couple days.

23

About four hundred years back, Spaniards came to seize Queretaro. The Otomis there saw the fiery guns and horses and figured they couldn't whip that arsenal. So they challenged the Spaniards to a fistfight. The macho Spaniard captain decided to punch it out first and shoot later, if they lost. So the two armies duked up and down the hills, until after a day or so, when thousands of men lay beat up and delirious, a vision of Saint James appeared in the sky, and gave a TKO to the Spaniards.

The stoic Otomis went and got some sleep. Later, the ones who didn't like having Spanish patrones hiked south to make their home in the Mesquital, a desert so harsh nobody would fight for it.

Now a band of Otomis lived in the shantytown. They were small folk with delicate features, watchful eyes, sad, dark, brooding faces. Back home they were the tenders of the maguey plant, from where you get tequila, mescal, and pulque. They used to drink a lot of pulque but here all they had was the stinking river water, and their food was garbage the cook at a restaurant saved for them, and tortillas they cooked over a fire on an old fender. They were ready to go home to the Mesquital, but two thousand miles was a dreadful walk. They'd ridden up here on a bus, eleven men and four new wives, because a couple months after Pearl Harbor a guy came and told them there were plenty of jobs in Tijuana, serving the great city of San Diego, which had boomed on account of the big war. This fellow got paid to spread the word, so more folks would come begging for work and keep wages down, like the Okies used to up north.

Only one Otomi knew a few words of English. Most knew a little Spanish. Hickey gathered them around in the shade of their homes made of cardboard and two Plymouths. Then he had to go meet Leo. Tito stayed as the recruiter.

Since it was too late to drive back over the mesa, he crossed the river on a stone bridge and walked fast toward the gate, his eyes panning around, looking for cops or strange cars.

He didn't know any of the gate guards. But as he neared the walk-through gate, the MP, a lanky, freckled boy, got big-eyed and grabbed his revolver. Hickey said, "Hey, I'm gonna call the colonel and turn myself in." He kept walking, through the gate and fast toward a block past the office where Leo's Packard waited at the curb outside Sally's Café. The MP followed. So Hickey whipped around, pointed a finger south, and snapped, "Get back to your post, fella."

The boy stepped closer, his gun raised, and gaped his mouth to shout for help. Hickey moved in closer, thinking he might dodge left and smack the gun hand right and then gut-punch the kid. But Leo got there first.

He came puffing, running from the north, and flashed the L.A. badge he still carried, his souvenir. "Weiss. San Diego PD. Thanks."

He rushed Hickey off before the kid could find his wits. They hustled over to the Packard, jumped in, and sped out of there.

"You got bored, needed some excitement, so you tried the gate?"

"Yep," Hickey said. "Smythe treat you right?"

"Hell, Smythe ever treat anybody right?"

"For a price."

"He got us the grenades and a couple cases of ratty Springfields, look like they had to fight their way outa Russia. I got 'em in the trunk. Tom, this'd be a good time to quit, before we get caught with an arsenal and shot for being conspirators or something."

"I found Tito," Hickey said. "Turn here."

Leo wheeled right and grinned. "Swell news." Then soberly he asked, "Which ones got it?"

"Turn up that dirt road. The twins."

Leo gave a sigh and fell quiet. As they crawled in low up the dirt trail, the differential and muffler kept bottoming out. The high sun broiled the mesa and colored it reddish with heat waves, and the wind blew steadily, crackling, moaning through the arroyos.

Hickey sat braced against the dash and ground his teeth. It seemed they'd crash on a rut and land too hard, blow up, or suddenly get bushwhacked by Marines. Mexican soldiers. A company of Nazis. No telling who might be after them. The craziest dangers felt real when the Santa Ana blew.

But Leo kept to the least rutted trails, creeping in low gear, and they didn't spot another soul until they crawled off the mesa and neared the river. They reached the shantytown about 2 P.M. By then Tito had recruited five Otomis, sent out a guy to round up a few cars, another to scout the Casa de Oro and draw them a map of Las Lomas.

Hickey and Leo got a crate of old Springfield .30-caliber rifles out of the Packard and called the Otomis over. First Hickey showed them how to load the rifles. The sad-faced Otomis held the guns reverently as if they'd belonged to a saint. Then Hickey ushered them into the Jeep. Leaving Leo behind to deal with some English-speaking Kickapoos Tito had found, they cut along the river to the creek trail, up the side of Otay mesa, then a few miles southwest to a place Tito knew where Cárdenas's army used to train, so if people heard the shots they might not suspect anything. In the Jeep, the Otomis sat still at first, frightened, holding tight and yelping every time they crossed a rut or tipped a little along the sandy bank. But soon they chattered and hung loose as monkeys, leaning out over the sides.

They stopped near a grove of wild olive trees. Hickey tore a spare shirt he'd brought along, clipped a piece of it to a tree with some loose bark, then called the Otomis to line up. He gave Tito some rules, and the cabbie translated, barked them out—they had to stay together, not even wander off to piss without asking, and swear to follow orders no matter what. They picked a sergeant, a young guy named Guillermo, with an egg shaped nose and pointed teeth, the only one who wanted the job. Finally Hickey showed them how to aim the Springfield and hold it right, how to snap on the bayonets, how to fire.

They blasted away gleefully until the last shreds of Hickey's shirt wafted toward the sea.

Checking them out on the Springfields took until late afternoon. Then they drove back across the mesa, with the Otomis sitting taller as they held the guns in both hands and didn't look quite so sad as before.

At the shantytown, Leo and the Kickapoos were gathered on the riverbank, eating. The Kickapoos were small, wiry, wore their hair in single braids. Their smiles were quicker than the Otomis without giving up the fierce glint in their eyes.

The tribe had long ago got driven out of Wisconsin, Oklahoma, Kansas, Missouri, Texas. Finally a gang of them landed in Mexico where the government gave them territory in Cohuila, in exchange for help fighting off wild Texans. Sometimes the Kickapoos rampaged over the border, until thirty years ago they made a treaty that let them pass freely both ways as long as they'd quit pillaging—so now they could work harvests in the States and winter down in Cohuila. A week ago, these Kickapoos headed northwest, to pick carrots in the San Joaquin valley or maybe try working in a factory. They'd only stopped in TJ to check out putas.

The oldest of them was twenty-five, named Jack. He wore a baseball cap with the St. Louis Browns insignia. He wanted to hear more about the Nazis and the gold. Hickey talked, mostly the truth, except he made speculations sound more like fact—while the seven Kickapoos squatted in a half-circle in front of him. The Otomis stood behind, eyeing a leftover plate of tacos. Finally Hickey gave one of them ten dollars and sent him across the river to the coffee and taco stand. Then he and the Kickapoos squeezed into the Jeep with a pile of weapons, and drove up the creek bed toward the mesa.

169

The Kickapoos knew how to shoot already. In less than an hour Hickey had checked them out. He showed two of them how to use the Thompson light machine gun McColgin had carried into Hell, and instructed two others how to activate and sling grenades. Finally he sat them down in a circle and talked awhile about the gold and the dangers—how they needed to strike and get out before the Army could react, since Cárdenas had a battalion less than two miles away. "And, truth is," he confessed, "I got no proof about the gold, only the word of a mixed-up girl and a German who's so scared and drunk he might be seeing guys from Mars, too."

He left the Kickapoos to pow-wow, walked to a high place and looked off the mesa, over the town to the ocean and the Islas Coronados and a hundred miles farther across the water to where it appeared the Santa Ana had blown the most glorious desert sunset out to sea. A thousand shades of rose and deep as eternity. Hickey stood there feeling mighty. Immortal. When Jack shouted, "Hey, Chief, we gonna do it," hot shivers ran from his groin, along his spine, all the way to his skull.

Back at the shantytown they found most everybody clustered around a couple vendors who stood bent over their carts, dealing out tacos fast like cards to the ragged children and their mothers, to the bums, grandmas, thieves, the cheapest whores in town. Leo rested in the Packard's rear seat. When Hickey came over, the old guy said, "You can feed a whole village of moochers for fifty bucks, why not? Too damned hot for 'em to go out scrounging." Leo gazed around at the sorry crowd of Indians. "Some damn army you got, Tom. Those Nazis better look out." He grimaced. "How about we go on home and call it a draw?"

"Naw," Hickey said. "We got some tough boys here."

He enlisted a swaggering Kickapoo named Renaldo to run and check out the border gate, see if an old Chinese man was there.

By 9 P.M., in Leo's Packard, Hickey'd gotten passed through the gate by Mr. Chee and Alvarez, driven to his attorney's place,

signed real-estate papers, come away with $750 cash, and made it back to the Surf and Sand motor hotel. To visit Wendy Rose.

As they stepped out of their room and crossed the gravel toward the sea wall, the red wind gusted furiously, howling around the apartment buildings and bending palms toward the sea. Their dry fronds sounded like rattlesnakes. The moon had risen. The tent city, a mile down the beach, swayed, fluttered, whole walls torn up and slashing through the air like flags. They climbed over the sea wall. In front of them, beachcombers walked along the shore looking down for treasure, their hair streaking out behind them. A few small, lighted boats fishing or dropping lobster traps past the breakers, teeter-tottered on the swells.

Wendy kept quiet. She made as if to reach for Tom's hand and walk closer beside him, but then she held back. If she touched him—he was a man, like Pa and George, Franz and the devil's Captains—all the men except Clifford. What men did was petted you softly at first, till the heartbeats banged in your ears, then they squeezed you and pinched and scratched and tried to tear your legs apart till you cried from how it ached and burned then they socked you and pounded you—Ma said men want you to be perfect, give them everything they want. When you don't, they hate you. It must be the same reason they fought a war, Wendy thought. Somebody doesn't give them everything, they hurt somebody. She wanted to ask Tom not to go to the war. Maybe—if he stayed—he could be her brother. The only man she could trust to hold her—like Clifford—and never beat her, not for anything. If Tom got killed tonight, she wouldn't have a brother. Nobody would take her to Heaven, and the Devil would come. He would dash out of Hell and carry her back there. He would burn her and slap her, bite her skin, smear her belly with . . . She walked stiffly. Her legs and arms were hard with goosebumps and frozen through. The wind had blown her eyes shut. But she didn't cry, or yell out, or ask Tom Hickey to stay home from the war. Her ma used to say that men do what they want and only get mean when you ask for things.

"Magda's gonna sleep with you, in case you get scared," Hickey said. "That's good, huh?"

171

"And when I wake up, you'll be back." She looked up at him, making it a question.

"Maybe." He nodded and watched her eyes fluttering as if every instant they switched between wanting to see and deciding not to. Then out of his mouth came the strangest, unexpected thing. Without thinking, or knowing what all he meant, he said, "I sure love you, Wendy."

She almost touched his face with a finger, but pulled it away and whispered, "Yes. Like my Clifford."

Hickey watched the glow of her eyes, the quiver of life in her skin, the lips poised to speak but afraid to. He thought about Tijuana, his army, the gold, the Nazis. All that seemed madness now. Outlandish dreams like those mescal gave you.

But once you set things up, if you turn back, you're a goner. Hickey learned that long ago. You had to do things in a certain order. First you think, then you decide, then act. If you try to do one of those when it's time for the other, you always get tragedy. So he walked the girl back to the Surf and Sand. He said goodbye to her, to Magda and Violet. He promised Vi that Leo wouldn't join any battles. Finally he looked over at the dresser where he'd set a letter, addressed to Elizabeth, that Vi would find when she straightened his things up if he didn't make it back. He'd tried to write some advice but it looked silly on paper, so he just told what would've happened – he'd stumbled upon a good war, and gone out fighting.

On the patio, he warned Nels and McColgin to look alive. Then he walked to Mission Boulevard and climbed into the Packard, with about forty minutes to reach the border while Alvarez and Mr. Chee stood guard.

24

At the shantytown, Hickey found Leo asleep, wedged into the backseat of Tito's Ford. The night had fallen quiet. Now and then you heard a moan or laugh, a child's whimper, a chorus of rasps from the crickets. Hickey sat on the riverbank, smoked, and missed Wendy. Or the man he felt like around her. A kinder fellow, less polluted by the world.

The way he saw her life, there was a child too sensitive to bear cruelty, who saw it everywhere. To escape she started dreaming herself off to better places and wouldn't come back until she felt safe. Probably she only felt safe around Clifford. Then the Army took him away. And Hickey got him killed.

Finally he woke Leo. The old guy half-sleepwalked to his Packard and dumped himself into the driver's seat. "It's a nightmare, is all," he groaned. "Tomorrow there won't be Nazis in Tijuana." He fired up the Packard and lurched away.

Hickey curled into the back of Tito's Ford. The cabbie was sleeping in front. A few snores rattled out of him. Then Hickey was gone, walking a beach holding hands with somebody. Elizabeth. Wendy. He couldn't see. His gaze was locked on the ocean where boats with loud-colored sails glided toward something big and dark, maybe a carrier, or an island. It didn't matter. What mattered was that somebody needed him. He woke feeling strong. Anxious to move, to settle things.

By 7 A.M. he'd bought the whole shantytown churros and coffee, and started up the mesa with the Yaquis Tito had gathered yesterday, handsome guys with squarish faces and leathery skin. All of them knew Spanish. Their sergeant was a big Yaqui named Carlos who'd lived in Phoenix two years ago. Now he'd been on his way to try to enlist in the U.S. Marines. All six Yaquis could shoot. In twenty minutes they blasted every leaf off an olive tree. Hickey drilled them to reload fast and to use the bayonets. Whooping, they charged tumbleweeds and sage.

Back at the shantytown, Hickey found Tito on the riverbank drinking coffee with Arturo, a bucktoothed man he'd sent to scout the Lomas, who said it looked like business as usual at the Casa de Oro. By 4 A.M., most of the ricos and whores had gone to bed, the gamblers had pulled away in their big sedans and limos, the guards snoozed.

When Arturo left to get some cars, Tito and Hickey studied the maps, talked over schedules and strategies until the Packard drove in and Leo came waddling toward them. The old man's shoulders slumped inches and his head drooped as though he wore an iron hat.

"Metzger told one thing straight, Tom. They're after the girl, or us. The way I make it, a gang of pachucos busted into my house about dawn, crashed windows, ransacked the place, dumped out Vi's china closet. Later they got to our office. Looks like they had a bullfight in there. The girls are okay. I gave McColgin and his pal two Brownings."

Hickey gazed around, at the east mesa, at the bridge, the high roads that led to Revolución. Anyplace up there, a guy could be watching through a sight, planning an execution or a massacre.

"There's more, Tom. I finally got through to Finnegan, in the flesh. I told him from word one. Even how we snatched Wendy outa Hell, except I blamed it on some anonymous guys. All right, Finnegan says, not to worry, it's all sewed up tight, he says, account of Lázaro Cárdenas won't stand for monkey business, and he's got

174

Baja under his thumb. Not a cork gets popped down here without Cárdenas hears about it. In other words, Finnegan says thanks for the dope, but we got our own problems."

Hickey squatted like an Indian and muttered, "What's it mean?"

"I figure, if Cárdenas has got things that tight, not only's he gonna smash you, but most of the gold won't be at the Casa, because del Monte's the wrong man. Cárdenas must be the Presidente the girl talked about. See, Tom, it all clicks, once you allow Cárdenas is a crook. Could be he outlawed the Agua Caliente Casino just so he could steal the gold. You thought about that?"

"Yeah," Hickey said. "I don't buy it. Cárdenas might be on the take. But he's not the Presidente. Because if he is, I only got a few hours to live." He motioned toward the huts and the river. "Same as a lot of these guys."

"Unless we scat outa here, pronto."

"Naw. Too late." Hickey stood, laid a hand on Leo's shoulder, and started walking toward a Kickapoo hut where he could borrow some shade. But Leo called him back and handed him a letter. From Elizabeth. He stared at the envelope a minute, and then folded and pocketed it. She hadn't written in weeks, and the letter would disturb him, take his mind off business. He walked to the shade and squatted there, thinking how the fortune in gold was Wendy's story. And people called her a moron. Besides her, he was trusting Juan Metzger, who might lie for a dozen reasons. To set them up for the kill. So Hickey'd sneak the Metzger clan across the line, like he'd done. It could be what scared Metzger wasn't the Germans but what Hickey might do in revenge.

Hickey imagined Indians running down a hill toward the sea, smacked with bullets, blasted apart with grenades. It took him half an hour to discharge those visions.

By then he was back on the mesa teaching the Browning machine gun to Carlos the Yaqui and Kickapoo Jack, and two other Kickapoos, the biggest ones, swaggering Renaldo and Desmond who wore thick glasses. He gave a lesson, then stepped back to watch them practice. The noise rattled his head. His mind drifted. It didn't take long to find Wendy.

He saw her laughing, jumping over tiny waves, in a pretty red bathing suit with a ruffled tutu skirt. Her skin glowed white as the sun. She turned and saw him, and ran across the beach with one arm out, vibrant with joy, enough to warm a ghoul's heart. He went to the Jeep for his thermos, shot down a jolt of café con leche, gazed back over his troops, and got a warm feeling about this ragged army of his—like a band of peasants during the Crusades. A smile possessed him. He admired these Indians. They were brave or else they wouldn't go this far from home. And desperate for loot. One share, say a hundredth of the gold, and maybe an Indian could set up his family with a few hectares of land or a small business, break into capitalism—maybe they'd do better than he'd done. These fellows had plenty to win, damned little to lose, so he figured they wouldn't run from the heat, and they'd follow orders for fear of getting him mad. Surely they knew that when a white guy got mad at Indians, he gypped them out of their money, at least.

Besides, some of these Indians had ancestors who cooked their enemies, fed them to lions. And the ones who'd been Christianized, their churches were lavished with pictures of bloody Jesus hung on a tree, saints being mangled, witches and heretics burning. Maybe he should translate Nazis as heretics and make this into a holy war. Hickey'd read a few books about the Mexican revolution, enough to know that once these peaceful Indians rose to vengeance they might cut the heart out of every rich guy and German in Las Lomas.

Hickey left the Indians on the mesa, drove back to the shantytown to meet Tito's friends and deal for a taxi and three other cars. They bargained until Hickey'd bought the Fords for fifty dollars each, the Studebaker for seventy-five, and traded a couple Springfields for the taxi. When the dealing finished, Leo walked Hickey down by the river, and on the way he muttered, "I might go with you, Tom."

"Forget it."

"Naw, I could use another shot at those Nazis. All this making ready's got my blood stirred, my heart slam-banging. If I just sit

176

around and worry the damn thing's gonna blow. Anyway, I figure, who wants to die like some old farmer, slow and with plenty of time to stew about what I oughta done. I been around. Magda's almost grown. Today, I got no beef with saying adiós, long as I'm not screaming loud as Franz Metzger did. He was looking into Hell, Tom."

Hickey's throat locked. Weakly he said, "You gotta stay out of it, just in case. Somebody's gotta take care of the girls. Both of 'em." His eyes drifted off to the hills. Finally he lay a hand on Leo's shoulder, mumbled, "Thanks anyway," and turned back to the Jeep.

By the time Hickey drove to the mesa, picked up the Indians, and got back to the shantytown, as the sun dipped behind the west mesa and the low sky flashed red and gold, Leo had ordered dinner for a few hundred. He sat in his Packard with the door open, paying cart vendors for tacos, coffee, sodas. When they left him alone he counted money, to keep busy so as not to get spooked when the wind climbed to a howl. Or when the Indians stared too long and made him feel like a freak show. Or else he got to worrying that these half-assed troops would desert and steal the guns, directly after suppertime.

Hickey and Tito went to the Olmec jacal where El Mofeto still lay on his side, facing the wall, on the straw mat left of the door. With his wrists tied and wrapped behind his head and his legs still bound at the ankles, it looked like all his muscles had shrunk and drawn him up small as a mummy. His hands looked dark purple. Tito kicked him in the back and waited a minute for the body to stir, before he rolled the skunk over.

Where they expected a face writhing in misery, a weird, gleeful countenance appeared. The mouth spread wide in amazement as if he'd just seen a great spectacle. Then he started laughing and muttering, loud, fast.

Finally Tito said, "He don't tell us nothing, boss. *Puro loco*. He don't hurt nobody, no more."

Hickey stepped outside, got a beer from a soda vendor and slugged it down, went and found a taco and tried to eat but couldn't stuff it down. He got one more beer, sat on the riverbank while dark fell. The air remained summer hot, only harsher, drier, charged with brutal energy. If you listened close, the wind grew louder and wilder until it was all you could hear.

Then from four miles northwest at Ream Field, the air raid siren blew. Everybody in the shantytown turned that way and froze still. The siren quit. Blew again. And stopped. So it was only a red alert. There could be a sky full of Japs speeding this way and a brigade of Nazis sneaking up the coast toward the border, but probably it was only a night of spooks like they'd gone through before, every full moon since Pearl Harbor.

If you'd been a cop in this part of the world, you expected the worst on those rare nights when the full moon met the Santa Ana. One time, a whole squad got bushwhacked in Chinatown. The cops had gone there on a riot call. A grocery and restaurant had got looted, but all the cops found were hecklers they chased into a park, grass and shrubs around a Buddhist shrine. Guns blazed. Eight guys died, only two of them Chinese. Another hot, windy full moon, some looney torched a movie house. Thirty folks got trampled. Morticians grew rich on nights like this. It was a natural law.

From his pocket, Hickey grabbed Elizabeth's letter. It was only two pages long. She missed him. She'd gone to a dance at the country club Mr. Castillo had joined, and met a boy named Marshall Green, a golf champ who drove a British touring car. Next year he'd be a naval officer. She wrote, "I still want to visit you this summer, but Mom says where would I stay since you live in the barracks, and I'd probably get bored while you're at work all the time. I'd go mad thinking of Marshall dancing with other girls. Maybe you can take a leave and visit me." Her mom was happy, Elizabeth claimed. They both liked New Jersey now that winter had passed. She closed with love.

Hickey stuffed the letter into his pocket. Then he ripped it out again, wadded it tight, and threw in into the stinking river.

25

From the crest of Las Lomas, you could see all around. The high moon's beams glowed bluish-white off the white mansions. A red hue still washed the sea, from the shoreline a quarter-mile out, and the Islas Coronados five miles off looked so close you could see caves in their hillsides. About three miles north lay Tijuana's downtown in its dim, smoky light.

Hickey, Tito, and two Yaquis sat in the Jeep, on the crest trail a few hundred yards above the del Monte place. They had evaded the private cops who stood sentry at a gate on the road to Las Lomas by driving farther south, then four-wheeling straight up the hillside.

The Yaquis shared a Coca-Cola. Tito sat holding one of the two-way radios, a pack the size of a lunch box that hung from a strap with a phonelike receiver. He started bouncing his chin rhythmically.

Hickey put on his glasses.

There were a dozen mansions spaced across Las Lomas and half of them belonged to old del Monte and his sons. Big, square colonials with lots of ironwork and balconies, and a couple low-slung joints, like mausoleums. Each yard had a tended garden of an acre or so, surrounded by a high block wall. Between them spread dry land covered with tumbleweeds and sage, except on the east side, where the fairways of a golf course ran up the hill, beside the resort hotel at the hot springs, where the Agua Caliente Casino used to be. Just down from that lay the paddock and stables of the racetrack, a quarter-mile from where the Lomas road crossed Revolución—by the supper club where Leo's Packard waited.

The radio crackled, then Leo's voice barked, "Get moving up there, huh? It's almost breakfast time."

Hickey grabbed the radio mike, squinted at his watch. 2:50. "Nag, nag. We got ten minutes to go."

"Well, I got four cars full of Indians and they're acting like they never stayed up past dark. Crispín's right here snoring like a bull."

"Pinch his nose."

"Tom, my heart's been thumping too loud, too long. It'll be tenderized if we don't get moving soon."

"Nervous, huh?"

"Sure. I figure if we die and go to hell, it'll stink like the Club Paris."

"Okay. Let's move, then," Hickey said quietly. "We're gonna wait until you get past the gate and start up the hill. Listen, keep yourself out of the battle, old man—if I get it, you hafta run this crusade. Right? Hey, and you gotta take care of the girls, so the least thing goes wrong, or looks wrong, you bail out. Hear me?"

"When'd you get so bossy?"

Hickey switched off the radio. He grabbed for his pipe, in a hurry to catch a last smoke, but the wind blew out every match he lit, until finally he slung the lousy briar fifty feet into a sage bush. Then he switched the radio back on and relayed orders to the Yaquis he'd sent to keep watch on the west slope of the Lomas, in case the Army got alerted and started to move from their base on the coastal plain below.

"Matches?" Hickey asked Tito.

The cabbie sat munching peanuts. Now he rifled through the pockets in his dark brown and orange Hawaiian shirt and his khaki trousers until he came up with five matchbooks. He took out a cigaret, lit it the first try, and gave it to Hickey, "Maybe you a little nervoso, no?"

"No. Maybe you got better matches."

"Sure. I bet that's how it is."

Downhill to the east, Leo's Packard Phaeton crept toward the gateway to Las Lomas. A block behind came a Ford and a taxi. The Packard stopped at the gate. Suddenly all four doors flashed open. Bodies swarmed out and seemed to devour the guards. Then two Olmecs dragged the limp guards off the road, and the other Olmecs piled back into the Phaeton as the trailing cars caught up. All three cars came speeding up the hill.

The Yaquis and Tito piled into the Jeep beside Hickey. He pushed the starter pedal. The motor sputtered and caught. In a second they were bounding across the hill. They met the road seaside from the crest, just before the other cars got there. Hickey waved. All the cars rolled slowly, quietly down and pulled to a stop, single file on the shoulder about three hundred yards up the hill and around a turn from the del Monte place.

Hickey ran to the Packard and met Leo climbing out. The old man looked cooler than he'd sounded on the radio. He leaned over the door, resting his chin on the frame.

"Stay here," Hickey said, "and keep a few boys with you. If there's trouble and you need to take the Jeep, just do it. Don't think."

"Go on," Leo grumbled.

Hickey gave a glance around while Tito shooed the sad-faced Otomis out of the Ford. Two of them opened the trunk and took out a couple of thin cotton mattresses. Tito sent them down the road to cross on the far side below the estate and proceed in from the west. The Olmecs he sent straight across, with two mattresses, to scale the east wall. Hickey drew a long breath, then ran back to the Kickapoos, around the cab and the Studebaker. They looked ready, gassed up and primed, waiting for the spark. He said, "You all got the plan? Okay. Now, shoot if you have to. Make up your own mind. Let's go."

Hickey led the way. They ran across the road, started down

toward the gate along the eight-foot-high wall topped with shards of broken glass. About thirty yards up from the gate, they walked more softly, listening, and just before the gate, they stopped—at a sign from Hickey, two Kickapoos strapped their rifles across their backs, pulled hunting knives and set them between their teeth, took leather gloves from the pockets of their jeans and pulled them on. Hickey made another sign. Two more Kickapoos hoisted those first ones up the wall. One on each side of the gate. Light, wiry, and strong, the Kickapoos flew over the wall. They fell like ghosts beside the two blue-shirted mestizo guards at the door of the Casa.

One guard yelped, whirled, and fell with a knife in his back. The other, clobbered by a rifle butt, toppled against the wall and down. A Kickapoo threw open the gate. Indians with ropes and gags dragged the fallen guards into a garden of succulents and started binding them, in case they sprang alive, while Hickey clicked on his radio. "Send the rest of 'em in."

On the west side, the Otomis scaled the wall, over the mattresses, and dropped, quiet, barefooted, onto a patio beside an Olympic pool surrounded by statues of naked athletes and gods. The desert Otomis gazed in awe at the cobalt blue water. Finally Sergeant Guillermo whistled and waved. They scampered quietly over to the dark shadow of a bathhouse. They looked through a kitchen window and the open kitchen door, where a couple of servant women leaned over a sinkboard.

Guillermo talked softly into his radio and glowered at the thing a minute before he remembered to switch it on. "Capitán, we okay."

"You in the yard?"

"*Pues, si.*"

"Anybody there?"

"*En la casa.* Two señoras. It's all."

Crispín in the lead, Olmecs had scaled the north wall. The mattresses they crawled over shredded. But they wore huaraches, and with their short, strong bodies that had gotten fed the last few days since Hickey came along, they scaled the wall like gymnasts. Only a few tore their knees on the glass. They ran past the servants' quarters, shacks in a corner of the yard, past two cabañas, and through a grove of citrus trees. They huddled close to the house beneath a balcony on the bedroom wing. Somebody above them wheezed. Crispín clicked on his radio. "We ready, Señor."

On the porch, Hickey looked up from Tito's radio, and studied the faces of his Kickapoos. They stood pressed against a wall on the west side of the front porch. Something looked wrong. No resistance. It could be that the loud wind had given them cover. Or maybe a few platoons of Germans waited inside, with machine guns aimed at the door.

He turned to the cabbie. "Whatta you think?"

Tito stood hunched with his hands on his knees like any second he'd vomit. "Why you ask me? You the general."

A cramp jabbed Hickey's stomach, hardened to a knot. He wondered how a loser like himself had got to run this deal. Phony, he thought, you crazy faker. Who the hell are you, risking twenty lives?

When Guillermo yelped into his radio, "Here they going," Tito jerked up tall.

"Now, boss."

Hickey slowly flicked on his radio. "They bit, old man. We're going in."

The knob turned easily but the door must've weighed five hundred pounds. Hickey shoved hard. It swung and banged against a wall. He stepped inside. Behind him came Renaldo, the biggest Kickapoo, with a Browning machine gun. The rest jumped in and fanned across the entryway that led to an enormous white room. With not a soul in it.

A blue-shirted guard posted in the foyer had heard a shout from the porch, looked through a peekhole, seen Hickey and the Kickapoos. He'd raced through the main hall to the gaming room, chasing the ricos and women outside, the back way. They'd swarmed across a lawn, through the citrus grove to where the cabañas stood near the stables and the servants' quarters. About a dozen men in dress clothes, uniforms, or silk guayabera shirts staggered, cussing, while the women, in evening gowns and coiffed

183

hair studded with jewels, yelled and stumbled on high heels, until they saw the wild Indians. So many ricos and whores gasped at once, it sounded as if they'd rehearsed.

Dreadful Indians stalked toward them from both sides with bayonets raised, herding them across the citrus grove, past the cabañas, up against the wall. One man tried to flee. He sprinted east along the wall. Guillermo the Otomi kneeled, fired, hit the target just below his ribcage. The man hopped ten feet farther and fell. He pounded a leg on the ground.

Inside, the Kickapoos started crossing the great hall, which Hickey recognized—a replica of the ballroom, where he'd played sax, at the Agua Caliente Casino. The floor was a shiny mosaic of small wooden blocks, oak, teak, mahogany in patterns of stars, pyramids, and moons. In front of the sofas and chairs upholstered in velvet and suede lay fine Persian rugs. Tapestries and paintings covered the walls—Chinese landscapes, Renaissance merchants, a gaunt horseman by El Greco. The mahogany dining table, big as a dance floor, took up only a corner. In another corner was the bandstand. Glittering chandeliers of crystal and enough bulbs to wake a whole city hung from the ceiling two stories up. The mezzanine's railed landing stretched down the whole east side— from there the first three shots blasted.

Two bullets splintered the floor. A Kickapoo yelped. He dropped his gun, grabbed his shoulder, staggered back into a wall and let himself down. The other Kickapoos wheeled and fired.

A guard toppled over the rail and crashed onto the dining table. Another fell and writhed on the landing with a foot and leg sticking through the rail. But the last gunman escaped up a mezzanine hallway.

Hickey told a Kickapoo to tend the one who was shot. He sent two others and Tito to search the first floor beneath the mezzanine, through the doors that led off the great room. He ordered Sergeant Jack, Renaldo, and four other Kickapoos up the circular stairs to the mezzanine. Then he led the other three Kickapoos across the great hall. They spread out, peering behind sofas and chairs. They kicked over chairs and end tables, knocking drinks on the Persian rugs.

One picked up crystal glasses and threw them at the walls. Hickey walked slowly with an eye on the far doors.

At the end of the great hall, through one door on the right, was a powder room with three marble sinks and fixtures of silver and a small mauve alcove with a toilet and bidet. Another door led to the parlor full of stuffed velvet chairs and candlelight tinted gold from the shine off picture frames and candlesticks. Beyond the parlor, a long archway led to the gaming room, white carpet so fine and deep it looked like ermine, walls mosaiced in tile renderings of naked brown angels floating toward the sky. There were six card tables with maroon felt, two roulette tables littered with half-full drinks and stacks of chips.

Hickey and two Kickapoos stepped through a door on the left, into the kitchen that looked like an outbuilding. It had a floor of dark, splintery pinewood. Stained walls hung with cast-iron pots, stalks of chiles. Big sinks, long cutting tables, the smells of beans and masa.

They cut through the pantry and outside, ran across the back yard to Crispín and Guillermo. Hickey stood gazing at the crowd.

A few blond men. At least two—the short, gray-faced guy, and the older one with liver spots—Hickey'd seen before when they were wearing uniforms with velvety maroon hats and gold buttons, in Hell. The old fellow had collapsed. A middle-aged, portly doll, and an Indian beauty so young she might've been a kid playing dress-up, held the old man by the arms. Hickey scanned the whole crowd, looking for Zarp. Maybe the Devil stood at an upstairs window, drawing a bead on his skull.

But the rest couldn't scare a chipmunk, between them. They were a flock of tweety birds, now that a gang of poor Indians stood between them and their substance. Hickey turned to the nearest Kickapoo, motioned toward Crispín and Guillermo. "Tie these clowns back to back and throw 'em in the pool."

Two shots cracked. From inside. Hickey's army spun and aimed at the noise. But there was nothing to see, and all you heard now was shouts and the blustering wind. Hickey and the Kickapoos ran back to the house through the kitchen into the great hall and found Tito and his men with their guns aimed at the landing. Hickey ran up and yelped, "Who's shooting?"

"Don't know, boss," the cabbie whispered. "But you gotta see what's out there. A garage, so big like for trains. And six limousines. We don't find no gold, it's okay, hombre, we got six limos."

Hickey ordered them to follow and ran to the spiral stairs.

On top, two hallways led off the landing. Two bedroom wings, each with six carved hardwood doors. Hickey sent the cabbie and his band down the south wing, and started with his own squad down the north wing but as they got ready to turn the corner, his radio sounded.

"Tom, who's shooting?"

"That was five minutes ago. You just waking up, Leo?"

"I been on the other radio."

"Yeah. Well, we're okay, so relax."

"Relax, hell. I think we're in a mess, Tom. A cruiser's on the road. Our boys at the gate got 'em stopped but don't count on that for long. Find your damned gold yet?"

"Buy me ten minutes," Hickey said. "And get the cars down here into the yard."

"Right. I guess ten minutes you got. Maybe not a second more."

Hickey dropped the radio mike. He poked his head around the corner. At the end of the hall, a guy lay sprawled on the floor, his blue shirt stained like a bloody vest.

Hickey told the Kickapoos to each search a room. He took the closest door, on the right, turned the knob, and with his bayonet out, he kicked it open. The room was tinted soft pink and green, dimly glowing from a lamp beside the canopy bed where two señoritas in torn nighties lay tied with wound-up sheets. They weren't even squirming but their dark eyes followed Hickey like searchlights. Hickey gave them a quick bow. Then he looked in the bathroom and saw it had a door leading to the next room. He quietly turned that knob. Kicked through the door.

He almost got blasted by Sergeant Jack who was guarding two

naked women and one old man, Santiago del Monte. The Presidente, who might be as rich as Solomon, stood bowlegged in a corner, pissing down his leg. Both arms over his head, one hand flexed claw-like, he yelled a string of curses. Then he fell back into the wedge of the corner, dropping his arms and using them to brace himself there.

Jack aimed his Browning at the old fool and growled, "One more time he calls my mother a puta, boom."

"Who fixed that guy in the hall?"

Jack told him how the guard had stepped out of the last room on this wing, the one on the left with the locked door that you couldn't kick through. Desmond had blasted him.

Hickey nodded, and stepped out there. He walked to the last door on the left, stood a minute beside the dead guard, as three Indians gathered around him. They all stared at the door. Hickey knew exactly what he'd find in there. He could feel its power.

He gave orders that everybody should get herded out back.

A parade of whores and ricos began. They appeared out of rooms all along that wing. Kickapoos and Yaquis shoved them down the mezzanine hall, along the balcony toward the spiral stairway. The men, especially the police chief, Buscamente, proud as ever in his silk cowboy shirt and high-heeled boots, cursed and threatened everybody. Most of the whores looked amused, like they were going to a party with their long bare legs and bright silk underwear, hips rolling and twitching. Two of them pranced along the hallway applying lipstick. The Indians herded them outside, across the yard to the pool deck where the Otomis bound them together and drove them to join the others in the pool.

As he stood at the door of the last room on the mezzanine, Hickey's radio clicked. "Tom, that car's the goddamn Federales. I didn't hear any shots, but they knocked out our boys somehow. They're making time up the hill."

Hickey's overloaded brain popped and sputtered. *With this loco wind and moonshine. What was behind that door. Now, Federales.* "Okay, get yourself outa here. This minute."

"No. Listen to me, Tom. If you ain't found the gold yet, once

187

those cops get up here—they'll pin you down till the Army shows. We all gotta run now. Bring a couple hostages. Big shots. Forget the damned gold. It ain't there."

"Yeah. It is," Hickey said darkly. "I'm not leaving without it. But you are. You got Vi. Magda. And Wendy." With a cramp in his chest and his legs shuddering, Hickey switched off his radio.

The big Kickapoo Thompson gunner, Renaldo, Hickey ordered to stay by this door. He led the other two down the hall, back to the landing and along to the south wing. In the first room on the right, he found Tito chatting with a pretty mestizo who lounged on the sofa rubbing against him.

When Hickey glared, the cabbie snapped, "It's okay, boss. We got everything fine down here. I'm asking Malu here about this gold. You want me tell you where the gold maybe is?"

"I know," Hickey said. "Now, you take some drivers and get the cars off the street, on this side of the wall. There's Federales on the way."

The cabbie sat for a minute squeezing the girl's knee. Then, mumbling, he got up and hustled out. His boots clomping hard on the stairway echoed in the great hall. Hickey turned to the servant girl.

26

≡ ≡ ≡

"El cuarto de oro," Hickey said.

Pretty Malu nodded and walked ahead of him. As they started down the landing, she turned and doed her eyes. *"Por favor,* General, *da me una cosita de oro."*

"A little gold. Okay. You got a key? *Llave?* "

"No, Señor. *La unica llave es del diablo Alemagne."*

"That'd be Zarp."

"Oh, si."

They turned down the north wing. Two Kickapoos stood by the door at the end of the hall. They'd pushed the dead guard up against the far wall, out of the way.

Since Hickey outweighed the biggest Kickapoo by at least fifty pounds, he told them to stand back and cover him. He kicked the mahogany door, a full blast with his right sole that nearly busted the arch of his foot. The door didn't give. He told the Kickapoos to have at it. They hit the door with feet, elbows, shoulders. When they gave up, Hickey pulled his .45 and fired at the lock. Then he kicked again. Still wouldn't budge. Finally he shooed the others down the hall, unclipped a grenade from his belt, pulled the pin, set the grenade on the floor in the doorway, then let go and ran for the landing. In three seconds he made the corner.

The boom sounded far off, echoing down the hallway like out of a cavern. A moment of quiet. Then with a great thud the door fell, and three rifle shots from the room smacked into the wall across the way.

Dark, acrid smoke gushed up the hall on wind from the blown-out window. Hickey unclipped another grenade. He walked along the north wall, stepping softly, but to him it sounded loud as falling trees. Halfway, he stopped and listened. Heard nothing. Five feet from the door, he pulled the pin and lunged forward. He stumbled, almost fell over a hunk of crashed-in wall, and slung the grenade through the doorway.

As that blast hit, he slipped and skidded around the corner. The Kickapoos and Malu watched him with admiration, and he sat there a minute catching his breath, wishing his heart would ease down. The Kickapoo named Desmond reached to help him up, and stood beside Renaldo waiting for orders. Three more Kickapoos ran down the landing from the south wing. Hickey asked for volunteers to go in first, and got nobody. He thought of going himself—but you don't want to get the general killed—except all this mess was *his* big idea. He started around the corner. But Desmond touched his shoulder. "Me, sir."

Desmond took the lead, Hickey followed, then came Renaldo and the others. By now the wind had blown the smoke away, gusting hard, hot, down the hallway—you had to lean against it when you walked. But the room was still full of smoke like a reddish-golden fog. Walking on debris, Desmond used a sleeve to wipe his glasses, then he pushed through the fog, his head stuck forward, with Hickey just a rifle-length behind and to the left. When the shots boomed—two in a breath, and Desmond fell sideways as if he'd been cut in half, and Hickey got miraculously spared. He dropped behind Desmond, sighted at the blue thing moving through the smoke—he fired a whole clip, ejected, slapped in another and fired it clean. He might've squeezed off twenty rounds before he was sure all the noise came from his own rifle.

Renaldo and another Kickapoo stepped in, looked down.

Hickey looked too. At Desmond's guts and chunks of flesh strewn across the floor.

In a fury, Hickey leaped up, jumped over the body and a pile of debris, and kicked the blue soldier who lay twisted on the plush white carpet, ribbons of blood spurting from his neck. The Indian face looked about twelve years old. Still Hickey booted, kicking hate and fear out of himself. Then he wheeled and gazed around the room, eyes pulsing with his heartbeat.

Suddenly the smoke cleared and the room flashed at him like sunrise knocking you out of a hazy dream.

First he saw a wall about twenty feet long, of shelves covered with golden vases, candlesticks, statuettes, bowls. Beneath the shelves sat three trunks twice as big as footlockers. Cherry wood with golden hasps and braces. Along the east side, about thirty feet from the blown-out door to the corner, the wall was cluttered with paintings in golden frames and two big calendars, an Aztec and a Mayan, made of gold, and the cameo likeness of a schooner, all gold.

Then he gazed toward the corner, and saw the gold-framed bed and a gun pointed at his eyes.

Behind the long .38 pistol, lay Señor Zarp—his giant head, with the gray beard and tiny eyes, propped on a stack of pillows, his free arm clutching a golden thing. The voice was deep as ever, but tremulous. "Why don't I kill you right now?"

Hickey swallowed his breath. He tried to sound tough but only could gasp, "You want me to bring the girl back."

"Oh yes, and . . ."

Suddenly, a great yell filled the room, as Renaldo sprang up from the body of his cousin, spun and ran with his arms out toward the foot of the bed, and then dove head first and sailed through the air. Zarp didn't quite get the gun around before he fired two shots—as the Indian and then Hickey landed, Renaldo crashed Zarp's midsection with a rifle butt. Hickey tore the pistol away and crunched the big white face. Busted a cheekbone, and molars. Blood and teeth oozed out of Zarp's mouth.

Hickey backed away from the bed, grabbed the Kickapoo's arm, and both of them dropped onto the floor and sat breathing hard, shaking, with their eyes on all that damned gold. Soon the other Kickapoos came and stood by them, gawking.

After a minute, at the sound of a crackling radio, Hickey got up, walked out on rubbery legs, and found the servant girl in the hall holding his radio. Then Tito and two Indians came on the run. His face tightened like someone's swimming underwater, the cabbie shouted, "Man, we got one of those cars in, but no more. The goddamn pinche Federales got us stuck in here, hombre. What we doing now?"

Hickey motioned Tito and the others into the room. As they stepped that way he picked up his radio. "Leo? Where are you?"

Through the static, Leo's voice rasped, "Right out front. Me and these two Indians and six Federales so far. Tom, Cárdenas's boys'll be along any minute. Yaquis say the army's climbing the hill."

Hickey couldn't stand anymore. He sat on a pile of rubble, struck by a paralyzing melancholy in which nothing mattered because everything was doomed. All along he should've known the deal would end like this. Dreams always ended this way. At the climax. Then you wait to die. The only thing to do was go downstairs, find the liquor cabinet, and die like a man, stone drunk. If these buzzards caught him alive, they'd torture him trying to get the girl back. For Zarp. Unless he stepped in there now and wasted the freak.

He stood up. Looked at the doorway. At the radio, and wondered if gold could buy their way out of here. "Leo, anybody out there wanta listen to our side?"

"I'm giving it to 'em, Tom."

"Good, and tell 'em they oughta see all this gold."

He switched off the radio, dropped it on a pile of rubble, and stepped back into the room where five Kickapoos, Tito and Malu, all leered and plucked things off the shelves to look closer. The girl wore a necklace of diamonds and gold. Someone had dragged Desmond to the barest corner. Zarp lay panting through a mouth of blood and chopped, swollen tongue, as Hickey stepped over to

192

where Tito gripped a statuette in one hand while his other hand rode the servant girl's rump.

"Get back outside. Make sure we got Indians posted all around, up on the wall . . . C'mon, move! The Army's racing up the hill."

"Where he get all this much gold?" Tito muttered.

"Now!"

"First you tell me what we going to do."

Hickey grabbed the flowered shirt and twisted it into a noose. "Load the gold in the limousines. That's what."

Tito fiercely threw down the statue and marched out of the room. The girl stood petting the necklace, wagging her chin at Hickey, who turned to the Kickapoos and barked, "Start packing this junk down to the garage." Slowly, entranced, they went to the shelves, loaded their arms with vases and things. Hickey sat on the bed. He stared for a while at the mashed, bloody face, the hot eyes deep in puffy sockets, and a sharp corner of the gold thing Zarp still clutched to his chest.

"So you're the devil," Hickey mused. "Anyway the girl thinks so . . . Guess why I don't kill you, yet?"

The faint voice gargled blood. "You are afraid."

"Naw. But I'm a heck of a nice guy."

The radio sounded. Hickey jumped for it. "Tom, the commandante wants to see this gold."

"Send him up."

After a minute, Leo said, "He figures you oughta bring it down."

"Sure enough," Hickey snarled, then considered how much gold they could dish out and still have a gang of fortunes. Even so, for a second he broiled at the idea of letting any of it go. A weird possessiveness caught him, like this gold was his right and destiny. All his life he'd passed up chances, acting like a dupe, Madeline figured, too proud to bend far enough, always trying to stride like some hero through a world that treated heroes and clowns the same. Leo call his name a few times before he said, "Okay, then. Some guys'll be coming out pretty soon. The first shot fired, or any bad news, we open up too. Tell 'em that. Tell 'em how we got air support coming." He shut off the radio, mumbled, "Tell 'em any damned lie you can," and sat on rubble waiting for the Kickapoos to return from the garage. Trying to boost his spirits, he picked out items of gold, and estimated their worth. Renaldo came back first.

"You and somebody take a bunch of those candle things down front, heave them over the wall. Be careful you don't go near the front gate or the Federales'll chop you in half."

As the Indians filled their arms and left, Hickey stepped to the French doors and out to the balcony. Below, a dozen rifles wheeled and levelled at him. He dove back inside and heard shouts like Crispín yelling, "Es el Heecky!"

He got up from the floor, stepped out there, and looked over the backyard. The Indians on sentry paced, spooked like horses in the paddock, their guns up and gripped tight as they looked every way at once and tried to listen through the wind. Any second now, Hickey thought, one of those Germans or Spaniards could yell the wrong cuss word at the wrong Indian and cue the massacre.

He walked back and sat on the bed. Sank into the downy mattress and let a hand glide across the silk sheets. He listened for gunfire. For wheels rolling up the hill. Finally he looked at the bloody sorcerer, and after a minute the man stirred. Then he rose up just a little. Even with his face bashed-in, the tiny, greenish eyes looked catlike and ferocious. A gust of wind slammed the French doors. Hickey whipped around, then turned back. "Where'd all this gold come from? Besides what del Monte stole from Agua Caliente? He find the seven cities? Or did you alchemize the junk?"

Battered as it was, Zarp's face got animated, his slack skin tightened, eyes rounded, like he saw a chance to turn Hickey's mind. "You are interested?"

"Naw," Hickey said. "Just passing time."

The man started coughing, choking. Each cough, blood like raindrops shot out. His voice strained weaker. "In this room are coins four hundred years old, and jewels that belonged to the Empress Carlotta."

"Oh, yeah? Del Monte steal most of it?" The man coughed

194

another mist of blood, and Hickey said wearily, "How'd you get your claws into him?"

A shot, then a volley of screams issued from the backyard. Hickey jumped to the French doors and looked out. Over by the pool, Indians dragged a body along. The screams kept on, louder, wilder, and another shot cracked. Then the wind gusted viciously. Hickey turned back to the room, collided with a Kickapoo—a fortune clattered to the ground. He started to yell at the Indian but he clipped his words off and, muttering, stepped to the bed. Zarp reached out and tapped his arm with a bloody finger that left a wet stain. "Señor? Who do you believe will find more pain, less pleasure, for eternity in hell? You or me?"

"Guy like you believes in hell," Hickey mused.

"I have visions."

"Yeah, I bet." Hickey sneered. "Tell me more about the gold. That's what I'm here about, and we only got a minute."

Zarp collapsed into the bed and pillow as if the will had sapped out of him. Finally he said, in a voice mostly breath, "I can get you home alive, with half of the gold for your own."

"Not your gold, is it?"

"The spoils of war."

"War, huh?"

"A man is always at war," he gasped. "If not against another man, then against his nature." His mouth quivered, trying to speak, but his lungs couldn't raise the power.

"Half the gold?" Hickey muttered, and waited.

"All you must do is bring me the girl."

As that sank in, Hickey snarled weirdly, raised his arm high and smashed the bloody mouth with his elbow. Then he wiped his arm on the bedspread. Zarp lay still, sipping little breaths. The gold thing he'd been holding had fallen beside him. Hickey picked it up, the ornate gold frame around a painting, a miniature, an exquisite face, white and young with carved and polished features. Ringlets of real golden hair. Eyes of real gold. The same image as Zarp had worn in Hell, on his medallion. It could've been male or female. It transfixed Hickey, made him dizzy with staring. Lucifer, it was. The brightest angel.

If there was any truth to the tales of Christians and Jews, this one damned spirit inspired all the death and misery.

He tried to snap the thing with his hands. Then he slung it down onto the floor and reached for his M-1, fired on automatic, one clip then another until all that remained was the gold frame and gold chips that used to be eyes and hair. A dread silence had fallen. Even Zarp's breathing had stilled. Hickey sat on the bed waiting for judgement. Then he wondered if he'd shot anybody below, through the floor.

The Kickapoos ran in from the garage, and out toting their armloads of gold. Hickey told one of them to stay in the room on guard. Then he grabbed up his rifle, his radio, and walked out, down the hall to the landing and turned toward the front of the house, to see if he could get a look at the street. Electric bolts zinged up his spine and down his arms to his fingertips, as if he could start a fire just by touching. He turned down the south hallway and entered the first bedroom on the right, stepped to the French doors. With the moon low, behind the house, it was dark enough so he opened the door a little way, crept out, and hid beneath a potted rubber tree.

There were two black Chevys across the street. Behind them a Federale's head popped up now and then. Like in a shooting gallery. Somebody's hat blew off and bounced along the road downhill. No sign of the Army yet but they had to be close. He didn't see Leo or what had become of the gold the Indians had thrown over the wall. Finally he stepped back into the bedroom. He wanted tobacco or liquor, so he walked out to the landing, called one of the Kickapoos on his way downstairs with gold and told him to send up a cigaret. Then he went back and sat on the bed, the softest he'd ever felt. Maroon silk sheets. He picked up his M-1, and began stabbing the bed with the bayonet, easily at first, then harder until clouds of down flew and hung in the air.

Finally he tossed the gun, clicked on his radio. "Hey! Leo? What's going on out there?"

After a long moment of silence, the balcony door clattered— Hickey dove for his rifle, spun around, and almost started firing at the wind. He sat back, caught his breath. A few seconds later, the rumbling started. He jumped to the French doors and looked toward the sound, just in time to see the tank roll over the crest of the hill.

It stopped there, at the highest point in Tijuana. The turret swiveled. Then the gun flashed. An instant before the clap like an earthquake.

Hickey folded his hands and sat staring at the radio. He looked at his watch. 3:40. He wished that damned Indian would come back with his cigaret. And he wondered what things would be like in hell.

27

The shell flew directly over the prisoners and landed twenty yards beyond the wall, a warning shot. It blew flack and dirt, set off panic in the swimming pool. Santiago del Monte waved his arms, throwing curses at the sky, while the police chief and a burr-haired German ran to the edge and tried to leap out of there—an Olmec swung his rifle butt at Buscamente's head and conked him squarely. The German had to fish him out, hold his head above the water.

The Otomis—who'd lived so far out they didn't know much about such things—gaped at this monster on top of the hill, like a giant black roach with an elephant's trunk, spitting dynamite. Two Otomis ran for the wall and scaled it, would've jumped and fled down the hillside, across the plain toward the Playas. But first they saw about fifty soldiers climbing the hill and two Jeeps carrying turreted machine guns, one on each flank of the infantry. The Otomis dove back into the yard and squatted at the base of the wall. A Kickapoo ran out through the kitchen door and told Crispín that the general had ordered them to march all the prisoners inside, upstairs. Soon the ricos came wading to dry land. A woman with long, plaited hair towed old del Monte by one arm while his other arm splashed at the water like a swimmer.

Tom Hickey still sat on the down bed near the balcony in the southwest bedroom. He finished the cigaret, ground it out on the carpet, and looked at the radio. "How much more gold?"

Leo took a minute to consult the Feds, and came back, "How much is there?"

"Look," Hickey growled, "first I wanta know does the commandante believe you? About the Nazis."

"He's thinking it over, Tom. But the colonel just stands there. Looks like the son of Zapata by Goliath."

A Kickapoo ran in with news of the soldiers climbing the hill. Hickey barked, "Get everybody on the wall—Crispín tells 'em when to start shooting." The Indian ran out. "Leo? Tell 'em this gold makes the Pope's collection look like a dime store. And I'll dish out a fortune, soon as you get in here with the rest of us."

His voice high, straining, Leo answered, "I better stay here awhile."

Hickey stiffened, wondering if his partner could sell him out, if he thought all of them inside were doomed anyway. But if he couldn't trust Leo, he couldn't trust anybody, including himself. Then life was a sentence he didn't care to serve. Finally he said, "Tell 'em to get that tank outa sight, and they'll get more gold."

He switched off the radio, hung it over his shoulder, and stepped into the hall where he ran into some Otomis herding the last of the prisoners, Santiago del Monte and two of his sons. The old man lunged at Hickey with claws out and shouting gibberish in a stiff, gutteral language, maybe Russian.

Hickey turned toward the landing. "Where's Tito?"

"*Con el oro,* Señor," an Indian said.

Hickey walked slowly, listening to the fading yells of old Santiago, eerie wails like a Moslem praying. In the gold room, the shelves and the wall sat bare and all that remained were the bed, a pole lamp, and the three trunks. Somebody had busted the locks off the trunks, and Tito stood there with his hand hitched into the back of Malu's frock as they bent over looking into a trunk—at a lode of brooches, pendants, coins, bracelets, letter knives, daggers. When Hickey stepped near, Tito startled and wheeled around. They all turned to gawk at the trunk, and up at each other, and Hickey

199

muttered, "You figure most of the Indians want to risk it, or try to get out of here with their skins?"

As he contemplated, Tito unhanded the girl and lit a smoke. "I think they crazy, boss. Like a man, or a dog, don't matter, he gets beat all the time but he don't fight back until one time he does and then it sure don't matter if he gets killed, not to him anymore. Maybe that's how the Indios thinking. Maybe so, maybe no. Who knows these Indios? But for me, I think it don't matter, boss. The Army got us surrounded, we going to die, we don't got something to lose no more."

"How many cars we got?"

With a rapturous grin, Tito declared, "Oh man, we got some cars. We got two Cadillacs, five limos, a pickup truck, and that old Studebaker."

"Fire 'em up, make sure they're gassed and ready. Then load up all the gold. Don't make any one of 'em too heavy." He waved at the bed where Zarp lay gulping air. "Take the Nazi too. Let's bring enough big shots for one in each car, use 'em for shields."

The cabbie clicked his heels, saluted.

"And give me another smoke."

Tito passed over three brown cigarets and a gold cigaret lighter, then hurried out to round up his Indians. Hickey lit up and kept flickering the lighter as he walked out, up to the landing and down the spiral stairs, across the great hall to the kitchen. There he sniffed out the liquor cupboard. Scotch. Brandy. Cognac. The best Cuban rum. Spanish liqueurs. Not a drop of mescal. Rich folks didn't go for that swill. It'd give them nightmares, Hickey thought—sweet dreams were mostly for the poor. He settled for a half-empty liter of cognac.

Then he walked out back, waving his arms and shouting, "Soy Hickey," so the wild Indians wouldn't blast him down. They stood positioned every twenty or so feet along the wall, on ladders, tables, stacks of chairs. Hickey sat on a bench by the path that led to the citrus grove. The wind looked dark reddish. All but a thin slice of moon had dropped behind the hill. In a half-hour or so it'd be down, and then they should run—in that darker span between the last of the moon and the first glow of dawn. Maybe there'd be an hour of dark. Until 5:30 or so. If they could speed out of here by 5:00, they'd reach Otay mesa before first light, when they wouldn't likely get chased by calvary.

A siren bellowed. He spooked, as if from a trance. Its wail carried across the wind, picking up an eerie vibrato. From way up there in another land, at Ream Field, nine miles away, four miles over the line. Hickey gazed out over the sea, and thought how weird it would be if the Japs showed up right now. Then he thought, No, it'd only make sense to attack when daylight was near and the lookouts off their guard, just after the full moon dropped on the hottest night of a Santa Ana. There couldn't be a more perfect time.

When he heard noises like the German Army rumbling over the coastal plain toward the border, Hickey dashed around the pool, climbed the diving board ladder, and looked down the hill.

The only army he saw was aimed at him. The tank up the hill. Artillery down the hill. And about two hundred soldiers lying in position all around.

He stood a long time, and thought—What if they got captured, and Zarp still wanted the girl so bad he'd trade for a ton of gold? What if it came down to choosing between a million and Wendy?

The wind's noise making him shudder, he climbed down and stood by the wall, lit a cigaret, and imagined Wendy sleeping with just a sheet over her, shoulders bare, her head to one side, eyelids fluttering, her bottom lip pushed out slightly like it always was, a little crooked with worry.

With a sigh, he turned back to the bench, to the cognac and the radio, and sat down wishing that lousy siren would quit before it torched off the last cool nerves and his army and the Mexicans started blasting each other and everything in sight just for relief. He lit another brown cigaret and took a long slug of cognac. As a rule, he didn't like rich guys for much. But their liquor was okay.

He sat there awhile figuring out how they'd die as they tried to break through that army. Or if they gave up now, they'd rot dead in a slimepit Mexican prison. There was no way out of here alive, it

201

seemed, without giving up all the gold. And then, the Mexicans would probably slaughter them anyway. Twenty dead men. Himself deadest of all. There might not be a hell for folks who minded their own business, but wise guys like Hitler, Mussolini, Tojo, and Hickey would sure get burned. He took another slug of cognac, thought once again about Wendy. He saw the two of them in a big car driving up a mountain. She was leaning on his arm and shoulder. She breathed like kisses.

Damned if he was ready to die.

An idea struck him. A simple one he must've had before. He thought—you go along being a loser, but just win big one time, only once, then you're no loser anymore. One big score can carry a guy through his lifetime. Like a big enough loss can finish you.

He couldn't see the moon but he sensed when it fell behind the mesa.

The radio clicked. "Tom, I got their terms. A split of the gold, and they're leaving it to your honor."

"Think it's a ruse?"

"Ten to one."

Hickey only pondered a second. "Well, I'm sending out a car full of gold. Soon as you and your boys get over the hill, past that tank. Then they're gonna move the tank off the road. Clear so far?"

"Yeah."

"Okay, then—we're holding the del Montes and some other big shots. They're going for a ride to the border. Tell the colonel we're a bunch of crazies, Leo, and if they want to start shooting, tell 'em I don't give a damn."

For a half-minute the radio sat quiet, before Leo croaked, "Guess you made up your mind."

"That's a fact." Hickey switched off the radio, strapped it to his shoulder, picked up the cognac, and walked toward the house, wishing to Christ that siren would quit screeching like the high end of a buzz saw. He lifted the cognac, stopped, looked at it a moment then smashed it on the ground, cussed, and walked inside.

He passed through the pantry and kitchen to the garage that ran down the whole east side of the building. There stood a Chrysler

limo and two Cadillacs, with motors running, Indians perched all over the hoods and fenders. Tito leaned against a tangerine-colored limo, flanked by his servant girl. He threw a grimace at Hickey. "What you think about this—we got two more cars than we got pinche Indios that know how to drive."

"I'll drive one. You drive one."

"Sure I'm going to drive. That makes one more we need."

"Teach somebody, quick. We got five minutes. And send up for a prisoner to drive the old Studebaker, and fill it pretty good with gold. About half the junk. That's our ticket outa here. Give 'em the biggest stuff, chandeliers and all that. We'll take what's easiest to carry." He nodded toward the servant girl. "She going with you?"

"She's wanting to, all right."

"You tell her we're probably gonna die?"

Tito rolled his eye. "You don't have to tell a woman every-thing." But Hickey kept staring. Finally the cabbie turned to Malu and talked in Spanish. She bowed her head a little, then raised up and grabbed tight hold of the cabbie's arm.

Then the radio sounded. "Tom?"

"Wait a second," Hickey snapped. He called over a Kickapoo and told him to get a few guys and race around and bring the troops, and make sure all of them got out here. The Kickapoo ran off and Hickey said to the radio, "What?"

"I'm in the Phaeton, Tom. Getting ready to take it over the hill. But damned if I could tell you what these Mex guys plan to do. They're yelling at each other. Be easier if the saps talked English."

"Listen, pal," Hickey said. "If I don't make it, do right by Wendy, will you? Instead of just figuring she's a moron. Give her a chance."

When he got no answer, Hickey wondered exactly what that could mean. Then he heard the Packard start before the radio fell silent.

Soon the Kickapoos ran in with the Otomis and Olmecs, and a minute later, Indians sat pointing guns out all the windows of five cars, while Hickey and his captain walked around giving the drivers

instructions. Then each of them jumped into his car. The first one, Tito's limo, pulled out. Stopped in front of the gate. The others lined up behind. Hickey's Chrysler came fourth, behind the Cadillac driven by the Kickapoo who'd just learned to drive. At the end of the line, the fifth car, was the old yellow Studebaker, a del Monte chauffeur at the wheel. It scraped along the ground from the weight of a trunk and backseat full of floor lamps and parts of a golden bedframe.

A couple Otomis threw open the gate, which squealed above the wind, and scampered back into the tangerine limo. Hickey yelled, "Go on," and the cabbie pulled out.

Keeping half an eye on the row of heads that poked up behind the two police cars, he swung a sharp left up the hill and eased along, riding low, an inch off the ground from the weight of his Indians and gold. Then the second car pulled out, turned left and stalled, right across the road from where the Mexican colonel and the commandante of Federales crouched in hiding behind a Jeep. For a moment, while the Cadillac was stalled, between revs of big motors you could hear the men shout roughly at each other.

All up the road to the crest, Mexican soldiers kneeled in a line about an arm's length apart with guns readied, eyes flashing, their fingers trembling and set to bust free and get with the killing. On the field behind the soldiers sat two troop-carrier trucks, another police car, and a Jeep with a bazooka mounted.

Finally the stalled Caddy moved, lurching up the hill after Tito's limo. The third car pulled out jerkily but made the turn all right and started upward. Then came Hickey. And in the limo's middle seat, old del Monte kept trying to scream through the gag Renaldo had lashed so tightly that blood ran down from the corners of his mouth and the gag or his fury had turned him purple, with his eyes bugged out and red tears streaking down his face.

Hickey idled through the gate, made the turn, and stopped. He leaned over two Kickapoos to the shotgun window and yelled, "Hey! Who there speaks English?"

"We hear you," someone in hiding, a baritone, shouted.

"Okay. Gold's in the Studebaker back there. But see, we also

planted a bomb in the car. And another right next to the ladies and gents we left tied up in the Casa. See, I got a radio hooked up to the bombs, so if anybody's gonna shoot, he better plug me first, or they're gonna lose a bunch of gold and the cream of high society. *Comprendes?*"

When no answer came, Hickey shouted, *"Adiós,"* and pulled away.

Creeping along, then stopping to wait for the cars behind, Tito's limo finally neared the crest, a quarter-mile up the grade. Twice more the second car stalled and rolled back a little before it fired again and lurched up the hill. The third car bumped the second car.

Mexican soldiers drew beads on the heads of Indians and Indians aimed back at them, while almost everybody cussed loudly and shouted threats and challenges.

Hickey got halfway to the crest idling the big Chrysler at five mph. From eight guys in that car, the only sounds were Santiago's muted squawling. A couple of words sounded French but the rest were too slurred to tell. The men at the windows held tightly to their guns. Those in the middle, and Hickey, pressed forward, staring through the windshield at the M-4 Sherman tank. With its 75-mm gun and the three machine guns below, it looked like a battleship on top of the hill.

Suddenly the big gun turreted right. Hickey stomped on the brakes. The Cadillac behind knocked them a good jolt, drove them ten feet up the hill. The tank's tracks moved. Stopped. Inched forward.

The monster turned right—and crawled away into the field.

28

As the tangerine limo took off like a missile over the crest of the hill, the whole motorcade sped after it. With whoops, prayers, battle cries, blasts on the horn, they flew out of Las Lomas, swung left, and zoomed like a hot-rod funeral down Avenida Revolución, a straight shot of two miles to the river bridge. Some Kickapoos broke out rum, bread, oranges they'd swiped, passed the loot around for inspection, and laughed like the next stop was paradise. In all the cars, Indians chattered and dreamed about the farms, machines, and women they'd buy.

But Tom Hickey just drove, smoking his last brown cigaret, looking out for an ambush while he tried to figure what had saved them. What had made the Feds and Army act reasonably? Why the Mex officers had allied with gringos and Indians against their own kind.

Finally he slapped the dashboard then switched on the radio beside him. "You there, Leopold?"

"Just across the river, Tom."

"Swell. Say, you know what got us outa there?"

"Sure. I figure it was Cárdenas. Means he's on the level."

"You bet."

"Some damn general he is, too. Let us handle all his dirty work, break up the coup, deliver his boys a ton of gold."

"Yep. We played to his hand, like dopes. And all we got to show for it is a million or so."

"Damn shame. Say, how much you figure he knew about del Monte?"

"Probably a bunch," Hickey said.

"So, why'd he let it go on so long?"

"Figured he oughta wait till they did something besides talk and hocus-pocus. That'd be my guess. Suppose he had it under his thumb, like Finnegan said, ready to squash 'em the second they made their move. If it was like that, it was him that gave us half the gold."

"Swell guy. Think I'll invite him over to dinner."

After a minute, when Hickey didn't talk back, Leo said, "You okay, Tom? Something bothering you?"

"Yeah. The girl."

"Aw, some guys never learn."

He thought about the girl while they raced through downtown past Indians scavenging through the gutters and sidewalk litter, into and out of the acrid smells, alongside the nightclubs where pimps and whores stood beneath rotting signs and broken windows, hustling even in the last hour before dawn. When they turned toward the river and the town receded behind them, as he saw it in the rearview mirror, Hickey mused—TJ was some place. It had everything. As if it spanned the border between heaven and hell. In TJ a guy might find his precious dream dancing on the same stage with his nightmare. One side of a street might be stacked with tons of garbage while across the street lay a mountain of gold. This place had it all. Terrible, wondrous, obscene. Anything you could dream, all the world was there, usually standing naked, sometimes in disguise.

Fords and limos raced over the bridge, tooting horns and waving at the shantytown until naked kids and women wrapped in threadbare serapes crawled out from the jacales and from beneath derelict cars with eyes so bright you could see them shining all that way.

Hickey pulled his limo up in front of Coco's Licores. He jumped out beside a bus driver and a laborer who'd been standing there, and offered them each a pistol and twenty dollars for an errand—to deliver seven prisoners to the border and tell an old Chinese gringo to throw these wetbacks in a cage, since Tom Hickey'd caught them trying to jump the line.

When he'd gotten all the prisoners out and marching, Hickey thought about a pint of mescal, to celebrate. Except he didn't want to celebrate. He wanted peace.

He waved. The tangerine limo shot across the road. It led the way, bounding on a trail up Otay mesa.

29

≡ ≡ ≡

Forty-two miles inland, a mile north of the border, not far off the Campo-to-Tecate road, Hickey's gang rested. The oak log cabin belonged to a friend of Leo. Twenty men squeezed into the one room crowded with gold and smelling like an old wild dog. Leo had to drag the trunk he sat on to the window. Then, on his clipboard and paper, he scribbled the name and tribe of each Indian, before letting him grab some big stuff, or a half-lunch box full of coins and jewelry out of the open trunk. Outside, the Indian bundled his gold into a gunny sack or stashed it in one of the limos or cars that waited in the pasture.

Hickey sat in the dirt beneath an oak, leaning back, feeling as loose as a sober man could. He watched the Indians. Now and then he got a vision that rushed back from last night. For a while he crumpled and tossed up some dry oak leaves and watched the specks drift a few yards on the spent wind and fall. He smoked a cigaret and daydreamed of Elizabeth.

The two of them stood on the patio of a swank nightclub. Havana sparkled across the bay. Inside, the orchestra struck up a tango rhythm. Elizabeth wore a gold tiara, a slinky dress, gold bracelet and rings, a gold mesh necklace. Stunning. A princess. Like Madeline used to be. Except his daughter's lips had an uppity turn.

Convinced of her charm, with a steady gaze, she turned toward the ballroom as two gentlemen came strutting her way. They made Hickey want to puke.

About fifty feet away, in the backseat of the tangerine limo, Tito and Malu sat cuddling. He'd already packed his gold in the trunk. After Leo, he'd gotten first pick and taken candleholders, vases, a few nude figurines, a gold rosary, two large pockets full of coins. Now he sat with a hand up Malu's frock, on her thigh, dreaming of a classy four-room house in Matamoros. He felt her fingers tighten on his arm and wondered if maybe he should leave her behind. Already she looked plenty older than last night, with puffy eyes and her makeup running. But she'd be a hot one, better than the putas who were all he'd known since El Mofeto carved out his eye with the razor-sharp point of a switchblade.

He'd drive to a hidden place and wait and have this Malu rubbing his huevos all day. Then at dark, he'd feel safer—what you think about when you're going to cross a thousand miles of borderland in a stolen limo with a trunk full of gold. Good thing a couple of those tough Yaquis would be riding with him. His Yaquis sat on the hood of the limo. One of them kept looking inside over his shoulder. Finally Tito pried himself away from Malu and jumped out, told the Yaquis to get off his car, before they scratched the paint, and make ready to leave in a minute or two. He walked around some cars, squatted next to Hickey.

"What you did with your gold, General?"

"Didn't get it yet. Later."

Tito looked the man over. He didn't like the way Hickey's eyes wandered—when he used to stare right at you. "Boss, you feeling sick?"

"Naw. I feel swell."

"I don't think so."

"Lay off," Hickey snapped. "When I don't eat, I get a little dizzy, maybe."

From his pocket Tito pulled a Hershey bar and a bag of peanuts. Hickey only took the peanuts. He ripped the bag and chomped a big handful while the cabbie scrutinized him, and finally

210

said, with a shy smile, "You know, maybe someday I going to have this son, call him Heecky Pacheco.

Hickey blushed at that one. Tito donned his sunglasses, stood up, unwrapped the Hershey bar. He munched and promised that when he got to Matamoros he'd write down his address and send it to the place on el Weiss's business card. Because Hickey better come to Matamoros pretty soon, to meet the wildest chicas in Sonora.

"Maybe when I get out of the Army," Hickey said.

"Army? Man, you know, they going to hear what we did, and they going to make you a general maybe with four stars, and probably they send you for an invasion. I think Tokyo."

"Ugh." Hickey chuckled and yawned. "You better scram."

"Okay. I'm going now. And you better get your gold, boss, or the pinche Indios will steal it all."

He walked off, hollering to the Yaquis. In a minute the limo bounded away across the field. Hickey wadded the peanut sack, tossed it into the breeze, leaned back against the oak, and shut his eyes.

He saw Wendy, in a blue sleeveless dress, sitting in a pile of leaves beside a redwood tree where a streak of sunlight angled through the shadows. Her hands and fingers made a little dance on the side of her face.

A motor fired. Springs creaked and metal scraped the ground. A Cadillac and limo pulled away—the rest of the Yaquis heading east. Hickey slapped his head, looked around, and saw that the Olmecs and Kickapoos had already gone—maybe he'd dozed off awhile. The only Indians left were the Otomis standing near the cabin. All six of them. He wondered why they weren't inside grabbing their gold. So he got up, walked past the smiling, sad-faced Otomis, and stepped inside.

The only gold left was in one trunk. Leo was on his knees sorting through it. He sifted the coins and jewelry that looked most valuable, piled that left of the trunk, and put the stuff that only looked worth its weight on the right. He looked up at Hickey. "About time you give me a hand here, loafer."

"What're you doing?"

211

"Plucking out your share and getting the coins for the little fellas out there. They gotta have small bundles, since they're riding the bus home."

"Got a smoke?"

Leo took out his Luckys, lit one, passed it to Hickey, and grumbled, "My back's sore as hell."

"Go on, take a walk. I'll finish up here."

After Leo trudged out, Hickey knelt in front of the trunk and looked at the treasure. He picked up a heart-shaped locket. He saw it on a gold chain against Wendy's skin above her breasts. It looked splendid—but when he gazed up to her face, her mouth twitched and her eyes closed against the terror. Then he saw Zarp laying naked and blubbery atop her on that golden bed. Her hands reached for the sky. Finally he remembered the altar in Hell, as Wendy stepped to it, threw back the sleeves of the scarlet robe, and lifted her arms. A big golden knife fell, into George's heart.

Hickey growled, spat, shook his head, and commanded his mind not to wander so far. Then he thought of sending Elizabeth a pile of money that Castillo or Madeline couldn't get their mitts on. Maybe having her own would turn her away from the snobs. She might delight him, do something fine like give a heap of money to somebody who needed it. But he knew her better—she was more like Madeline than anybody in the world, and Madeline would never leave the snobs. She needed to feel singled out that way, like one of the chosen.

Hickey'd known plenty of rich guys, but only a few he could bear. It'd take a giant, he figured, to get rich yet stay true.

For a while he stared at the treasure and thought about where it came from. Finally he grabbed a handful of coins and small jewelry, held it there over the trunk, feeling mean, low as Paul Castillo. Only worse. Not just a thief, a murderer too.

He knelt, rapping a knee on the floor, breathing smoke, haunted by at least nine dead people. Maybe eleven. And two madmen, El Mofeto and old del Monte, who probably weren't so crazy before. He dropped the junk and stared where it fell until the cigaret burned down to his fingers. Suddenly he jumped up and booted the trunk—in three kicks the side gave in and collapsed under a pile of gold trinkets. Then he grabbed up the bust of some old dame and heaved it against the wall. Finally, seeing he couldn't break the stuff, he turned and stomped outside.

Around back of the cabin in the oaks, he found Leo pissing. When he started to talk, nothing came out. He steadied himself against a tree and rasped, "I got what I wanted outa there. Go take some more, for what I owe you, and enough to pay Smythe and Boyle. Give the rest to these Indians."

Quickly he turned and walked away, as a high, silky voice like Madeline's came out of nowhere, saying, "Tom, oh God, you're such a loser." His step faltered, like something was pulling him back toward the gold. It took all his will to move his legs toward the limo.

The limo would give him a thousand or two. It'd be a start. That was all he wanted. He dropped to the cushiony seat behind the wheel and watched Leo amble over.

When his partner gave him a nod of understanding, put a hand on his shoulder, told him to wise up and take his fair share, Hickey said, "Okay then, grab me something that'll bring a few grand. But do like I say with the rest. Just get me enough so I won't feel like a perfect chump."

"You sure oughta feel like that."

Hickey shouted, "Do like I say, huh."

Leo jerked back his hand, took a step away, and stood there with his face scrunched up like at a bad joke. "You're acting like a nut, Tom."

"I got my reasons." Hickey turned the key. Pushed the starter. Threw the limo in gear. "I'll tell you all about 'em someday."

30

■ ■ ■

From the window of his cell, you could look over the warehouse across the street and see the tops of a dozen battleships with masts like oil derricks, crows nests on top above the highest big guns, and the stars and stripes flying everywhere around the harbor. Sometimes a B-24 taking off from Lindbergh Field, or a seaplane lifting off from the harbor, shuddered across the sky.

Leo had brought him a new pipe, a good Kentucky briar, a pound of Walter Raleigh, a stack of books. *The Decline and Fall of the Roman Empire*; *Undercover*, a new book about Nazis on the home front; Bernal Diaz's *Discovery and Conquest of Mexico*.

There'd be plenty of time to read, once the guards quit pestering him. They kept nosing around, asking to hear his story. The WAC typists looked in on him, bright-eyed. All the brig personnel treated the old, busted private like a hero, on account of the rumors that with a few pachucos he'd wiped out a company of Nazi troopers on their way to a hit-and-run attack on Ream Field. Hickey didn't straighten them out. The less the Army knew the better. So far, they'd only charged him with AWOL.

The San Diego cops, where Hickey and Leo had friends, didn't care a damn about what they'd done in Mexico. And nobody down there had called to gripe. The del Montes, Zarp, and the rest had got sent home after a couple days. Old Santiago couldn't talk a word of sense anymore. He'd kept shouting his mixed-up language and he'd got lost in time—he spent whole nights in jail screaming at his dead mother. Zarp, with his head and face wrapped in bandages, seemed a changed man, quiet, lost—maybe building a world of his own somewhere, like Wendy did. And since Boyle decided not to charge Hickey with kidnapping, on account of they were old friends, he said, and there was no use stirring up the past, it looked like Hickey might get out of this joint someday. For now, he only wished the window was bigger, sunnier, that they'd let him send out for grub to the Pier Five Diner, and allow him visitors, one anyway.

But nobody got all he wanted. And that was okay. Life would be smooth enough if he could just quit thinking about that money.

Leo had paid his debts, got him the bayside cottage back for what the flyboy had paid him plus five hundred, and dropped seven thousand into a bank account for him. Sometimes he felt like a thieving mercenary. But it was only a tenth of what Leo and Tito had bagged, a twentieth of what he could've grabbed. He wondered if he'd done right. Not about the killing. All that blood, those years somebody wouldn't get to see—he'd be grieving that a long while. But the money—if he should've kept his share—that was the puzzle. He tried to remember his reasons. Maybe he'd gotten too tired, forgot to eat, and fatigue or something had kayo'd his mind—a million dollars worth. He wondered so much it made his guts churn.

The only escape was to think about the good—how ten days ago it seemed he'd failed perfectly, played every note until it went flat, and left himself sapped, wasted, powerless to turn anything around. He'd let everybody down, even his own little girl. Then Wendy appeared.

Which gave him plenty more to think about. Like how does a guy his age handle a nineteen-year-old doll who can hardly read, who thinks like a kid, and who, every time she gets spooked, flies up into the heavens. He figured he must be a sleaze, a pervert, considering a few urges he'd gotten about her. He couldn't decide what to do with her. Send her to a nunnery or asylum? Find somebody else to take her? Or play like her dad, teaching her modesty, manners, and such, then marry her off to some kid? He couldn't feature any of that.

There seemed no end to questions but hardly any answers. Still, what to do with a beautiful, innocent girl who's devoted to you—Hickey knew he shouldn't bitch too loud about having to solve that one. Besides, he didn't need to rush. She'd room with Leo for the duration. After the war they could go up to Tahoe and spend a summer building Wendy a house on that lot she owned. Fishing for rainbows. Walking on the beach, swimming until they got numb. Climbing the high peaks and looking down at the lake on one side, desert on the other. Maybe they'd get a little sailboat.

But damn, he thought. You're almost forty. In a couple of years your chest will sag, eyes droop, teeth cave in. Your glasses will get an inch thick, and your little scraggle of hair might turn gray. Almost forty, he thought, and so far a map of your life would look like a two-year-old's scribbling. All you need is to go off playing house with the kid. She'll either bore you crazy or run out and leave you a bitter, nasty old fool.

Toward evening on Thursday, six days after the battle, a lieutenant allowed Hickey the visitor he wanted.

She came into the brig on Leo's arm. When Hickey heard the old man's voice out there, he jumped to the bars and tried to get a look through the door. It was nearly closed. But Leo said her name. A minute later they stepped in, behind a guard and his keys. Out in the lobby an MP whistled. A different guy yapped, "What a babe!"

As they walked toward the cell, Wendy's free hand covered her eyes. The guard used his key and the door creaked open. Wendy let go of Leo, dropped her other hand, and seemed to float into the cell. She stood there in Magda's yellow dress with butterflies, with her lip slightly raised on the left side, and her hands out halfway toward him. Her eyes wandered all around before they caught Hickey's straight on. They stopped and sparkled. Flecked with gold. They didn't even blink anymore.

She wanted to say something. But first Hickey stepped near and wrapped his arms around her waist. He pulled her so close her breath came out a sigh. Just one note that moved him like a whole symphony. Sure as hell, he wasn't going to leave her.